Praise for **That Slippery**

'Look out Marion [...]
on the block . . . a h[...]
New Zealand Woman's Weekly

'It's frothy, funny and forthright.'
Next

'[This book is] a joy, funny, rueful, slightly
shocking and bang up to the minute.'
Wairarapa Times-Age

Praise for **Famous**

'Grab a latte, turn off the cellphone and enjoy
the read.'
Otago Daily Times

'Chick lit at its snazziest, wittiest and frothiest
. . . funniness that rivals a *Friends* script.'
New Zealand Herald

'Irreverent and laugh-out-loud funny.'
Hauraki Herald

'Naughty, hilarious and highly entertaining.'
Citymix

'Kate Langdon has cemented her place as the
pioneer of quality New Zealand chick lit.'
Dominion Post

By the same author:

That Slippery Slope
Famous

making lemonade

kate langdon

Dear Suz
Hope it makes you
laugh!
Lots of love
kate xx

HarperCollinsPublishers

For Petra, Lauren and Atlanta,
three top chicks

National Library of New Zealand Cataloguing-in-Publication Data
Langdon, Kate, 1975-
Making lemonade / Kate Langdon.
ISBN 978-1-86950-624-7
I. Title.
NZ823.3—dc 22

First published 2007
HarperCollins*Publishers (New Zealand) Limited*
P.O. Box 1, Auckland

ISBN (10-digit):1 86950 624 3
ISBN (13-digit):978 1 86950 624 7
Cover design by Sarah Bull – Anthony Bushelle Graphics
Internal text design and typesetting by Janine Brougham
Printed by Griffin Press, Australia.

50gsm Bulky News used by HarperCollins*Publishers* is a natural,
recyclable product made from wood grown in sustainable plantation
forests. The manufacturing processes conform to the environmental
regulations in the country of origin, New Zealand.

Jools

I hung my head in shame as they wheeled me across the gangplank and onto the boat. Well, after they stopped the boat and turned it back around that is, someone finally noticing that I was still sitting on the jetty. I'd been hoping they'd forget about me and leave me there forever, so I could quietly wheel myself off the side and into watery oblivion.

'Sorry, lady,' said the Fijian man, as he pushed my wheelchair too close to the side of the boat and banged the cast of my outstretched broken leg against it.

I grimaced at the searing pain that shot through my foot and up my left leg, but somehow I managed to refrain from crying. This was only because I was so totally hungover and thoroughly dehydrated that my tear ducts appeared to have shrivelled up and died. Every ounce of moisture in my body made its way to my tongue so that I could swallow and the sheer gargantuan size of it wouldn't suffocate me to death.

There they were, sitting around the deck of the boat in the blazing sunshine, the fifty or so people I had spent the past four days with. The people who had flown in from Australia and New Zealand for our company conference. And there he was, The Bastard, in animated conversation with two of the Aussie girls, not even glancing my way, let alone acknowledging my crippled presence. A couple of people ventured a 'hello' and gave me a little wave as I was wheeled on board, but they were by far the minority. The rest just stared at me as though they, too, had been hoping I'd be left on the jetty.

'Where shall we put you, lady?' asked my wheeler. 'Over dere in the shade?'

Yes! screamed my body. Yes God, please! The shade!

The blazing sunshine, coupled with my ground-breaking hangover, was making me feel as though I'd been locked inside a sauna for three days, prior to being run over by a lorry.

'Yes, thanks,' I replied. 'Lovely.'

As if there was anything remotely lovely about my current situation.

So there I was deposited, parked in the shade in my wheelchair, alone, on the opposite side of the deck from my colleagues. My suitcase was wheeled on and plonked down beside me.

Who was going to wheel me off? I wondered. Perhaps I would be left again? Left to catch the ferry back and forth to Nadi until the end of all time.

I took a book from my handbag and pretended to read, eventually turning it the right way up. I sneaked the odd glance at him through my face-eating dark glasses. He was like an antipodean Tony Robbins, so charismatic that every man, woman and their brown-nosing dog fawned to sit on his lap, in the vain hope that a smidgen of it would rub off. But I'd seen through him. He was nothing more than a good-looking used-car salesman who would give you the flick (literally) if he thought you were shadowing his star.

The bump of the waves underneath the boat made me want to cry. But I couldn't. I wasn't even supposed to have gone to Fiji. I was a contractor at the company, and contractors didn't get to go to the annual company conference. It was only because I was sleeping with him that I was here. He thought he was doing me a favour by wrangling my attendance. Some bloody favour that turned out to be! And now of course everyone knew I'd been sleeping with him: the chief executive, the big boss, absolutely everyone.

For some reason, I was the one to blame. Not him. Even though he was married with three kids and I was the single, available one. Some people are addicted to reality telly, chocolate-covered cashews or internet shopping. I am addicted to affairs with married men. It's not as though I sniff them out, hunt them down and beat them into cheating on their wives. It just happens that every man I'm attracted to and start dating is married. Yes, I should stop dating them the minute I find out they're married. Yes, you're right, this would be the sensible and morally correct thing to do. But when you've been staggering through the desert for many long months in search of a well and finally meet someone who has a direct mainline to the Nile, this is a very difficult thing to do. What can I say, I was low on self-control. It seemed to me there were no attractive and single men in this city, but there were *plenty* of attractive married men who thought they were single.

Anyway, it seemed nothing could tarnish his gold-plated image. It had been difficult to keep our affair a secret once word of the bicycle incident got out. It was tricky to explain why I'd been sitting on the handlebars of a bicycle being ridden by him across the resort at 2 a.m. that morning, in a direct beeline for his bure. If only he hadn't ridden straight into the rock. And if only I hadn't been flung from the handlebars onto the stone path. There would have been nothing to explain.

It was incredible how quickly word had spread amongst our colleagues. In a remarkable example of Chinese whispers, the story now included me naked on the handlebars, yodelling at the top of my lungs, swigging from a bottle of Lindauer and giving him a blowjob. Simultaneously.

One long hour later we docked at the Nadi marina, the bump of the boat against the jetty sending fresh waves of pain cascading up and down my leg. It was by far the longest ferry ride of my life. The longest plane ride of my life dangled in front of me, like a mouldy carrot. My colleagues piled off the boat without even a glance my way, let alone an offer to push the wheelchair. I hadn't the energy to wheel myself; I was scarcely managing to breathe on my own.

Once the flocks had filed past me, one person remained standing on the boat. Him.

'Bloody great,' I muttered under my breath as he walked towards me.

It is very difficult to look both aloof and severely pissed off when you are sitting in a wheelchair with a broken leg. The best I could do was to avert my eyes downward, which made me look even more pathetic.

'How are you feeling?' he asked.

'*Me?*' I replied, looking over my shoulder for wounded emphasis. 'Oh, just peachy. Thanks for asking.'

'How's the . . .' he stalled, pointing at my leg.

'Oh, it's perfectly fine. They put it in a cast for the hell of it. Thought it might be nice and soothing in the forty-degree heat.'

'I see,' he replied. 'Broken then?'

For someone who regularly prided himself on his intelligence, he was currently a firm contender for village idiot. I declined to reply.

'I'm sorry for leaving you at the reception desk last night . . . I didn't know how I could explain my . . . my presence.'

I stared up at him, fury blending with my hangover, giving my eyes a lovely deranged appearance.

'I didn't realize it was that serious,' he continued. 'Otherwise I would have . . .'

'Would have what?' I asked. 'Waved as you rode off?'

'C'mon, Jools. You know I can't be seen with you.'

'Well it hardly matters now, does it?' I said, raising my eyes towards the jetty. 'It's not like they haven't all seen the movie.'

'Let's get you on da bus, lady,' said the Fijian man, as he released the brake and wheeled me off the boat.

I wasn't in any position to protest. Not unless I wanted to miss my flight and take up a permanent position as the boat's maimed mascot.

'I'll bring your suitcase,' Gary called after us, hoping I'd take this as some sort of chivalrous gesture.

It was the bloody least he could do. The *very* least.

The kind Fijian man carried me onto the bus, banging my head loudly on the doorframe as he did so. The pain was indescribable. I could feel the sea of stares before my dazed eyes could focus on them. They stared at me like the circus sideshow I was.

Thankfully there were two vacant seats at the front of the bus so I was spared being carried down the Aisle of Hell. I would be able to sit sideways and lay my leg across the other seat.

'Dere you go, lady,' said the man, plonking me into the seat, but thankfully not bumping either my leg or my head in the process. 'I hope your leg be getting better.'

'Thank you,' I replied, somehow managing a smile.

9

He'd been so lovely to me. So much more lovely than the asshole who was currently putting my suitcase into the luggage hold. If only I'd been of able body I would have told him to shove the suitcase up his arse. But instead here I was, A Cripple. A cripple who needed someone to carry her luggage if she'd any hope of bringing it home with her.

He climbed onto the bus and had the audacity to smile sweetly at me as he walked past.

I hope he trips and impales himself on an arm rest, I prayed. Unfortunately no screams were forthcoming.

I could feel the stares and whispers hit the back of my seat and echo around the bus, while every bump and pothole (too many to count) sent excruciating pains flying up my leg and around my head. I needed water. Desperately. It was the longest twenty minutes known to woman.

We arrived at the airport, a devastating hour and a half before our flight was due to depart, and I was once again deposited into a wheelchair by the kindly bus driver.

'You have anyone to help you, lady?' he asked.

I looked around but Anyone appeared to have grabbed their suitcase and scarpered into the terminal.

'Er, no,' I replied.

'I will help,' he said sweetly, somehow managing to both push my wheelchair and pull my suitcase inside the terminal, where he recruited an airport staff member to take over.

I could see my colleagues queuing at the check-in counter ahead.

Bastards, I thought to myself. And then I said it.

'Pardon, lady?' said my new female helper.

I fished in my handbag and handed her my passport.

I wondered what the hell to do with myself for the

next hour. It was Nadi after all — there was no Jean Paul Gaultier or Ralph Lauren to lift my spirits and cripple my credit card.

'We put you over dere,' said the lady, making my mind up for me. She wheeled me towards a roped-off area beside the check-in desks and then, much to my surprise, lifted up the rope and wheeled me under it.

'Dere you go. I be back,' she said, wandering off.

I looked around at my new surroundings. I appeared to be the only human in the roped-off area; the rest of my companions were various pieces of luggage, including some very big boxes with the word *oversized* emblazoned across them. The rest were suitcases and the like, all sporting a sticker that said *lost*.

It took me a moment to realize I had been left with the oversized and lost baggage. Which meant, in all likelihood, that I was considered to be an oversized or lost piece of baggage, too.

I looked across at the queues of people waiting to check in, including my conference colleagues, who were all, it's fair to say, staring at me with what could only be described as unashamed abandon. Some were trying their very best not to laugh, and the rest were staring at me with nothing but pity.

I hung my head and took a moment to ponder my situation. I wondered, *really* wondered, if life could possibly get any worse than this. I strongly doubted it could.

What shall I do? I thought. Keep hanging my head and pray that I will suddenly be blessed with the ability to teleport to another dimension? Realize that I will never be blessed with the ability to teleport to another dimension and turn myself around to face the wall? Or hold my head up high, get my book out, and act as though it is the most natural thing in the world for me to be parked in a roped-off area surrounded by lost baggage and it's no skin off my nose, no siree.

While I tried to make up my mind, I kept my head down and stared intently at a spot on the floor in front of me, as though it were the most fascinating spot I'd ever laid eyes on. There were plenty of spots on the floor to stare at (it wasn't the cleanest floor I'd ever seen). Perhaps I could just keep doing that?

Where the fuck is my helper? I wondered. Having a cup of tea? Standing outside having a ciggie?

I suppose I could have wheeled the chair myself and escaped under the rope, but it all seemed like too much hard work. I was sweating enough from the combination of stifling humidity and violent hangover without adding to the cause.

'You want drink or eat?' asked my lady helper, who had finally remembered where she'd left me.

'Yes, please,' I said, fishing in my handbag for some coins. 'A juice.'

There was a very audible rumbling coming from my stomach, but I decided it was more likely to be the processing of alcoholic toxins than a need for food. The wrong conclusion could have disastrous geyser-like results.

Once again I was left alone in the roped-off area, as people continued to walk by me and either stare or smile sympathetically, which was worse. I was the girl who'd gone on holiday and come a cropper. The girl who was returning home maimed. Their stares and smiles said it all: bloody glad it's her and not me!

I could see my colleagues now gathered at the seating bay in the middle of the terminal, sitting and chatting amongst themselves or reading magazines. Thankfully half of them soon boarded a flight to Australia, so the number of evil stares diminished significantly as they headed towards the gate. Plus, it appeared the rest were beginning to tire of staring at me and whispering behind raised hands. (Actually, most of them had stopped whispering behind raised hands fairly early in the piece and had instead been having very audible face-to-face conversations about me.)

The lady arrived back and handed me my juice. I all but wrestled the cold can out of her hands and threw it down my fur-lined throat.

'Sorry,' I said, after emptying it without taking a breath. 'Bit thirsty.'

'OK,' she smiled, forgiving me my rudeness. 'I come back and get you for plane.'

And with that she was gone again.

'But,' I called after her 'I need to go . . . toilet.'

It was too late. She had waddled out of earshot.

I have often wondered why it is that when you feel the urge to pee and you're near a toilet, you take your time and hold it in for a while, no problemo. When you feel the urge to pee and you can't, however — for instance if your leg is broken and you're stuck in a wheelchair behind ropes — you are simply incapable of holding on. It really is one of life's great mysteries.

Approximately thirty seconds later I could take it no more and had to take action.

But even if I manage to break through the barrier, how the hell am I going to lift myself onto the loo? I wondered.

I wheeled myself to the edge of the ropes, beside the check-in counter, and — after subtly trying to get the attention of one of the check-in staff and then giving up and hollering out 'Hello! Down here!' — I was paid some attention, voiced my urgent requirement, and my female helper was paged back.

'You need something?' she asked.

'Yes,' I replied, teeth gritted with the pain of desperately trying not to wet myself. 'Toilet.'

She lifted up the rope and wheeled me out of the cordoned area and around the back of the check-in queues, to the toilets.

This must be what it's like to be an old person, I thought, as the lady helped me to stand on one leg, pulled down my skirt and knickers, put her large arms under my shoulders and hoisted me onto the toilet. No privacy or dignity to be had.

'You yell me when you finished,' she said, closing the door behind her.

The relief was indescribable, although the results were nothing to write home about. It was a miracle I'd managed to pee anything considering my advanced level of dehydration.

'Finished,' I called out, meekly. But no one was forthcoming.

'I'm finished!' I called, louder this time. Just like I was three years old, had done poos and needed my mummy to wipe my bottom.

'Sorry,' said the lady, opening the door. 'I go toilet, too.'

Pants back up and me back in the wheelchair, she wheeled me out of the toilet and across the terminal. I presumed I was heading back to the baggage.

'On plane soon,' she said. 'We go for little walk 'til then.'

No more ropes. This was good news.

Until she wheeled me straight past my colleagues in the seating bay, who were gathering their things ready for the boarding call but who, despite this, still managed a final stare and loud whisper as I passed.

Please, God, I prayed, don't let me be sitting beside any of them on the plane. Surely I've suffered enough?

But it appeared God had his hearing aid turned down, because, when I was wheeled and then carried onto the very full plane fifteen minutes later, I was lucky enough to be sitting in the front row, with room for my broken leg, but unlucky enough to be sitting directly beside Him. He looked just as surprised to see me.

'Oh for fuck's sake! What are the odds?' I muttered, as he stood up and assisted my carrier to deposit me into my seat.

'Do *not* touch me,' I hissed, pushing away his helping hands.

Bloody hell, I thought, four hours of sitting next to Him. What've I done in my past life to deserve such rewards? Murdered my mother? Conned old people out of their retirement funds? Slept with a priest?

'Jools,' he whispered, once we were left alone, 'I know you're angry with me, but you have to understand, I had no idea how serious it was. And I couldn't have stayed with you at reception last night . . . what if someone had seen us together?'

There'd been just so many other people riding bicycles around the resort at 2 a.m.

'Gary,' I snarled, spelling it out as slowly as I could, 'In case you had-n't no-ticed e-ver-y-bo-dy KNOWS we were SHAG-GING!'

'Not everybody,' he whispered, clearly delusional. 'My wife doesn't.'

'Not yet,' I replied. But it was only a matter of time.

'Jools . . .' he said, reaching for my hand, but checking for spectators before he did so. I'd never seen him look so nervous. In fact I'd never seen him look nervous. Ever. He obviously thought I was going to spill the beans to his wife. But I had no intention of sinking that low, not just yet anyway.

'You know I think you're a top girl . . .'

A top girl? What a fucking wanker.

'. . . and I wouldn't have left you alone last night unless it had been absolutely necessary . . . for both of us.'

'Gary,' I snarled again, whipping my hand away from his, 'I was just wondering, if perhaps you would consider going and *fucking yourself?* Or at the very least shutting the *fuck* up?'

I plugged in my headphones, in case he didn't get the message.

Four long hours later we finally landed at Auckland International Airport, where I was carried to a wheelchair by airport staff and pushed through Customs. Gary had wisely decided to leave me in peace for the rest of the flight, but only after I put on my eye mask and pretended to be asleep. Usually I stay on full alert during a flight until the food comes, in case the unthinkable happens and the trolley passes me by without stopping, but I just didn't feel hungry. My stomach was far too busy churning with embarrassment, shame, anger and the remains of twelve pina coladas to process any food.

I was so glad to be off the plane and free of evil stares that I didn't mind all the fresh pitiful stares which greeted me. *Poor girl! Went and broke her leg on holiday.* I was glad not to be relying on The Bastard to carry my suitcase, who had finally had the good sense to make himself scarce. I asked my helper to wheel me very slowly so my colleagues could steam on ahead. With any luck I wouldn't have to see them again; well, at least not until I was back at work.

Work. How was I going to get there, let alone do any? Sick leave, I comforted myself. But it was a fleeting moment of comfort, because I quickly remembered that, being a contractor, I wasn't entitled to paid sick leave, or any leave for that matter.

Thankfully, Francie had kindly offered to pick me up from the airport, so I was spared the agony of catching a taxi with Gary and his faithful flock, who had congregated outside the terminal.

I'd texted Francie from Fiji with minimum details of my physical demise, so I was spared a stare of horror and a loud gasp as I was pushed through the arrival gate towards her. The pathetic look on my face warned her not to erupt in fits of hysterical laughter either, and she read it well.

'Hell's bells,' she said, taking the wheelchair from my helper. 'Let's get you out of here, babe.'

I bestowed her with the full gory details on the car journey home.

'Wanker!' she agreed. 'Arse-licking bastard!'

Francie was one of my oldest and dearest friends. And just like all best friends, she was unfailingly loyal and more than willing and eager to hurl abuse at any man who dared to upset or cross me. Francie was a hand model. There were only a few professional hand models in the country and Francie was one of them. Naturally, she had truly lovely hands. Smooth and soft and wrinkle-free, with long slim fingers and perfect nails. Of course there was a lot of work involved in keeping her hands in such pristine condition. Weekly manicures and massages, only the best and most expensive hand creams, concocted from the sweat off a newborn emu's brow, among other ingredients. And, for the love of God, no direct sunlight. Not to mention the insurance premiums she paid to safeguard them.

Finally I was back at my apartment after what had been, without any shadow of doubt, both the worst trip and the longest day of my entire life. Francie helped me to unpack and then kindly went to the supermarket to get me some much-needed provisions. She also offered to stay with me for a few days, which was a godsend.

I hope he gets mauled by a stray rabid dog, I thought as I hoisted my throbbing leg up onto the sofa. I really, truly do.

Sally

I watched from the front row as he bounded across the stage and took the hand of a tiny, grinning, grey-haired, slightly stooped old woman. The cameras followed his every purposeful movement as he slid towards her. Vincent the Saint.

He should audition for *Dancing With The Stars*, I thought to myself. He'd be perfect.

She clutched at his perfectly manicured hands, fawning over them as though they were the Crown Jewels themselves.

'Bless you,' she said, tears in her eyes. 'And bless the Lord.'

'Thank you,' he replied, meeting her gaze and flashing his oversized and blindingly white teeth at her, and then the camera. His teeth hadn't always been so big, or so white. Once upon a time they had just been normal teeth, average-sized and with slight imperfections like everyone else's.

'And may God bless you, my dear,' he replied.

I had seen this exact routine so many times, yet it was still agonizing to watch. He always made a beeline for the old people and children.

He walked back to the centre of the stage. The cameras followed.

His thick auburn hair was slicked back, leaving a

crest at the front of his prominent low hairline, which was at least two inches high. You could have balanced a three-tier wedding cake on the top of it, it was that hard. He used more hair product in a week than I'd used in my entire lifetime. The gels, the conditioning colour treatments, the anti-frizz, the mountains of spray. Not to mention the beauty treatments. He'd had more beauty treatments than any woman I knew, and far more often.

'I have to look my best, Sally. It's part of my job,' he'd tell me, whenever I complained about the cost.

The facials, the waxing, the sunbeds, the plucking, the manicures (yes, the manicures). And the botox. An injection into his forehead once a month, rendering it completely immobile, just like his hair. It wasn't cheap to be plucked, waxed and injected on a regular basis.

'Our Lord is here!' he yelled to the audience. 'Right here! Right now!'

Wasn't that a line from a song? I was sure I'd heard Davey playing it in his bedroom. Fat boy something-or-other?

The crowd roared and clapped.

'In this very room!'

And let's not forget the clothes, I thought. He used to dress like a normal man. Jeans, shorts and polo shirts on the weekend. Plain, well-tailored suits and ties at the office. Nice, inoffensive clothes. But ever since his foray into television, he'd begun to resemble a cross between a used-car salesman and a pimp, with his pin-striped suits and coloured silk shirts, open wide at the collar to reveal a small tuft of dark brown hair. His black patent-leather loafers were so shiny it was a small wonder the reflection of the many studio lights didn't blind him permanently.

I glanced across at my children sitting beside me. They looked as bored as I felt.

Davey desperately didn't want to be there.

'Do I *have* to go?' he'd asked me that morning, as he did every Sunday.

'Yes,' I'd sighed. 'You know you do, sweetheart.'

'It's not fair,' he whined.

'I know,' I'd agreed. 'But it won't take long and we can go out for a hot chocolate afterwards.'

'O-*kay*,' he sighed, reluctantly changing into his pressed fawn trousers and white dress shirt.

All Davey really wanted to wear was his cargo pants and a T-shirt, like every other thirteen-year-old boy did on the weekend.

It's important for the kids to look smart, Vincent kept reminding me. They need to set a good example. He meant that it was important for me to set a good example, too. I got changed into my conservative tailored navy suit, pale-pink blouse and black pumps. I reeked of conservatism. Of good, strong family values.

It was a battle getting Hannah into her white sundress, too. She would rather have stayed in her shorts. For an eight-year-old she had very strong opinions on fashion — comfort and practicality winning every time. Except on Sundays. It was very difficult to ride a bike and climb trees in a dress, she pointed out. But at least there'd been no tears that morning, for once. Elizabeth, on the other hand, loved wearing dresses and was the only one of the three who ever got dressed willingly.

I glanced across at her and watched as she stifled a yawn, putting her hand over her mouth. Good girl, I thought. Don't let anyone see you. Especially not Vincent — not that he'd be looking at the kids. He was far too busy looking at the cameras.

'He is with us!' he bellowed. 'In our skin! Our eyes! Our hearts!'

There was something in my eye all right, a small gritty something scraping against it when I blinked and making it water, but I doubted it was God. I dabbed my handkerchief at my eye again in an attempt to flush whatever it was out. Finally I retrieved it, only to look down at my handkerchief and find it was nothing more than one of my eyelashes. It amazed me how something as small as an eyelash or a piece of dust could feel so enormous when it was trapped in your eye.

'He is listening to us! Right now!' he yelled.

I tuned back out. His words cascaded off me like buckets of water. Once upon a time they had drawn me up, made me listen, and desperately made me want to believe.

Once upon a time.

'God is here. In this child!' he cried, snapping me back to the present.

He was down on his knees now; crouched beside a small and very bewildered blond-haired boy, whom he had handpicked from the audience and led onto the stage.

'In this very child!' he cried again, one arm wrapped around the boy's shoulders and the other pumping the air. He reminded me of Tom Cruise . . . only his teeth were whiter . . . and bigger.

The audience cheered and clapped. There was nothing like a small child on the stage to really get them going.

I felt my attention slide as he started his rant about children, and families, and the importance of a mother and father to a child's success and well-being. As though he was in a position to comment on successful parenting. Surely you had to spend time with your kids to qualify?

I refocused on the stage.

Oh God, I thought, if only you could see this . . .

though I honestly hope you can't. Surely you would despair at what has become of all your hard work?

He had the palm of his right hand pressed against the forehead of a middle-aged woman.

'I can feel the Lord in you,' he said. His eyes were closed in sheer concentration, as though he actually could feel something other than the woman's slightly clammy forehead.

He hadn't done the forehead-pressing thing in a while; I thought even he had realized how completely ridiculous it looked. Obviously not.

'You are full of the Lord and His good ways,' he continued. 'I can tell.'

The woman looked at peace knowing she was full of the Lord. The peaceful face of someone who had finally got their money's worth.

I glanced across at Davey, who was staring at Vincent with a mixture of embarrassment and . . . what was it? Pity? Surely not?

I tuned back out again and made a mental grocery list, until I was confident the end was in sight. The children could tell the end was near, too, and began to shuffle in their seats.

I gave them a look. Not stern — more of a hang-in-there-not-much-longer-I-promise look.

'God bless you all! And God bless my family!' he cried, gesticulating wildly at the four of us.

It was over. *Praise the Lord.*

I let out a small sigh of relief and then caught myself just in time, as he gallantly gestured towards us once again and a camera swept across our faces. I smiled sweetly, the smile I reserved especially for Wednesday evenings and Sunday mornings. I looked at the children, who also gave their very best fake smiles. They should be child stars, I thought, they're brilliant.

He flashed the teeth one last time for the cameras.

Five thousand dollars to get his teeth looking like that, I thought. Five thousand dollars that could have been spent on a family holiday. Or a new fence that would have kept the children in and the neighbourhood animals out.

I watched as the children visibly relaxed. It was over for another week and they were free to be normal kids for the rest of the day. Well almost. There was just the procession to go. They followed me up onto the stage and we stood in a line beside him, the united family front. Every single person in the audience, all two hundred of them, walked onto the stage to shake his hand. Just like a royal line-up. The cameras were off but our fake smiles remained. Some of them wanted to shake my hand, too, and the children's. I couldn't help but think about the multitude of germs being passed around. I was looking forward to washing my hands.

Why don't they want to rush home and read the Sunday papers? I wondered. Or do some gardening? It's a lovely day outside.

Finally we were free to enjoy the weekend. The children and I went out for a hot chocolate, and Vincent stayed behind to work on his sermon for Wednesday night. There was no rest for the television evangelist, as he often said. I was glad he didn't come with us. He would have wanted to talk about the service, go over every tiny detail for our benefit, even though we'd been there. Plus, it was nice to have this time with the kids by myself. Time to catch up on their week, to talk about school, their friends, sports, television, celebrities and whatever else they wanted to talk about.

After our hot chocolate and gossip at our local café,

the children and I arrived home. Davey and Hannah immediately got changed into jeans and T-shirts. So did I. Only Elizabeth remained in her dress. I walked into the laundry and closed the door. It was good to be home. And free.

What has happened to my life? I wondered, as I stood on my tiptoes and reached up into the top cupboard, behind the Spray & Wipe.

I worked. I taxied the children from A to B. And I spent every Wednesday evening and most of every Sunday in church. That was my week. Every single week.

Hell, I couldn't remember the last time I'd sat down and had a glass of wine at night, without getting told off for it.

'You shouldn't drink in front of the children, Sally,' he'd scold. 'We must teach them the evils of alcohol and drugs.'

The evils? I didn't remember alcohol or drugs being that evil when we were young; in fact, if I recalled correctly we'd rather enjoyed them. Wasn't he the same person who'd got me stoned for the first time?

What has happened to him? I thought, as my hands found the bottle of vodka and shot glass and brought them down on top of the washing machine.

I wasn't an alcoholic who had several bottles of vodka hidden in various locations around the house, if that's what you're thinking. It was just the one bottle in the laundry cupboard, which I visited a couple of times a week and very slowly worked my way through. I would have preferred a glass or two of white wine instead, but I didn't fancy drinking it warm. It was only because it wasn't worth the wrath of Vincent to drink in front of him that I found myself hiding in the laundry at all.

People change, I reasoned. But do they change as much as he has?

It's hard to pinpoint exactly when his foray into religion had begun. When I'd first met him, he'd wanted to be an actor which, I guess, to all intents and purposes he was — an actor on his own reality-television show. His parents weren't religious, so I'd no idea where he'd got the urge from. He said it was because they'd named him Vincent, a saintly name. I often now wished they'd called him Trevor or Bob.

We had married young, too young, when we were both twenty, after meeting through mutual friends at a rugby match. He was playing in the same team as my friend Susan's boyfriend. He was working in a marketing and sales job, selling audiovisual equipment. I was studying to be a nurse. At first he had started attending the odd church service, nothing out of the ordinary. And then he had met Elvin. Elvin was a new-generation preacher. He drove a flash car, wore expensive suits and travelled the country staying in upmarket hotels and preaching, largely to the already converted. Elvin was married and had six children. He also had no fewer than three mistresses.

Under Elvin's influence, Vincent was drawn to and fostered in the way of the preacher. He was baptised, and so were the children and I.

Five years ago Elvin had stood down from his role as head preacher of Divinity Church, to move to America and 'break' into television evangelism.

Vincent was appointed new head preacher of Divinity Church (where he was commonly known as 'Mr D' by the congregation, which pleased him no end), and three years ago, under Elvin's guidance, Divinity Church also broke into the world of television.

That there was anyone at all, let alone as many people as there were, who wanted to watch a man preaching the word of the Lord on their television screen was beyond me.

Davey had caught me in the laundry once, the bottle of vodka out and shot glass in my hand.

'Can I try some?' he'd asked. I passed him the glass and he took a tiny sip.

'Yuck!' he exclaimed, screwing up his face. 'That's gross!' He handed me back the glass. 'Don't worry, Mum, I won't tell Dad.'

Vincent hadn't caught me yet. The last place on earth he'd look for anything was in the laundry cupboard. I don't even think he knew where it was. Cleaning was part of my role after all, and providing was his. I'm not sure how he classed my job as a geriatric nurse, but I'm sure it wasn't *providing*. A hobby, perhaps? An indulgence he permitted in order to keep my brain working? In any case it was the one part of my life that was keeping me sane.

Asshole, I thought, surprising myself that I actually meant it. Vain asshole.

But I always got angry whenever I sat on top of the washing machine, having ingested a large shot of straight vodka. And then I just carried on as though nothing had happened.

Is this what I'd wanted for my life? I thought, as I poured another shot.

Kat

My life could be subdivided into three distinct categories. The life I should have had. The life I had. And the life I have.

It was now February. I was supposed to be pregnant in February. That was the plan. *Our* plan. But I wasn't. Instead I was violently rearranging the furniture in the living room, for the fiftieth time that week, desperately trying to erase any trace of the *life I had*.

I probably should have sold the house, and maybe I still would. But at the moment I wanted to stay put. I needed to stay. I figured I'd said goodbye to so many things lately, without having to say goodbye to the home we'd spent so long redecorating. The home I loved. I'd closed the door to the small bedroom which would have been the nursery. There were some things I just couldn't face. Not yet.

Gus and I had been together forever. Well, for sixteen years anyway. We had met in our first year at university, on the annual pub crawl to be precise. He was studying engineering, I was studying accounting. Four years on, and, just as we had planned, he was an engineer and I was an accountant. And we were still very much in love. We moved out of our parents' houses and into a flat together, with their combined blessing. My parents loved him, and his me. We were one big loved-up extended family. Our parents even loved each other.

Two years later, after saving as hard as we could, we bought our first home. We were the first of our friends to buy a house, a rundown villa in a respectable suburb. We slaved nights and weekends, too many to count, painstakingly doing it up. And three years later, true to our plan, we sold it while the market was still thriving, for a healthy profit. We were doing well for a couple of young 'uns, or so our parents said. Then we rented for a year, waiting for the market to settle down, before we bought what was going to be, with some much-needed renovations, our *dream home*. The home we would happily stay in for the next ten to fifteen years. The home we would raise our two children in. The home in which I was currently yanking things across the floor, leaving angry welts in the polished floorboards.

This was something I never would have done in the *life I had*, largely because there would have been someone else there to lift the other end of the couch. But it felt good. It felt right. If I had to suffer, then so should the floorboards. The floorboards Gus had sanded and polished to perfection.

'Why me?' I yelled angrily at the floorboards, tears steaming down my face. 'Why? Why? *Fucking why?*'

By now you probably assume Gus is dead. You're right, he is. Well, he is, as far as I'm concerned anyway. Although most other people would probably tell you that he's very much alive and well and living in a trendy warehouse apartment in the city. With his New Love. And they would be right too. I just prefer to think of him as dead.

Gus hadn't mentioned selling the house. I think he figured that letting me keep living there was the least he could do. Plus, he was probably far too busy being in love and having hot sex to give it much thought. Oh

God! I thought, as The Image flashed before my eyes and I pulled the couch a little too vigorously onto my foot.

'Fuck it!' I screamed, to no one in particular. Naturally it was Gus's fault that my toe was throbbing. I kicked the couch, which didn't help matters. If Gus had been there I would have kicked him instead. Hard. But he wasn't. I was alone. *All alone.*

I was about to kick it again when there was a knock at the door.

Knocks at the door were about as scarce as hens' teeth these days, most people preferring to keep their distance, which suited me perfectly. It could be only one person. The one person who was willing to believe I would one day become a normal, functioning, social human being again.

'Hi, gorgeous,' said Izzy, giving me a kiss on the cheek as she whizzed past. 'Hmm . . .' she said, noting the haphazardly parked couch. 'How about we pop out for a drink?'

'I'm busy,' I replied, raising my eyes at the couch. As if it wasn't perfectly obvious that I was in the midst of some very important furniture rearranging.

'No, you're not,' she said, smiling. 'Plus, if you rearrange the living room tonight, what are you going to do tomorrow night? C'mon, go and pop a bit of lippy on. Thatta girl.'

I sighed. She was interrupting my madness. Going out for a wine was the last thing I felt like doing.

'*Please*, Kat,' she sighed.

'No.'

'C'mon.'

'No.

She plonked herself down on the couch (the one I was in the throes of moving) and gave me a sweet smile.

The cow.

If I stayed at home she would keep sitting on the couch, like she did every bloody night, and I wouldn't be able to move it anywhere.

I let out an annoyed sigh and trudged off to the spare bedroom. I sat down on the spare bed and let out another long, annoyed sigh.

And then I stood up from the bed and very reluctantly yanked on my dark denim jeans and knee-high brown boots. I put on some lippy, as instructed. I didn't brush my hair. Really, what was the point?

'Crikey,' said Izzy, jumping up from the sofa. 'Are you *really* . . . ?'

'Yes, really,' I replied. 'But you'd better be quick or I'll change my mind.'

She lunged for her handbag, her eyes giving me the once-over and resting on my hair. To her credit, she didn't say anything. It was no small feat getting me out of the house at night, not dissimilar to moving a volcanic isthmus, and she didn't want to jeopardize her progress. In fact, it was the first time she'd succeeded in getting me out since The Incident.

We drove to a new jazz bar downtown, no doubt carefully picked by Izzy because it was new and there was no chance that Gus and I had been there together (i.e. no happy memories to make me weep uncontrollably, smash my wineglass on the bar and attempt to slit my wrists with the shards). Although bars weren't somewhere Gus and I had frequented in recent years; we were far too busy having barbeques and dinner parties and taking holidays with our other married friends. Somehow my single friends had slipped by the wayside, apart from Izzy of course. I probably should have made more of an effort to keep in touch, I suddenly thought. But doing things with other couples was just easier. Hiring a holiday house, playing a game of doubles tennis, even numbers at a dinner party.

Not anymore, I thought, a sour taste materializing in my mouth.

Izzy succeeded in keeping me at the bar for an hour and two glasses of wine before I insisted she drive me home. I had furniture to abuse and things to smash.

Surely you can find something of his to destroy? I challenged myself. Considering all he's taken are his clothes and toiletries? So far I'd been annoyingly unsuccessful in my quest. I'd thought about smashing his prized white Versace dinner plates and minimalist sculptures. Torching his precious paintings in the front yard while the neighbours gathered outside their houses and discussed whether they should be calling the police or a vet carrying horse tranquillizers.

But the truth was I liked his things. I had to admit he had good taste. If only he'd left his prized rugby jersey I could have mercilessly hacked it with the scissors, before stuffing it with Little Lucifers and watching it burn to a crisp. But he didn't play rugby. He played tennis. With Dan. Why couldn't he have appalling taste like a normal bloody bloke?

Jools

I took the week off work and spent it sitting on my couch, watching talk shows and being waited on by Francie, when her hands weren't required elsewhere. She was brilliant. She happily let me sulk in silence, only interrupting me with cups of coffee or plates of food. My mother was also a modern Florence Nightingale, turning up with homemade soup and apple pies, and texting me every hour when she wasn't there.

I had made the mistake of buying my mother a mobile phone for Christmas (purely for selfish reasons, of course — on the very rare occasions I wanted to track her down, to ask her worldly advice on how to cook a ham, remove a large red-wine stain from the carpet, or revive a dead plant, she was my woman and it annoyed the hell out of me when I couldn't get hold of her). But I'd no idea she would take to texting the way she had, with such unabandoned enthusiasm. Her texts were so abbreviated they were positively cryptic, and it usually took me a good half-hour to decipher what the hell she was talking about. It astounded me that a woman who was such a stickler for grammar and pronunciation was happy to text away like a thirteen-year-old schoolgirl.

'What on earth did you buy her a phone for?' asked Richie, my older brother, who had been receiving his fair share of cryptic texts too.

'There's no way I'm getting one,' said Dad, who relished the fact that no one knew where he was most of the time.

Mum, however, was thrilled. 'Now I can text my friends!' she cried.

To be honest it surprised the hell out of me that someone who was yet to successfully operate a video player, let alone a DVD player, had managed to master a mobile phone.

'Oh Lordy!' said Mum, walking through my front door, chicken pie in hand. 'I'd no idea conferences could be so dangerous!'

It was the affair with my married boss which had spelled danger, but this was superfluous information given on a need-to-know basis, and my mother most certainly did not need to know. So far as she was concerned, it was simply an unfortunate and innocent bicycle accident.

'How about moving back home for a while?' she suggested. 'Until your leg's better.'

I am very fond of my parents. As far as parents go they aren't too shabby. But I'd no desire to live with them again. Ever.

Plus I'd learned to shower myself, with great difficulty, and had also become reasonably steady and capable on my crutches.

The following Monday I had no choice but to go back to work, maimed though I was. I had bills and a mortgage to pay, and, aside from those two rather large obstacles, I also had a job to do. I had condoms and lubricant to sell. I was assistant brand manager for these two products, because not only were they under the same brand, but they also, in the words of the company, 'complemented each other'.

Mum, my virtual taxi, dropped me at the office.

'I'll help you in, love,' she said, making a move to exit the car.

'No!' I practically screamed. 'I mean no, thanks. I'll manage.'

The last thing I wanted was to walk back to my desk, shame-faced and limping, with my mother holding me up.

The only saving grace was that no one from my immediate department had been at the conference, although I was sure they would undoubtedly know every tiny embarrassing detail by now, true or otherwise. It was an office, after all, and the devil's spawn (email) was present. Usually I loved email. I was its number-one fan. I loved the way it was possible to organize your social life/ book your holiday/pay your bills and still look as though you were up to your armpits in work. I also loved the way it enabled you to keep in touch with every acquaintance you'd ever met, but only see the ones you wanted to. But email had suddenly become my arch enemy. It spread embarrassing news faster than the plague. I was sure every employee on either side of the Tasman would be infected by now.

Unfortunately a marketing meeting had been scheduled for me in the afternoon, with senior management. As Celia, the office secretary, had access to my diary, I had no choice but to attend.

Bloody great, I thought. I had so far managed to avoid Gary (who thankfully didn't appear to be in his office) and the last thing I felt like doing was sitting in a meeting with him.

At two o'clock I hopped along to the boardroom to find the executive director (aka Big Boss) and his trusty sidekick, Rory, sitting at the table. Big Boss's name was

Ivan Butterworth and he was nothing short of completely intimidating. He was approximately sixty years old and had taken over the company from his father, an equally intimidating man as legend had it. He had shoulders as wide as a healthy-sized canyon, a large beefeater nose, and thinning steel-grey hair, always with a steel-grey suit to match. I had been in his presence only a handful of times, due to the fact that he was based in Wellington, and each experience had left me twitching like a freshly electrocuted farm animal. He was one boss I had absolutely no intention of ever bedding.

Why isn't Gary the Bastard at this meeting? I wondered. I had no desire to lay eyes on him ever again, but considering it was a meeting with Ivan, surely he should be here?

Big Boss and Rory greeted me and beckoned me to sit. I rested my crutches against the boardroom table and eased myself into a seat opposite them.

'Right,' began Ivan. 'Shall we get started?'

It appeared we weren't waiting for anyone else. This revelation caused my palms to immediately erupt in a cold, clammy sweat.

What can they want with just me? I wondered.

I was about to find out.

'You realize that your contract with us ends at the end of this month, Julia,' said Ivan. It was more of a statement than a question.

'Yes,' I replied.

Although surely it would be renewed for another three months, as it was last time?

'Well . . . unfortunately we won't be renewing your contract here at Sure & Pure,' he continued.

What?

'We're restructuring,' he explained. 'And we have one

more assistant brand manager than we require. And since you were the last to start here at the company . . .'

Last to start, my arse. This was nothing to do with restructuring, or an overabundance of brand managers. We were overworked as it was. No. This was all because I had been having an affair with my boss. They were firing me for shagging my boss. *The bastards!* Didn't women all over the world shag their bosses and keep their jobs? In fact, not only keep their jobs but get obscenely large promotions and whopping great pay rises as well? Wasn't that the way it was supposed to work?

I should have said: that's awfully strange, management were just saying last week how there was a shortage of brand managers in the company. Or: that's rather fortuitous because I was head-hunted by Johnson & Johnson yesterday and was just about to hand in my resignation. I realize they're your direct competitor but they pay so much better, you understand.

But I didn't. Instead I sat there like a Mongolian monkey and let them fire me without uttering anything apart from 'Um, OK.'

Truth be told, this wasn't the first time I'd been fired for having an affair with my boss. It was, in fact, the third. The first time, I'd been twenty-five years old and a marketing assistant for a cereal company. The second time, I'd been thirty-one years old and assistant brand manager for a liquor company. (Although, in fairness, I doubt I would have had an affair with my boss unless there'd been a ready supply of premium alcohol on tap, he wasn't exactly in the running for a stand-in role on *Baywatch*.)

I wasn't completely without morals. I held doors open for the elderly, I let small children pick up a stray coin from the footpath (providing they saw it first), and I gave generously to crippled humans and homeless animals, or vice versa. But when it came to drawing a line between work and pleasure or married and single, I was incapable. Of course, aside from the very real possibility of losing my job, I felt incredibly guilty for having an affair with a married man. But I was powerless to stop myself. You'd think I would have learned my lesson the first time, wouldn't you? Well, I was a slow learner. I should only have taken jobs where the boss looked like the back end of a bus, but unfortunately most of my bosses had been attractive, charismatic, and more than willing to seduce me. And married. What can I say? I'm a sucker for the combination of power and a stylish suit.

'If you decide to leave your role before the end of the month, we will of course pay you for the full term,' declared Big Boss, snapping me back to the present.

They're so keen to get rid of me that they're going to pay me to leave? That's really rubbing salt in the wound, I thought.

Although what was the point in sticking around waiting for the chop? I might as well be at home sulking in solitude.

'You do understand, Julia?' he pressed.

No, you fucker, I don't.

'Of course,' I lied.

'I'm sure there will be plenty more contract work out there for you to get your hands on,' he smiled.

'Yes,' I replied. And plenty more bosses for me to shag.

It had taken me three months to find this contract and I was currently up to my ears in debt with an enormous mortgage, but, yes, sure there'd be loads more work out there. Asshole! I seethed, as I awkwardly levered myself into a standing position (without so much as a murmur of assistance), picked my crutches up from where they leant against the table, and hobbled out of the room and back down the hallway to my desk. I levered myself behind my desk and contemplated my current situation. It appeared that I was now not only crippled, I was also unemployed. Again. It is fair to say that, at times, life is not a peachy ride on the ferris wheel followed by an enormous stick of candy floss. In fact, sometimes life is nothing short of a gigantic red boil which sprouts in the middle of your forehead and refuses to die. And just when you'd have it lanced by the doctor and it's healed enough so you can venture out in public, it grows straight back again (for no apparent reason, of course).

Can things get any worse? I despaired. This is always a pointless question to ask yourself because of course they can. Much, much worse.

That evening I phoned my friend Jeremy, a lawyer, for some advice.

'Did they terminate your contract before it had finished?' he sighed, clearly a little dismayed that I'd lost my job again. He always asked me the same questions.

'No,' I replied.

'Was it up for renewal?'

'Yes.'

'So. They chose not to renew your contract then?'

'It would appear so.'

'Because they're restructuring?' he guessed.

'Yes.'

'And are they?'

'It would seem so,' I replied, recalling the memo that had been conveniently sent out to staff about the 'restructure' the day I was fired. 'Or at least they're pretending to.'

'Look, Jools, if they restructure the company and

make your position null and void, then there's not much you can do about it, I'm afraid. Again.'

'But they're firing me because I was shagging him!' I cried. 'And they're not exactly going to fire him, are they?'

'No,' sighed Jeremy. 'They're not.'

And then he patiently listened to me bleat on for another fifteen minutes about what an asshole Gary was. How women all over the world get the short or raw end of the stick, or whatever the saying is. How they cooked and cleaned for their husbands only to have scalding acid thrown in their faces (I'd read this in *Marie Claire*). How far too many bras were burned for absolutely bloody nothing! Et cetera, et cetera, et cetera.

The following day I went back to work, unable to concentrate on anything apart from the fact that I was unemployed again. That evening I stayed in my office until seven o'clock, until I was positive I was the only person left in the entire building. Then I packed up my desk, into one miserly cardboard box, ordered a taxi and hobbled out of the building, never to return again.

Sally

'It's a long way to Tipperary . . .' bellowed Henny. 'It's a long waaay to go.'

Henny, short for Henrietta, was another full-time nurse at the home. She looks like an adult Pippi Long-stocking, with her long, wavy red hair, freckles and beautiful rosy-red cheeks. She is the funniest woman I know, somehow managing to turn every situation into a full-blown comedy skit. She also has the wonderful ability of making others laugh at themselves. The oldies love her. So do I. She is a breath of fresh air.

'To the sweetest girl I know,' I joined in.

I'd brought a CD of old ballads into work with me that day which was going down a treat. Most of the residents had congregated in the lounge room and were singing their hearts out.

I watched as Henny began to march on the spot as she sang, swinging her arms like an over-zealous soldier, eliciting several smiles from the surrounding armchairs.

I gently massaged moisturizer into Ada's hands as she sang along enthusiastically, pausing only to smile across at me. She loved having her hands and feet massaged, as many of them did. And have their faces made up with the make-up Henny and I brought along for them. They missed the touch of another human, the contact of skin. They were all wonderful people who'd led amazing

41

and full lives, people who deserved to be treated with love and respect in their final years. It broke my heart that so many of them had so few visitors, it was almost as though they'd been forgotten about. I liked placing photographs of them when they were young on the shelves beside their beds, in the hope that any visitors would be reminded that their relative was once a young, fit person, full of vitality and life, much like themselves. Even though they didn't look it on the outside, most of them were still very much young at heart.

I remembered the last time Vincent had come to the home, about a year before. He'd arrived to pick me up, wearing one of his expensive shiny suits. Elsa, a resident who was a sucker for anything remotely tactile, had sat down beside him in the reception area and begun to stroke his suit jacket.

From the office, where I was gathering my things, I could see Vincent shift uncomfortably in his seat, at one point attempting to brush Elsa's hand away. But she was very persistent and had taken quite a liking to his suit.

'That's Elsa, our in-house lint remover,' said Henny, as she walked past Vincent and winked at me. Vincent had immediately looked down at his suit, presumably to see if there was in fact any lint on it, heaven forbid. Of course there wasn't.

Vincent hadn't been back since. I think the suit-touching, coupled with the fact none of the residents had any idea who he was, had kept him away.

On the way home, I realized that my body was desperately crying out for a glass of wine. Knowing there wasn't any in the house, I stopped and bought a bottle.

Once the dinner was on, the children were busy with their homework and I was alone in the kitchen, I pulled the bottle of Chardonnay from the fridge and gingerly placed it on the kitchen table, unscrewing the cap. It had been recommended by the man in the store and had a few award stickers on it to back him up. For some reason I felt like I was fifteen years old again, sneaking a bottle of gin from my parents' liquor cabinet.

I could hear Vincent's steps as he entered the kitchen and feel his reproachful stare drilling into my back before I could see him.

'What on earth are you doing?' he demanded.

'I am pouring a glass of wine, Vincent,' I replied, as calmly as I could. 'Would you like one?'

'The children . . .' he said, waving his arm in the direction of the living room 'are right in there.'

I walked to the doorway and stuck my head around the corner to see Hannah and Elizabeth lying across the floor, textbooks in front of them, and Davey sitting on the couch texting, his homework to one side.

'Yes, you're right, so they are,' I replied, pouring myself a large glass.

'And?'

'And what?' I replied, sitting down at the kitchen table and taking a big gulp. It tasted lovely. Even with him staring at me like he was.

'What on earth has come over you, Sally?' he hissed. 'You know we don't drink in front of the children!'

I ignored him and took another large gulp.

What has come over me? Let's see . . . quite a bit, actually, I thought. A hell of a lot, in fact. I felt the taste of anger and determination mix with the taste of the wine.

Every cell in my body willed him to bugger off and let me have my drink in peace.

But he wasn't budging. 'Are you deliberately breaking the rules of our family?' he asked, sitting down at the table opposite me. He looked at me and then the glass of wine, as though together we were surely going to be responsible for plunging the entire family into the depths of darkness.

I sighed loudly, took another gulp, and stared back at him. I wasn't giving in to him, not this time.

It's now or never, I decided, the wine giving me the confidence I'd been waiting for.

'I don't want to go to church this Sunday, Vincent.'

I was sick to death of spending every Wednesday evening and Sunday in church, watching him bounce around the stage like the fifth member of the Wiggles. Sick of keeping up appearances, sick of smiling for the cameras. Sick of going to strangers' weddings, baptisms, blessings and funerals.

'You have to come, Sally,' he'd say, whenever I'd mention that, just this once, I'd really like to stay home and relax. 'We're the leaders of the church forgoodnessake!'

You are the leader of the church, Vincent, I'd think to myself, sighing and getting changed into my church outfit. I am simply the wife of the leader of the church, a woman who would do anything for a normal life, or at the very least a weekend to herself. A woman who had no bloody idea of the circus act she was marrying.

'I beg your pardon?' he said, once he'd taken a moment to digest my words.

'Church. I don't want to go,' I repeated, taking another big gulp.

'Why on earth not?' he hissed, standing up and closing the living-room door, lest the children hear their mother utter such completely insane words.

'Because I am tired, Vincent,' I sighed. 'And I'm sick of spending every single Sunday in church . . . and so are the kids.'

'The kids?' he asked, incredulously. 'I doubt that very much!'

Was he completely oblivious to their grumbles all week and their ten-yard stares of boredom as they sat in the front row? Obviously he was.

'It's what we do, Sally,' he continued. 'We are preachers!'

'You are a preacher, Vincent. I am a preacher's wife. And the children are the children of a preacher.'

'Yes, but we're a team. We must keep a united front.'

'Well I'm sick of keeping a united front. I need a break.'

For the first time in at least three years, he looked at me as though he could actually see me.

'Have you lost . . . lost your faith, Sally?' he asked, desperation creeping into his voice.

Have I lost my faith? Perhaps I have.

'No,' I replied, although I wasn't entirely sure. 'I just can't . . . do this anymore. Every Wednesday and Sunday, you expect the children and me to go to church for hours on end. To sit in the front row while you preach. To listen to the same old crap. To smile at the cameras on cue, to line up like a royal procession, to shake people's hands.'

'*Crap?*' he cried.

'Yes. Crap.'

'Are you saying that I talk *crap*, Sally?'

'Sometimes. Yes, you do.' Actually, most of the time, I thought, if not all.

'The Lord will forgive you your sins, Sally,' he said, shaking his head.

My sins?

'I'm going out,' I sighed, picking up my handbag.

'Where on earth—?' said Vincent, eyeing the dinner cooking on the stove.

'To the . . . supermarket,' I replied. It was the only place I could think of at short notice.

What I should have said was: I'm going out to drink myself into a hazy oblivion at numerous swanky bars around the city, and then I'm going to check myself into the Hilton for the night. Just so I don't have to listen to you.

But the sad truth was I didn't know any swanky bars.

'Why?'

'To buy groceries, Vincent.'

Twenty minutes later I found myself standing in the baking-needs aisle of the supermarket, staring at the shelves of dried fruit, with absolutely no idea why I was standing there.

It must be for a reason, I decided. I must be out of something. Sultanas? Apricots? Dates?

I stood and stared as shoppers pushed their laden trolleys past me. Mine was still empty.

It's happened, I thought. It's finally happened. I'm having a crazy-in-the-supermarket moment.

I'd heard about them, but I'd never had one myself. Women who come to the supermarket, stare at the shelves, and then go home empty-handed. The combination of marriage, children and work rendering them incapable of completing a simple task such as grocery shopping.

'Sally?' said a beautiful, well-dressed woman with long, blonde hair, stopping her trolley beside me. 'Hi!'

She appeared to be talking to me. Interrupting my staring.

'It's Greta,' she said, her very familiar pretty face smiling at me.

Greta? Gorgeous, vivacious Greta? Was it really?

I hadn't seen her for, God, it must be nearly twenty years. Not since I'd left school when my parents shifted us to Wellington. Greta, Jools, Kat and me, we'd been the best of friends at high school. Inseparable. The Fab Four. Greta the adventurer, Kat the responsible one, Jools the trouble-maker, and me, well, I wasn't sure what I was. For some reason we'd lost touch over the years, although I couldn't remember why. If only it had been the email age; perhaps we'd still be friends.

'How are you?' she asked, leaning in and giving me a big hug. 'It's been so long!'

'I'm good,' I said. This was a lie at that current point in time, but there was no need to scare her.

'You look fantastic!' she said. This time she was the one lying.

'Thank you. So do you.' And she did. She looked amazing. With her shoulder-length blonde hair, olive skin, bright blue eyes and gorgeous smile. She looked just like she always had.

All at once the memories came hurtling back into my head: the scorching-hot summers, the school days that seemed to drag on far too long, the boys we had undying crushes on, the teachers we hated, the bicycles we rode, the lemonade we drank, the movies we watched, the nights the four of us would sneak out of our bedroom windows, meet at the bus stop and head into town. It felt like a lifetime ago. It was a lifetime ago.

'You're married,' she said, glancing at the ring on my left hand.

'Yes,' I said. 'A long time. And you?'

'About seven years now. Children?'

'Three,' I replied, telling her their names and ages. 'You?'

'Two, a girl and boy. Four and six.'

'It's so funny,' she said, smiling. 'We were practically children the last time we saw each other and here we are, with kids of our own!'

'But we thought we were so grown-up.' I smiled back.

'God, didn't we!'

We chatted away for about ten minutes, pushing ourselves hard up against the shelves so trolleys could manoeuvre past. We talked about our jobs — Greta worked in advertising — and about Kat and Jools, both of us wondering what they were up to these days.

'We had some great times, didn't we?' I found myself saying.

'Did we ever!' replied Greta. 'Wouldn't it be amazing to get the four of us together again?'

'Absolutely,' I agreed.

'It's been great seeing you, Sally,' said Greta, as she said goodbye. 'Really great. How about we meet up for a wine or dinner sometime soon?'

'I'd love to,' I replied.

'Well, here's my card. Will you give me a call?'

'Yes,' I replied, giving her a hug goodbye.

As she walked away I grabbed a few packets of dried fruit from the shelves, threw them into the trolley and headed for the checkout.

'This is serious, Sally,' said Vincent, when I returned

home. 'You seem to be losing your faith. You need to see someone. Immediately.'

With that he left me to go to bed in peace.

But he wasn't finished. Not by a long shot.

The next morning I found him sitting at the kitchen table, telephone in hand, trying to find me an appointment with a shrink. An urgent appointment. It seemed my desperate situation warranted the assistance of more than a preacher.

'There is nothing wrong with me, Vincent. I just don't feel like going to church for a few weeks,' I explained, in between his phone conversations. 'All I need is a bit of a break.'

It seemed he was struggling to find me a free appointment before the following week.

'There is everything wrong with you, Sally,' he replied. 'You have Lost. Your. Faith! And if you don't get it back,' he continued, 'your helpless despair will rub off on the children.'

Helpless despair? Surely he was overreacting?

'Well, I've got to go to work now,' I sighed, lifting my car keys from the kitchen bench. 'Good luck.'

'We will get your faith back, Sally!' he called after me. 'I promise you!'

Sometimes all I really wanted was for him to just shut up.

He called me at work later that afternoon, having made me an appointment with a psychologist in the city for Friday afternoon. Two days' time.

I couldn't be bothered arguing, so I agreed to go. 'Are you going to come with me?' I asked, hoping he wasn't.

'I can't, Sally,' he replied. 'What if someone sees me walking into the place? I've got to think of my profile.'

Kat

I'd had my vague suspicions Gus was having an affair. But they were just that, *suspicions*. I hadn't come across any incriminating text messages or emails, à la Posh Spice or Jennifer Aniston, but I had noticed some subtle changes in his manner and appearance. For one, he didn't seem all that interested in ripping my clothes off any more. I'd put this down to the fact we'd been together so long that we were bordering on Old Married Couple in the scheme of things. Surely there was a natural point at which we'd slip into the sex-once-a-week category? Although, to be honest, it had been more like sex once a month, for about the past year at least, and only if I undressed and launched my completely naked self on top of him.

And there was the Pubic Hair Situation. Or rather, the Lack of Pubic Hair Situation. Gus had suddenly decided that he no longer wanted any, so he'd shaved it off. 'I hate the way it gets all sweaty down there,' he'd explained. I thought it was the beginning of some new sexual awakening for us and was quite excited by the prospect. Surprisingly, I found his new smoothness a real turn-on. But contrary to my hopes, it didn't equate to a sexual revolution. At least not with me.

These may have been glaringly obvious signs of a cheating spouse to anyone else, but not to unassuming, trusting, few-beats-behind-the-drum me. Plus, Gus didn't sneak away for weekends with the boys, or work late several nights a week. In fact, aside from the few days a month I spent at the firm's Wellington office, the two of us were together most of the time.

But occasionally my suspicions still bugged me. Maybe he's seeing someone while you're away? I thought. I decided there was only one way to put my increasingly suspicious mind at ease once and for all, and that was to arrive back early from my next work trip. So, as ridiculous and pathetic as it made me feel, that's what I did. I told Gus I was going away for four nights, but instead I went for three.

Once the plane landed and I was driving home in the dark, I knew I was being a hypersensitive and over-hormonal psychopath. It's Gus, I told myself, he loves you. You know that, so what the hell are you doing?

I had no idea what I was doing. It felt so wrong and foolish.

As soon as I pulled up outside our house I felt even more foolish. There was Gus's car parked outside as usual, and there behind it was Dan's car. Dan, who had been best friends with the two of us forever, since university. Good-looking and charming Dan. Ladies' man Dan, always with a different, annoyingly beautiful girl on his arm, although none of them ever seemed to live up to his expectations.

'I'm looking for perfection, Kat,' he'd say. 'Nothing more and nothing less.'

'Perhaps you should consider lowering your expectations?' I'd suggest. 'Just a tiny notch or two.'

'Look, Kat, just because you settled for Gus doesn't mean that everyone wants to rummage in the discount bin,' he'd joke, at which point the three of us would erupt into laughter. He has such a great sense of humour, it's no wonder so many women find him irresistible, I thought. So had I when we'd first met, and for quite some years afterwards if I were to be completely honest.

How can you possibly think Gus is having an affair? I thought. When all he's doing is catching up with Dan while you're away?

I suddenly felt very angry with myself. How could I have been so pathetic? Everything was fine, and I should just be happy I had a husband like Gus.

I grabbed my suitcase from the boot of the car and rushed to the front door. I hadn't seen Dan for a few weeks and was looking forward to catching up with him. I stepped through the front door, suitcase in tow, calling out hello as I did. There was no reply.

They must have gone out for a few beers, I thought disappointedly, plonking down my suitcase. Of course they'll be at the pub. Ah well, I'll unpack and run a nice hot bath instead, I decided. And reflect on what a complete psycho-woman I've been. The fear and anticipation of my unfounded suspicions had completely worn me out.

I walked down the hallway to the bedroom, carrying my suitcase. And then, in very-quick-and-undoable succession, I did two things I would regret for the rest of my days. The first was to open the bedroom door (which in itself wasn't so bad; it was my second action which immediately turned my life into a living hell). Secondly, I flicked on the light switch. My eyes were immediately catapulted into a scene so surreal it would burn my innocent female retinas for years to come.

There was Gus, lying on our bed. And there was Dan, also lying on our bed. And for some strange reason they had both misplaced their clothes. And there were two busty blondes straddling them, yelling 'Give it to me, cowboy . . . yeah!' Right? But the funny thing was that there were no busty blondes in sight. Not one. The other funny thing was they didn't appear to mind the fact that they'd misplaced their clothes. In fact, they seemed to be rather enjoying it.

'Kat!' cried Dan, who was the first to see me.

'Shit, Kat!' cried Gus, turning around. 'Wait!'

But it was too late. I ran out to the street, jumped into my car and sped off as quickly as I could. But I needn't have hurried; they were going to have to put some clothes on before they could run after me.

'And they w-w-were . . .' I blubbered, sitting on Izzy's sofa, the tears and shock making me choke on my words.

Izzy looked back at me with the pained expression of someone who wanted their best friend to get everything off their chest but would much rather they didn't have to hear what she had to say. Poor Izzy, she had absolutely no idea what was going on. I had simply burst into her apartment like a wounded bull, screaming and crying, simultaneously, and collapsed in a terrifying heap on her sofa. She naturally assumed that someone had died. And perhaps that I had killed them.

'F-f-fu . . .' I stammered.

Her eyes pleaded with me to say no more. But every woman at the height of despair has the unspoken right to make their best friend feel completely uncomfortable.

'. . . ucking!' I finished. 'In my be-e-edroom!'

Are you done? her expression beseeched me.

I could tell she was still attempting to process the information I'd just given her. I watched as the revelation missile abruptly hit its target, the impact sending her body into turmoil. The result was a rather unattractive expression of pure disbelief and shock which slowly engulfed her face. I watched in slow motion as her jaw dropped to the floor and seemed to stay there for a couple of years, before she picked it back up to speak.

'It. Can't. Be,' she managed.

'B-b-believe me,' I stammered. 'It was. I saw it. With these right h-h-here.' I poked at my eyes for emphasis.

'Dear Jesus!' exclaimed Izzy, trying her best to compose herself, which in all fairness was virtually impossible under the circumstances.

I was well aware I had just shocked her beyond the realms of any news I'd ever delivered in our fifteen-year friendship.

'Perhaps it was just a oncer?' she ventured. 'Something they both wanted to . . . y'know, give a go . . . just the once?'

Although her less-than-hopeful expression didn't exactly fill me with confidence, maybe she had a point? Perhaps it *was* a one-off occurrence, an experiment which I'd been unfortunate enough to stumble across thanks to my crappy timing? But, then again, maybe it wasn't.

'Were there any . . . signs?' asked Izzy.

'You mean that my husband has been fucking a man? A man who, coincidentally, is also our closest friend?'

'Well . . . yes. Or that Gus was into . . .' I could see Izzy picking her words *very* carefully, ' . . . blokes.'

I tried to think back. Had there been any signs?

'No. Well, maybe . . . I don't know,' I replied.

'Well, what did the two of you get up to in the . . . ah . . . sack?' she asked, tentatively. Surely she knew what we got up to in the sack? She was my best friend after all. I must have filled her in? Although there hadn't been much to fill her in on lately.

'The usual,' I replied. 'Although he was quite fond of doggy style.'

In fact the few times Gus had instigated sex recently, it was always from behind.

Izzy gave me a strange, searching look.

'And he liked me to wear the boots,' I added, although I probably shouldn't have.

'The boots? You mean your lovely knee-high black stilettos?'

'Ah, no . . . his . . . um . . . boots.'

'*His* boots?'

She was really staring at me strangely now. 'He's got a pair of stiletto boots, too?'

'Ah, no. His workman boots,' I explained.

More staring.

'You know, steel-cap, lace-up type of thing?' I continued. 'The ones he wears on site visits.'

Down went the jaw again.

'And you didn't think this was *slightly* odd?' she hissed, the words sounding all strange as she desperately tried to stop herself from screaming them.

'Well, not at the time,' I whimpered. 'But now . . . yeah, I guess so. Oh Jesus!' I wailed, beginning to sob again. 'I've been such a fool!'

'No, you haven't,' comforted Izzy, although her tone suggested that yes, indeed, I had been a complete fool.

'How could I have been so blind?' I cried.

'Oh, Kat, don't blame yourself. How could you have known what was going on behind your back? Plus, Gus seemed . . . well . . . he seemed so *straight*.'

'You know what this means?' I sobbed. 'This means I've turned my husband gay. What kind of woman *am* I?'

'Sweetheart . . .' said Izzy. 'You can't turn someone gay. They either are or they aren't. If he wants to be with a man it's no fault of yours,' she continued. 'Absolutely *none*. Not at all!'

Oh God, I thought, as The Image popped into my head again. If only I hadn't come home early, I never would have found out.

'Look at you!' said Izzy, leading me to the mirror and pointing at my reflection. 'You're absolutely gorgeous!'

Izzy was used to pointing at reflections in mirrors; she was a top beautician at one of the swankiest salons in town. People waited for months just to get their pores steamed open, their bodies waxed or their eyeliner tattooed on by Izzy.

I stared at myself, but all I saw was a pair of red, puffy eyes looking back, and hair in desperate need of a brush.

'Perfect size-ten figure,' she continued, gesturing down my sides. 'Beautiful long blonde hair, clear skin, stunning blue eyes. Hell, even your teeth are perfect! Do you know what I'd give to look like you! If he's not into this right here, then he's as gay as a personalized numberplate.'

I gave a pathetic excuse for a nod.

'Seriously, Kat,' she said, turning me around to face her and clutching me firmly by the shoulders. 'This is not your fault. Not one bit. You *have* to believe me.'

I wanted to believe her, but it was impossible.

I stayed at Izzy's house that night. The following morning, under her strict instructions and after calling in sick to work, I had phoned a very nervous and tired-sounding Gus and told him to pack a bag and get himself the fuck out of our house by lunchtime. I was coming home and there was no way in hell his carcass should still be in the vicinity. And then I'd hung up. He should be the one to move out, just until you sort things out, said Izzy. It was in his best interests to do so, I agreed. There were no guarantees I wouldn't hack him to death with a stray ice pick if he stayed there.

Jools

I was wallowing in self-pity. Wallowing in it good and proper. Nothing could cheer me up. Not even the fifty-six missed calls from Gary on my mobile.

'Why don't you just answer it and abuse him?' said Francie. 'It'll make you feel better.'

I doubted it. The only thing that would make me feel better was him being a victim of a random and obscene act of violence. And I feared even that would only cheer me up for a little while.

On Francie's insistence I phoned around a few recruitment agencies to get a feel for how much contract work was available. The replies were all fairly similar. Not much.

'How about applying for some permanent positions?' suggested Francie.

There were even fewer of these around. Interest rates were on the rise and businesses were tightening their belts and shedding staff by the pound. Especially marketing staff.

'Maybe Sure & Pure did fire you because of restructuring?' said Francie.

'Like hell,' I replied. It suited me to believe it was because of the affair.

Crucial to my wallowing was the fact that I currently had no income, yet I had a mortgage and bills to pay. I rang the bank and lowered my repayments, but there was only so long I could continue to pay even this amount.

'Something will come up,' promised Francie. 'I just know it will.' She even organized an Accident Compensation payment for me, which alleviated some of my worry. She was a godsend.

Saturday night rolled around and Francie insisted that we 'go out and get trolleyed' (her words, not mine). She added something about me moping around home in a right state, and just because I had a broken leg and was unemployed didn't mean it was OK to sit on my sofa twenty-four hours a day looking like the dog who'd had the bone stolen straight out of its mouth.

'I am taking you out and I am paying,' she insisted. 'There will be no excuses. We are going to drown your sorrows.'

'But I have a broken leg,' I replied petulantly.

'So what? You can't sit in a bar and drink because you've a broken leg?'

She had a point. Sitting and drinking was about all I was good for.

'But I'm no company. Look at the state of me.'

'You're right. You're not. But at least if we go out I'll be able to ignore you and talk to someone else.'

Fair play, I decided. There was only so long I could keep her trapped in a silent couch vigil beside me. I had run out of excuses.

I lay in bed and waded through the embarrassing memories of the night before, what few there were. I vaguely recollected drinking a thousand glasses of wine. I was so drunk that, for the first time ever, the bartender told me 'last drink'. I think I was coming on to him, but I can't be sure. He was just unlucky enough to be standing in my three-centimetre line of sight at that point in time. I was officially a sad old desperado.

I thought about hobbling along to the shower, and tentatively lifted my head from the pillow. But it was just too painful. It's best to stay still, I decided. *Very* still. I will never drink a thousand glasses of wine ever again, I swore to myself. Not for the love of God. Not even for money.

Eventually I managed to piece together a rough summary of the night's events, embarrassing detail by embarrassing detail.

Francie and I had started with a couple of glasses of wine at my place. Or maybe a couple of bottles, I can't be sure. We had then caught a taxi to McDougall's, a new Irish pub in town. This was our only stop, as I wasn't in any fit condition to be bar-hopping. This was probably my downfall, I decided. If I'd been of able body, the fresh air would have (at some stage) made me realize exactly how drunk I was and, upon realizing that I was in fact very drunk, I would have quick-hobbled myself into a taxi and headed home. At least, that was my theory.

Eventually, exact time unknown, I had come to my battered senses and decided to go home. The only problem was that I couldn't walk on my crutches. It required an amount of co-ordination that I no longer possessed. Francie was busy chatting to the bartender who wouldn't serve me and was in no state to carry me a taxi. So the nice young man who'd been sitting beside me had obliged. All fresh-faced and ruddy-cheeked with short, spiky brown hair. All I know is that he looked young, far younger than me, but old enough to drink. That meant he was somewhere in his twenties. Mid-twenties I guessed. A sort of man-child.

Hang on, I thought to myself, as more details battled their way through the fog. He'd got in the taxi with me, hadn't he? And, I thought, as someone somewhere flicked on the light switch inside my head, he'd come home with me too. Lord above. And, I realized as my memory switched into second gear, I'd bloody well shagged him. How on earth had it happened?

Somehow (the details were a little fuzzy) he had ended up back at my apartment. I can only assume that someone had invited him back. Probably me.

We'd got all hot and heavy on the sofa. There may even have been some careless discarding of clothing at this point.

God knows what state the living room's in, I thought, as another searing pain did a couple of loops around my skull. Even my teeth hurt.

We had then progressed to my bedroom. Me hopping, him walking and propping me up. Things had rapidly become even hotter and heavier, to the Point Of No Return.

He was a fabulous kisser, I remembered. A perfectly teasing tongue and no nasty scratchy stubble.

God, perhaps he wasn't old enough to have stubble?

I tried to remember what he looked like (aside from the short spiky hair and ruddy cheeks), but unfortunately no details were forthcoming.

'Do you . . . ah . . . have a condom?' he'd asked, as we lay on my bed in a state of virtual nakedness, with him sort of lying on top of me but being very careful not to crush my leg. 'I'm very unprepared.'

There was something very sweet and endearing about a man who headed out on the ran-tan without a condom in his pocket. It was almost as though he didn't expect to get lucky. Or he had a girlfriend.

Did *I* have a condom? He had no idea who he was dealing with.

I directed him to my bathroom where he opened the bathroom cupboard and stared in awe, or perhaps it was shock, at the many boxes of condoms lining the shelves. There were pink ones, purple ones, triple-ribbed ones, glow-in-the-dark ones, super-thin-won't-even-know-I'm-on ones and silkier-than-a-set-of-satin-sheets ones.

I smiled back at him and then stopped, noting the look on his face.

'Oh . . .' I said, suddenly realizing how it might have looked. 'It's my job,' I explained.

Although this made him look even more uneasy, if this was possible. Clearly he thought I was a prostitute and he was going to be slapped with an enormous bill and a 'There's the door, honey, why don't you use it?' at our conclusion.

'I'm the account manager for condoms and lubricant,' I explained quickly. 'Or at least I was. They give me all the samples.'

He looked very relieved at my explanation.

'I must confess,' he said, sliding back onto the bed with a silkier-than-a-set-of-satin-sheets in his hand and giving me a cheeky adolescent grin, 'I've never had sex with a maimed person before.'

'You've no idea what you've been missing,' I said, pulling him down on top of me and shuffling my cast out to the side.

I vaguely remembered the sex. The few memories I had were good ones.

If I didn't currently feel like dying I would have been

very pleased with myself for managing to score a ruddy-faced young man while maimed. I would also have been very pleased with myself for actively attempting to wipe Gary the Bastard from my memory. A few more nights like this and I'd be struggling to remember his name.

I was startled by a small movement beside me. In my bed.

Mother of God! I thought, slowly turning my head. He's still here!

And he was. I looked across to see the eyes of a ruddy-faced young man begin to flutter open.

'Hiya,' he whispered, or rather croaked.

'Hi,' I croaked back.

'Big night, huh, Julia?'

'Huge,' I sighed. For the love of God, I couldn't seem to remember his name.

'You can't remember my name, can you? Don't worry, I won't take it personally,' he smiled.

'No, I'm so sorry,' I replied. 'Ashamed as I am to admit it.'

And I was ashamed. Forgetting someone's name when you've just shagged them and they're currently lying beside you in your bed wasn't exactly good social etiquette.

'It's Tom,' he said, smiling sleepily at me.

We lay in bed and talked for half an hour before he said he had to go. Mountain-biking or something equally uncalled for. I was glad I couldn't mountain-bike. I was also glad for once that I had a broken leg, as it meant I could stay in bed for the rest of the day and not feel remotely guilty about it. He wrote his phone number on a tissue and left it beside my bed.

'Give me a bell when the head's recovered,' he said, smiling and kissing me goodbye. But I knew I wouldn't.

The sex had been great, broken leg aside, but I had no desire to start dating or trusting another man. In fact I was seriously considering taking a vow of celibacy, or maybe becoming a lesbian. If only I was attracted to women. Plus, I decided, if he'd actually wanted to hook up again he would have asked me for *my* phone number.

My hangover lasted forever. It was a record-breaker in every sense of the word.

'I think you have alcohol poisoning,' said Francie on Thursday. 'You'd best go to the doctor.'

I wasn't vomiting. I just felt like vomiting. A continuous nauseous feeling that just wouldn't let up, no matter how much water I drank or Panadol I swallowed. The whole world had morphed into a flimsy life-raft bobbing in the ocean. I couldn't face food, aside from any variation of potato — boiled, mashed, roasted, fried — I didn't care, so long as it was potato. And I didn't feel like drinking, which was just plain odd. I'd never gone off the booze for this long before. In fact, come to think of it, I'd never gone off the booze before.

'Bugger the doctor. You need to go straight to the hospital!' exclaimed Francie, when I told her I still couldn't face a glass of wine.

After a further ten days, my hangover evolved into something far, far worse. I began to vomit, uncontrollably. Anything would set me off. The waft of salad leaves which had been left in the fridge a week too long, the sight of a mince-and-cheese pie at the service station, the smell of nail-polish remover. Anything at all.

After four days of this, Francie all but dragged me to the doctor herself.

'But I'm finally losing weight!' I protested, in between mad dashes to the toilet.

The only downside was having to bolt for the nearest toilet with a broken leg. Needless to say there were times when it remained just out of reach.

Francie sat in the waiting room, an unusually serious look on her face, as I was promptly ushered through to the doctor. I gave him a rundown of my various ailments over the past two weeks. The nausea, vomiting, tiredness. Even going off the booze.

'And the leg?' he asked.

'Bicycle accident,' I replied, which had become my standard reply and which was also, very conveniently, the truth.

'Is there any chance you could be pregnant?' he asked, jotting down my ailments.

Pregnant? Surely you had to have sex to get pregnant? 'No,' I replied.

He took my blood pressure, had a look inside my mouth, felt my glands. And then he suggested we do a pregnancy test, just to be sure.

He was obviously completely bonkers, but I was in no state to protest.

It was best just to humour him, I decided, as the nurse led me away to pee into a small white plastic cup.

Do they ever let you pee into anything else? A green cup? An orange cup?

Five minutes later I sat back in his office, while he sat at his desk holding a small white stick in his hand.

'Well . . .' he said, sort of waving the stick around.

And then he said something I didn't quite catch.

'I beg your pardon?' I replied.

I must have been hearing things. It sometimes happened when I'd just washed my hair; water gets trapped in my ears for extended periods of time. It usually suited me fine when my mother was off on one of her rants, but not when my doctor had just said something of great importance.

'You're pregnant,' he repeated.

'*Pregnant?*'

'That's right.'

He must have the wrong person. I looked over my shoulder, but I appeared to be the only other person in the room.

'Me?'

'Yes.'

'But *how?*'

'Well . . .' He looked a little unsure how best to answer me.

'I mean, I know *how* . . .' I said. 'It's just I'm not sure *how* . . . if you know what I mean.'

He stared back at me.

'I take it this isn't the best news for you at this time?' he asked.

He had no idea. I was pregnant. Quite possibly with Gary the Bastard's child. Or with the offspring of a man-child I'd met only the once — the night we shagged.

'No,' I replied, 'not really.'

More staring.

'We have a nurse here who's qualified to help people work through difficult news. Perhaps you'd like to have a chat with her?'

'What I'd like to do,' I replied, 'is to rewind my life to that night six months ago and never have slept with my boss. Or I'd like to rewind it to that night at McDougall's a couple of weeks ago and not have touched those thousand glasses of wine . . . at least not all of them . . . and to have gone back to my flat. Alone. One or the other.'

He stared at me some more, a look of confusion with a touch of fear in his eyes.

'He wasn't even good-looking,' I added.

I couldn't actually remember if he was good-looking or not, with both the night itself and the morning after being one great foggy blur.

'I see,' said the doctor. 'Not exactly planned, I take it?'

'No,' I replied. 'Not exactly.'

In fact it was about as unplanned as you could get, aside from being unfortunate enough to be walking naked across your kitchen floor, trip over your rubbish bin and land spread-eagled on an upright turkey baster filled with sperm.

'Ow!' I cried, doubling over in the chair and clutching my stomach.

'What's wrong?' asked the doctor, concern clouding his face.

'Just a . . . sharp pain,' I replied, through clenched teeth.

'Where?'

'Here,' I said, pointing at my lower abdomen.

'Has it been hurting for long?' he asked.

'Just now,' I replied. 'Bloody hell.'

How many times had I been in agony, only to walk through the door into the doctor's office and suddenly feel miraculously cured and dead keen on climbing a mountain? This was the first time I'd contracted an illness in his presence. It was perfect timing; twenty minutes later and I would have been in the car heading back home.

'Ouch!' I cried again, as another searing pain shot through my lower abdomen.

'Right,' said the doctor. 'I'd like to send you for a

scan just to make sure this isn't an ectopic pregnancy.'

'A what?'

He explained himself.

'When?' I asked.

'Now,' he replied, dialling the number of another clinic.

Francie was instructed to drive me to the nearby clinic.

'Pregnant!' she screamed, once we were safely inside the car. 'But *how* for godsake?'

'That's what I asked.'

After a fifteen-minute wait we were ushered into an examination room, Francie onto the chair and me and my broken leg onto the bed, with some assistance, to where the female doctor wheeled up a funny-looking machine and rubbed some cold jelly onto my tummy. She explained that sporadic pains weren't uncommon in the early stages of pregnancy and that they should go away in the next few weeks. A scan was the best way of making sure all was well.

'I can't seem to locate the baby,' she said, rubbing what looked remarkably like a telephone handset across my lower abdomen.

'OK,' I replied. This was good news. Maybe there was no baby to locate after all? Maybe the doctor had got it wrong and my life wasn't completely over?

I smiled at Francie and gave her the thumbs-up.

'I'd say that's because it's a wee bit small to be seen on the scan,' she added.

'Oh.'

'I think we're going to have to try another tactic. An internal scan.'

'A *what?*'

'It's a little camera, about the size of a tampon, which

we pop inside you, and it'll give us a much clearer picture,' she explained brightly.

'A camera?'

'That's right.'

'Inside me?'

'Yes.'

'It won't hurt a bit,' she promised. 'Just take your trousers and knickers off. It'll be over before you know it.'

With great difficulty and much assistance from Francie, I did as I was told and then clambered back onto the bed, watching as the doctor returned to the room with what appeared to be an enormous white dildo, with a cord attached, which she promptly plugged into the television monitor.

'What's that?' I asked, noting the look of complete horror on Francie's face.

'This?' she said, holding up the dildo. 'This is the camera.'

'*That?*' I asked, pointing at it and laughing.

This is hardly the time or place for humour, I thought. But perhaps she is just trying to put me at ease.

'Bit large for a camera, isn't it?' I smiled, playing along.

'Oh it's not that bad,' she smiled back. 'I promise.'

'You mean that really *is* the camera?' I asked in disbelief.

'That's right.'

'But it's . . . it's *big*,' I whimpered.

I had no idea what kind of prehistoric tampons she had tucked away in her bathroom cupboard.

'It's really nothing to worry about,' she comforted.

Somehow I doubted she was speaking from personal experience. Truth be told, I was afraid she was going to strap it on and have her way with me. It was that large.

The next thing I knew the dildo-camera was smeared with lubricant and the two of us were having intimate relations. Francie unsuccessfully tried to disguise her sniggering with a very loud and unnatural-sounding coughing fit.

Thankfully the experience didn't last long, once the doctor located what appeared to be a pulsating coffee bean inside me. A healthy coffee bean, she said.

'Do you know how old it is?' I asked, once I had my legs closed and trousers back on.

'Do you mean how many weeks pregnant you are?' replied the doctor.

'Yes.'

'Bit hard to tell at this stage,' she answered. 'But my guess would be anywhere between around two and four weeks. Very early days.'

I counted back the dates in my head. And then I did it again. Francie gave me a hand.

'Weren't you in Fiji four weeks ago?' she asked. 'With Gary?'

'Yes.' *Oh God.*

'But where were you two weeks ago?' she asked, looking utterly puzzled.

I gave her the Not Now look, which she completely ignored.

'Oh . . . that's right,' she said, suddenly remembering.

We picked up our bags. This was not a conversation to be having in front of a stranger.

'You'll need to come back for a scan in about six weeks, and we'll be able to give you a precise conception date then,' said the doctor. 'But if you'd like to know sooner, you can request a blood test from your GP which will give you a pretty accurate date.'

Did I want an accurate date? What was the point in having an accurate date when I had no idea if I was going to keep the baby or not? Not yet, I decided, it would make the baby seem too real.

We climbed back into Francie's car and the enormity of the situation hit me. I was pregnant. *Pregnant*. And not only was I *pregnant*, but I had absolutely *no* idea who the father was. Well, that wasn't entirely true. It was one of two men. But I had no idea which one. This was the stuff B-grade movies were made of. Down-and-out girl gets pregnant, shags so many blokes she doesn't know who the father is, pins it on the next one to come along. Or her brother/cousin/uncle.

But how could this happen to me? I wasn't a character in a B-grade movie and I hadn't shagged loads of blokes. Hell, Gary was the first man I'd slept with in over a year. Shagging two different blokes within the space of two weeks was hardly a regular occurrence. But, aside from all that, I had no idea how I'd actually got pregnant. I was careful. I'd been the brand manager for a condom company for God's sake!

'Weren't you on the pill?' said Francie, reading my mind.

'Yes,' I replied. I had been on the pill while I was having an affair with Gary.

'And did you take it?' she asked.

Yes, I had taken it. Well I'd taken it as often as I'd remembered to take it, which was every second day, or perhaps every third. Something like that. I'd always been erratic with my pill-popping, but I hadn't got pregnant before, had I? No, I hadn't.

'And what about with . . . what's his name again?'

I tried to remember. 'John . . . no that's not right. Hang on . . . Tim? What the hell is it? Oh, Tom. That's right, Tom! We used a condom,' I said. 'I stopped taking the pill when I got back from Fiji.'

'Well, how the hell did you get pregnant?' exclaimed Francie.

'I have no bloody idea,' I replied. And I didn't.

'I hope to God it's not Gary,' she said, reading my mind.

But it probably is, I thought to myself. It would be only fitting that he was still managing to completely fuck up my life when we were no longer in a relationship.

'Where to?' said Francie, starting the car.

'I need a drink,' I sighed, suddenly feeling the urge for the first time in weeks. But I supposed that was out of the question. God, no drinking, I thought. There were just so many things wrong with this picture.

'Home,' I replied, at a loss to think of anywhere more suitable.

I could tell Francie was refraining from asking the one question she wanted to ask. It was the same question I was currently asking myself. *What the hell was I going to do?*

'Don't make a decision now, sweets,' she said, reading my mind. 'You've got time to think things over.'

I. Was. Preggers. If I had a husband to go home and tell, no doubt this would have been wonderful news. *Hell* if I had a boyfriend, it probably would have been good news. But I didn't. I was single, solo, una persona. And I was also unemployed. And let's not forget the broken leg.

I was nearly thirty-five years old. What if this was my only chance to have a baby? What if I didn't meet someone to have a baby with? What if I met someone but couldn't get pregnant again? Could I live with the decision not to keep this baby?

71

So many thoughts, too many thoughts.

Maybe it's time for you to settle down, said my inner voice. Time for you to grow up.

But how would I support it? I currently had great difficulty supporting myself. I suffered from a bad case of financial bulimia. I haemorrhaged money left, right and centre.

You'll find a way, I told myself. If it's what you really wanted.

But what would be my chances of finding a boyfriend or a husband with a baby or small child in tow? Considering the only people I seemed to date were married men with children, this concern was possibly a little irrelevant. But this leopard really wanted to change her spots and surely a baby was single-man repellent? I mean, where the hell would I meet someone? It's not as though I'd be going out on the town, is it?

Don't be ridiculous, I told myself. People with kids are always shacking up. In fact I'd heard from my parent friends that play-centre committees were a virtual suburban fuck-fest. Plus, surely my parents would baby-sit. But how often? And how often was too often? God, I hadn't even had the baby and I was already wondering who was going to mind it while I went out on the plonk. I was an unfit mother already.

If I'd been ten years younger, the decision would have been easy. As selfish as it seems, I never would have compromised my career or partying years in order to be a mother. I wouldn't have felt guilty about my decision either.

'What would you do?' I asked Francie that evening, as we sat in front of the telly eating pizza.

'I've been thinking about that, but I honestly don't know,' she replied. 'It's a tough one.'

'No kidding,' I agreed.

'You know I'll be here to support you whatever decision you make,' she said, putting her arms around me and giving me a big hug. 'And I know you'll make the right decision for you.'

'Thanks,' I replied, smiling at her. She really was the best friend a girl could ever wish for.

'But at the end of the day only you can decide.'

She was right. It was by far the hardest decision I had ever had to make in my life.

I spent hours writing lists of the pros and cons. And then rewriting them. They always ended up even. I kept asking Francie for advice, but her response was always the same: only I could decide, and whatever decision I made would be the right one. But how would I know what the right one was? You'll just know, she said.

You'll just know.

What if I made what I thought was the right decision and it turned out to be the wrong one? What would I do then?

It won't be, she promised. Deep down you'll know what is right for you.

Sally

At two o'clock on Friday afternoon I found myself sitting in the office of Esther Molloy, clinical psychologist.

'Hi, Sally,' she smiled.

She had a lovely, warm smile. I guess she had to; it was all part of the service.

'Hi,' I replied, still a little unsure as to why I was sitting there.

We went through my details just to make sure I was Sally, and not some impostor who got their kicks out of showing up to other people's shrink appointments.

'I understand your husband made this appointment for you?' she asked.

'Yes,' I replied.

'Are you comfortable with that?'

'I'm not sure,' I replied, although I was there now so I might as well see it through. 'I guess so.'

'I just had to ask,' she explained. 'It's a little unusual for an appointment to be made by anyone other than the person I'm seeing. I don't want to hold anyone here against their will,' she said, smiling.

I found myself smiling back at the thought of this tiny woman shackling her clients to the chair against their will.

'How about we go ahead and have a little chat, Sally, if that's OK? And if you decide that you're not happy or comfortable talking to me at any stage, then please let me know and we can stop.'

'OK,' I replied. She had made me feel at ease already. She had a very kindly, caring way about her.

'Your husband — Vincent, is it?'

'Yes,' I replied. 'Vincent.'

'He mentioned that you have *lost your faith* . . . although, to be honest, I must admit that I'm not entirely sure what this means. Would you mind explaining it to me?'

'He thinks I've lost my faith in God,' I explained.

I briefed her on Vincent's position, even though he would have been completely horrified at me blowing his top-secret profile. And even more horrified that Esther had absolutely no idea who he was. Perhaps she had other things to do at 5.30 a.m. on a Tuesday morning when his show was on the telly?

'Do you feel as though you've lost your faith in God?' she asked.

'No,' I answered. 'I believe in a greater power — a God of some description — and Christian values. But I don't believe in a Jesus who requires my children and me to hold vigil every Wednesday and Sunday on public exhibition. Not to mention all the weddings and funerals where we don't even know the people.'

'Did you ever believe in this Jesus?' she asked.

I thought about my answer and it was simple.

'No,' I replied.

But I believed in making my marriage work and supporting my husband in whatever path he chose. Even if that path wasn't one I wished to take. I told her this.

'That's a perfectly normal wish, Sally,' she replied. 'To want your marriage to work and to want to support your partner.'

Normal. I didn't feel normal.

I felt a sudden and unusual urge to tell her everything, not just about Vincent, but about me too. It wasn't like me. I was usually so good at keeping things under wraps.

'Has Vincent supported you in your career?' asked Esther.

'No,' I replied, before I could stop myself. 'He would rather I didn't work at all.'

'What would he like you to do?'

'To stay at home. To do more work for his church. More work for him.'

'You say *his* church. Don't you feel as though it's your church, too?'

'No,' I replied. 'I guess I did once, when it was all new . . . but not now.'

I told her about the television cameras, the beauty treatments, the expensive clothes.

'Do you feel as though he's changed?' she asked.

'Yes.'

He most certainly had. Or perhaps he hadn't. He definitely wasn't the jean-wearing, beer-drinking, care-free young man I'd met sixteen years before. At least not to look at. But I guess he'd always been ambitious, even back then. Always a little too concerned about his appearance, with a knack for turning any conversation back to himself. He always enjoyed being the centre of attention, but I'd just put this down to his star burning a little more brightly than others. A little more brightly than mine. Plus, everyone we knew seemed to be drawn to his charm and charisma. I was no exception.

Before I knew it we'd been talking, or more specifically *I* had been talking, for over an hour. My session was up.

'I think you should come back again, Sally,' said

Esther. 'If you're OK with that? I feel as though we've spent a lot of time talking about your husband and his career, which is perfectly fine, but we also need to talk about you. What are your hopes and dreams? What makes you happy?'

My hopes and dreams?

OK, I replied. I'll come back.

I had enjoyed talking to her. It had somehow made me feel lighter. Not quite as though every step I took was filled with lead.

Vincent was waiting for me when I got home, obviously deciding that my current state warranted him arriving home early. He'd been in for another shot of botox, judging by the way his forehead remained in one place while the rest of his body moved on ahead. And his eyebrows were looking decidedly trim.

'How did it go?' he asked. 'Did she help you?'

Had she helped me? Yes, she had helped me to get everything off my chest, but not in the way he thought I needed fixing.

'Yes,' I replied.

'What did she say?' he pressed.

'That I should go back for another session. Next week.'

'Oh,' he replied.

He obviously thought one session should be enough to locate my faith again, especially since he was paying for it.

Kat

I spent the next few weeks rearranging furniture. It was the only thing which lifted my spirits ever so slightly, and gave me a small shot of satisfaction. I could move the coffee table, or the couch, to one end of the living room and they wouldn't suddenly leg it off into the dining room because they preferred it there. No. They'd just stay right where I'd put them, in an orderly fashion, until I wanted to move them again.

I also filled a significant amount of time eating. I had never been prone to bouts of comfort-eating in the past, but then I'd never been deserted by a gay husband either, so I guess there's a first for everything. Occasionally I wondered at the injustice of it all: that depression led to gorging, which was only going to make you more depressed when you finally took a good look in the mirror. But most of the time I didn't think about it, I just shoved another TimTam into my mouth and relished the momentary comfort it gave me. Plus, I had no desire to look in the mirror and see the sad reflection of a deserted wife staring back at me. I would far rather have smudgy foundation.

The only reason I stepped outside the front door was to go to work. My colleagues at the firm still had no idea Gus had moved out. The most feedback I'd had so far was 'You're looking a bit tired, Kat. Getting enough sleep?' from one of the partners. I desperately wanted to scream back 'No, I'm getting no fucking sleep at all, because my fucking husband is fucking a man!', but instead I smiled wanly and kept walking.

For the rest of the time, the world came to me (the world consisting of Izzy and Meg). Meg, like myself (until very recently) and unlike Izzy, was married. We'd been friends since we were at primary school. Meg was well-meaning and had a good heart, but she also had the annoying habit of offering 'good advice' and lots of it, regardless whether or not it was wanted. Izzy only barely managed to conceal the fact that she didn't like Meg and considered her to be a small-minded busybody. I, having known Meg for longer, agreed that she was a small-minded busybody, but she had also been a good friend to me over the years. However, she did drive me completely insane at times.

My job as an accountant, which I used to find so interesting and invigorating (much to everyone's amazement), now seemed dull and pointless. Everyone had wondered how I'd found accounting interesting in the first place. But I had. I'd loved it. I liked rules and regulations. And order. I found these things comforting. It was easy to make plans when rules and regulations and order were in place.

I'd known I wanted to be an accountant since I was ten years old, playing Monopoly with my parents and sister. Owning the most property didn't interest me, but working out who could and couldn't afford to buy the property did. Not once had I wished I'd studied another profession or thought I'd made the wrong choice. My aim had been to be made an associate of the firm by the time I was thirty-two, which I'd achieved at thirty. And to make partner by thirty-eight.

Being made a partner — the goal I was supposed to be aiming for — suddenly seemed so meaningless. What was the point in being a partner, of earning a huge salary and retiring early if I had no one to spend my money on or my retirement with? No children's education to pay for? No family vacations to Europe? I might as well keep working until I was eighty and then die. The sight of me, aged eighty, donning an out-of-date navy suit and hobbling into the office on my walking stick flashed before my eyes. 'Work is her life,' they'd say, 'ever since her husband ran off with a man, sad old duck.' And when one day I'd keel over in the elevator, on my way to the fourteenth floor, they'd probably even print it on my gravestone.

Snap yourself out of it, for God's sake! I told myself, grabbing hold of the coffee table and yanking it across the lounge again, in the hope that this might shake my thoughts from my own death. It didn't, but in moving the coffee table I noticed the mint green vase sitting on the mantelpiece and carried it into the dining room, placing it back in the middle of the dining table, where it belonged.

As I walked back out of the dining room, my eyes strayed down the hallway and spotted It. The Door. For the past four weeks the bedroom door had remained firmly shut, having hauled all my clothes and shoes into the spare room immediately after The Incident. There was a perfectly good en suite in there, not to mention a seriously lovely cleanser, my perfume, an electric blanket and a razor. The hairs on my legs were so long I would either have to plait them or ring Jim's Lawnmowing very soon. My underarms weren't faring much better. I was at very real risk of turning suburban feral.

How quickly my appearance has disintegrated, I

thought, as I stood at the opposite end of the hallway, staring at the door. Had it only been having a husband around that had made me show some self-respect? Was I now going to turn into a hairy old woman with no one to tell her that she'd a great wiry hair sprouting from the mole on her chin? Would I even care? Oh God, I thought in horror, maybe I won't care. That would be far, far worse. The image made me snap to my senses, something I hadn't been entirely convinced I still possessed. I had to open the bedroom door and retrieve that razor. I had to get a good old-fashioned grip.

Very tentatively, I walked to the end of the hallway and placed my hand on the door handle.

Don't think about it, I told myself. It's just your good old bedroom door. There won't be any naked men shagging on the other side of it, trust me.

I wanted to trust myself. Plus, I knew the odds of finding more naked men shagging behind the door were pretty slim, but still I inched the door open slowly, very slowly. So slowly that if there *had been* any naked shagging men in there, they'd have time to hear the door creak open, get themselves dressed, and position themselves at the wardrobe and French doors, respectively, as though innocently conducting a friendly conversation. But I was in luck: the room was empty, if a little musty-smelling and dusty. The bed was made to perfection: sheet folded over the duvet just so, and cushions nicely plumped. How could I not have known he was gay? What kind of straight man plumps cushions like that?

At that moment Meg decided to pay me an unannounced visit. Mind you, if she'd announced her visit I would have pretended I wasn't home as I usually did, in a vain attempt to avoid any unnecessary social contact. Only Meg and Izzy knew I was home (probably because I never went anywhere) and weren't likely to fall for the drawn blinds and deathly silence.

'You've opened the door,' noted Meg. 'Well done, pet. Small steps.'

I thought she was referring to the front door which I'd just opened, but she was looking past me, down the hallway, at the bedroom door.

It had felt like a pretty large step to me and one I wasn't keen to repeat.

As we sat down in the living room with a cup of tea, Meg started on her tirade of reason, advice and annoying attempts to make me look on the bright side.

'At least he wasn't cheating with a woman,' she sighed, having already said this to me several times before. For some reason she thought the revelation that Gus was cheating with a man should be easier for me to stomach.

But it wasn't. To me it meant our whole marriage had been a sham, that all our hopes and dreams and plans had been nothing more than small-talk.

'There's no way you can compete with a man,' added Meg. 'Nothing to be jealous of.'

But I was jealous. Yes, I was. Jealous of the intimacy that Gus and Dan shared, jealous of the fact that I'd lost my best friend in the world, the person who knew me better than anyone else, and jealous of the fact they had each other, while I had no one. I was insanely jealous.

Thankfully, Izzy arrived to save me from Meg's well-meaning but profoundly irritating words.

'I just got hit on by a preacher,' she said, plonking herself down on the sofa. 'Seriously,' she said, as Meg and I stared back at her.

'This guy comes in all the time for chest waxes and facials, even manicures. And so many sunbeds he looks like a tangerine. Anyway, he's always flirting with me, and today he asked what time I finished and if I'd like to go for a drink. God, he's revolting! His hair's got so much product in it that it feels like a slab of concrete. And the worst thing is I know for a fact he's got a family. When he first started coming in for treatments he tried to convince me to come along to one of his sermons, and said he could get me on telly.

'Think I'm gonna flick him on,' she continued. 'I can't stand him any more.'

'Maybe he was just being friendly,' suggested Meg.

'Yeah,' replied Izzy, sarcasm hanging from her words. 'He invited his wife and kids out for a drink with us, too.'

'I can't imagine Joe ever cheating,' said Meg, choosing to ignore Izzy and switching the conversation back to her. Joe was her husband. Tact had never been Meg's strong suit.

'And do you think Kat ever imagined that Gus would?' said Izzy, staring at her.

'Well . . . no . . .' replied Meg. '. . . that's not what I meant.'

'What did you mean?' asked Izzy.

'Well . . . I know Joe would never cheat with a man.'

'And how the fuck do you know that?' cried Izzy, losing her patience with Meg, which never took very long.

'I just know,' replied Meg.

'Just like Kat *knew* Gus would never cheat with a man?' said Izzy.

'Well . . . I never said . . .'

I sat on the sofa, tuning out the argumentative banter and glad I was being left alone.

'How was your date?' I asked Izzy, changing the

subject five minutes later, when it was obvious they weren't going to stop arguing about whether you'd know if your husband was gay and cheating on you or not.

Izzy had recently begun frequenting internet-dating sites in search of The One. Actually, it was fair to say she was addicted to internet dating. It's no small wonder that her fingertips hadn't fallen off with all the typing she'd been doing.

It's the perfect way to meet men, she'd say, when I questioned her sanity. You can safely vet them without the haze of a foggy bar and one too many vodka and tonics blinding your judgement.

It was almost as though she was addicted to the thrill of the chase. 'One day I'll strike gold,' she'd tell me. Though all she'd struck so far had been several bits of tin.

I was surprised she was willing to go on dates at all after the series of disasters she'd experienced. Number one was the Bed Wetter. She'd been out for a boozy night with a bloke she'd met through friends, one thing had led to another and she'd woken up at his place the next morning, both with ground-breaking hangovers and . . . a wet bed. She knew it wasn't her, which left only him, but he acted mortified and shouted and screamed about his flatmate's dog continuously choosing his bed to relieve itself on. Izzy had been completely repulsed by the thought of the dog weeing on the bed while she was asleep, but was at least pleased it wasn't her date. That was until she went out with him again and he stayed at her place, where she woke up with a damp leg again. Izzy didn't have a dog.

'It was ghastly,' replied Izzy, snapping me back to the present. 'His cue cards spilled all over the floor of the restaurant.'

'His what?'

'His cue cards. He'd written himself cue cards for our date and had them sitting on his lap. When we were leaving, he stood up and they spilled all over the floor.'

'Why did he have cue cards?' I asked.

'I have no idea. Because he was nervous and he'd forget what questions to ask, I guess. It would have been fine,' she added, 'if only he'd waited for me to finish my reply before asking me the next question.'

'Did you help him pick them up?'

'I had to, there were about twenty of the bloody things. The waitress picked up a few too.'

'You know, it's kinda cute,' said Meg.

At which point both Izzy and I looked at her as though she were completely bonkers. Which, to be perfectly honest, she was most of the time. There was nothing cute about a grown man who needed his conversation prompted by bits of cardboard.

Jools

For eight hours of the day, when I was sleeping, I felt fine. But for the other sixteen hours, when I was awake, I felt sick as a dog — an old dog that was not only on its death-bed, having contracted every canine disease imaginable, but was also unfortunate enough to have had its dog biscuits spiked with a fresh crop of salmonella the night before.

'Gonna throw,' I said to Francie, as another wave of nausea engulfed me and I levered myself from the couch and high-speed-hobbled to the bathroom.

'*Again*? But you've only just sat down.'

Our conversations used to be interrupted by our mobile phones, pausing to ingest food or alcohol or to appreciate a foxy man, or seeing an item of clothing or footwear we simply had to have. Now they were interrupted on a regular basis by me hobbling for the toilet and throwing up.

'So . . .' said Francie, as I leant my crutches against the side of the sofa and sat back down, '. . . as I was saying, he had the most beautiful hands I've ever seen, for a man. Exquisite.'

Francie had developed a severe crush on another hand model she'd been in an advertisement with.

'All tanned and smooth . . . impeccable cuticles and nails . . . just the right length.'

'What did he look like?' I asked. It was common knowledge that you didn't have to have a top-class face or body to be a successful hand model. Although Francie was one of those annoying women who had the whole package.

In between the relentless bouts of nausea, it became evident to me that I had to make up my mind, and soon. If I wasn't going to keep the baby then I had an appointment to make.

'I've decided,' I said to Francie, as we sat on her couch eating pizza and watching *Friends* reruns.

'*And?*' she replied, turning to me, eyes wide, respectfully holding the slice of pizza away from her mouth.

'I'm going to keep it.'

'Hurrah!' cried Francie, jumping up and throwing her arms around me. 'That's great news, babe! I can't believe it! You're going to be a mummy! A *mummy!* A yummy mummy!'

'Hell's bells,' I replied. 'Who would've thought?'

'I think I'm going to cry,' said Francie, as a tear slid down her cheek.

Now that I'd decided to keep the baby, it was only fitting to find out the identity of its father. I scheduled a blood test for the following morning.

When the following morning rolled around, I couldn't help but be nervous as all hell. I was nervous because there was a very real possibility the baby was Gary's. I would far rather it was Tom's. The thought that I might have a child who'd grow up to be as shallow and callous as Gary scared the bejesus out of me.

I sat in my doctor's office, the blood-test results sitting on his desk. This was all I was waiting for; he'd already checked my belly and blood pressure, declaring me fit and well.

The conception date is on this printout,' he said, handing me the piece of paper.

I refrained from looking at it until I was safely back in my car and out of earshot. If that date coincided with Gary, my piercing scream would surely alarm my doctor.

Nervously I unfolded the piece of paper and read the line at the top. *Date of conception: 22 February.*

I read it again, just to be sure.

'Well?' asked Francie, bursting through my front door at six o'clock, desperation in her voice. 'Tell me! Whose is it?'

'It's . . .'

'Yesss?'

I felt my voice breaking, betraying me.

'. . . it's not Gary's.'

I felt yet another tear of relief slide down my cheek.

'Oh, thank God! So it's the bloke from the pub?' she gushed.

Exactly how many men did she think I'd slept with recently?

'Yes,' I sighed. 'The bloke from the pub.'

'What's his name again?'

'Tom.'

'Wow. Hallelujah to that!'

I was relieved beyond belief. The prospect of being intrinsically tied to Gary the Bastard for the rest of my life had been terrifying.

'So the condom broke?' asked Francie. 'What are the chances?'

Actually the chances were even slimmer than that,

because, if my memory served me correctly the condom hadn't in fact broken, it just hadn't worked. And the chance of that, if you believed the statistics on the packet, was one per cent, i.e. not much of a fucking chance at all. How ironic that a condom had failed for me, of all people. It was lucky I wasn't still working at Sure & Pure; it would have been very difficult to keep my dedication to the product under the circumstances.

The next day the cast was finally removed from my left leg, exactly six weeks after it had been put on. A lot had happened in those six weeks. I had ended my affair with my married boss, I'd been fired, I'd had a one-night stand with a stranger I'd met in an Irish pub, and I was up the duff. My life was moving at a faster rate of knots than a *Shortland Street* script.

Nonetheless I was ecstatic to get rid of the cast. As ecstatic as a recently unemployed up-and-coming solo parent could be. If anything, it would make my job of running to the toilet to be ill several times a day that much easier. I was so happy, even the fact that my leg now resembled a KFC chicken drumstick that's been bleached white and left sitting in the bottom of the fridge for a couple of weeks didn't bother me.

'Let's celebrate,' said Francie, who had kindly driven me to the hospital for the removal.

Celebrating was a funny thing when it didn't involve the consumption of copious amounts of alcohol. It sort of plunged a couple of notches in my book. Francie managed to convince me that half a glass of bubbles wasn't going to kill the baby, but not having half a glass of bubbles was sure to kill me. I didn't take much convincing. Only the bubbles tasted terrible, much more like methylated spirits than wine. So I handed it back to the waiter and ordered another one, which tasted even worse. And then another one.

At this point he took a swig of the bubbles himself and said, 'Do you think there might be a little problem with your taste buds, madam?'

I ended up drinking sparkling water instead, which tasted exactly as it should.

Now that I didn't look quite so much like I'd been run over by a stray lorry, it was time for me to find myself a job. And some money. I could now leave the confines of my apartment without the aid of crutches and with only a slight limp. So, in between the waves of nausea which still engulfed me on a daily basis, I applied for jobs.

During my confinement an unexplainable phenom-enon had occurred. There were pregnant women all over the city. Every-bloody-where! It was like going out in public only to find a busload of people wearing the same frock as you. Or buying a new car and suddenly that particular model was the most popular one on the road. And babies — they were *everywhere* too. Small ones, big ones, bald ones, smiling ones, screaming ones. I'd never noticed them before. I'd just hustled past the pushchairs, cursing them for being so bloody enormous and wheeled at such a snail-like pace, and for taking up the entire width of the elevator/escalator/footpath.

I'd never glanced inside the pushchairs to see what might be lurking within. But now, oddly, I found myself looking, staring in fact. I couldn't help myself. It was only when the pusher abruptly turned it out of my path and glared at me with a mixture of pity and fuck-off-you-weirdo-baby-napper that I managed to look away. Sometimes what I saw was cute and smiley and well-dressed. Other times it looked as though it'd been given a good beating with the ugly stick, before being rolled in jam and snot and cruelly attacked with a red felt-tip. I also found myself smiling at other pregnant women, until they, too, took a step the other way and walked briskly past me. I'm not showing yet, I consoled myself; they aren't to know.

I was continually ravenous — if I didn't eat, I would self-combust. It was as simple as that. Any hint of social nicety would transform into impatient rudeness. Francie had quickly come to recognize what she called The Look. According to her, my eyes would firstly begin to glaze over, before beginning to ressemble a rabid dog. My shoulders would then sag and my body would appear to have had the life sucked out of it, with any pitiful scraps of remaining energy joining forces just long enough to hurl abuse at her. All this would happen within the space of about sixty seconds.

'Food *now*,' she would say, grabbing my arm and frog-marching me into the nearest café if we were out, or ice-skating across the floor to the fridge or pantry if we were at home. So perceptive was she to The Look that she had even started keeping snacks for me in her handbag. I think she was scared that if she didn't get me food, and pronto, I would start chewing on her arm, which was a justifiable concern.

And without consent, my bladder had metamorphosed into a kitchen sieve, unable to contain even half a glass of water for more than five minutes. I used to have an iron bladder, with the enviable ability to hold on in a rough-terrain car trip for at least two hours. There was no holding on now. The feeling went from slight pressure to *must go now* in the space of ten seconds. But at least I haven't lost control of my bladder yet, I consoled myself, after hearing pregnancy knicker-wetting horror stories. This pleasure was yet to come. I spent so much time on the loo that Francie had taken to following me in so we could continue our conversation.

'Is that it?' she'd ask, dismayed, as my pathetic two-second dribble came to a conclusion.

'Yep,' I'd reply. 'That's it.'

'But I thought you were busting?'

'I was. And I'll be busting again in another ten minutes.'

In between vomiting, staring at other pregnant women and at babies, eating and peeing, I earnestly searched for a job. Well, as earnestly as my current state would allow. What I wanted was a six-month contract, so I could finish up a month or so before the baby was born. But do you think I could find one? According to the ten or so recruitment agencies I met with, there was an unprecedented glut of brand managers, all looking for contract work. The best position on offer was a three-month contract with a toilet-paper company. A *toilet-paper company*. And this was without mentioning I was pregnant.

'At least it's in the same family as condoms,' said Francie, trying to put a rosy glow on the fact that I'd be spending the next three months up to my ears in poo tickets.

I wondered what I would do when the contract finished. How would I pay the mortgage on my apartment? Even if I took only three months off work to have the baby, I still wasn't entirely sure I'd be able to support myself.

'Something will come up,' said Francie, 'you'll see.'

But I wasn't so certain. Unless I miraculously stumbled across an available wealthy single bloke, who was desperate to get it on with a pregnant woman and father someone else's baby, or I won Lotto, it looked as though I'd be taking my fat ankles and belly onto the streets.

Sally

'I need to take a business trip,' announced Vincent, as he undressed, put on his maroon silk pyjamas, and climbed into bed beside me.

I put the book I was reading down on my chest.

'Where to?' I asked.

'Los Angeles . . . and the Dominican Republic.'

'*What! Why?*'

'For personal development,' he replied. 'And to build some networks. I'll be visiting some churches and meeting with Elvin and other pastors while I'm there.'

'I had no idea LA was a hub of Christianity,' I replied.

'You'd be surprised,' said Vincent. Perhaps I would.

'When are you going?' I asked.

'In a month's time, for two weeks.'

'And may I ask how you're paying for this trip?'

I hated to sound like a nagging fishwife, but the truth was we simply couldn't afford for Vincent to take a big trip like this, not with the way things were at the moment.

'Don't worry, Sally,' he assured me. 'The church is paying.'

'You mean the congregation is paying?' I corrected him.

'Well, the trip will be funded by the church and, yes,

some of the money will come from donations made by our congregation.'

Some of it? It was the unwritten rule of Divinity Church that to be part of the congregation you 'donated' ten per cent of your weekly income to the church. The small print read *if you can afford it the donation would be greatly appreciated by your church*, but it was unlikely to be a startling coincidence that those families who didn't make the 'donation' were no longer part of the congregation. They weren't exactly turfed out of the church on Sunday morning by a pair of burly bodyguards, just slowly ostracized and no longer made welcome.

For some reason our family was exempt from making the weekly 'donation'.

'I presume it won't be a family trip?' I asked.

'Not this time, Sally. Next time, I promise.'

But that was bullshit. The only business trips he'd ever taken the kids and me on were to Tokoroa (twice), Gore and Whangarei. Oh, and Christchurch, where the children and I had all come down with a vomiting bug and had spent three days shut in the hotel room tag-teaming the toilet bowl, while Vincent attended meetings, lunches and dinners and miraculously managed to avoid getting sick. This was probably because he'd checked himself into a separate suite because 'there's no point in all of us going down if it can be helped'. The children, who had been looking forward the plane ride and holiday, were devastated. Vincent had been quick to promise their dejected little faces that he would take them back in six months' time. That had been four years ago.

Why don't *you* take them? I asked myself. Whether he wants us to come or not. In fact, perhaps I could take them while he went on his business trip.

However, it appeared a few days later that there were

other reasons for his trip aside from 'business'.

'Hello,' I said, answering the phone as I prepared dinner.

'Hel-lo,' replied a thick American accent. 'Would Mr Vincent Sull-i-van be available, please?'

'I'm afraid he's not home yet,' I replied. 'Can I take a message? I'm his wife.'

'Well sure, OK then,' said The Accent. 'This is Dr Rader's assistant speaking, from the Lifespan Clinic. I'm just confirming that we've received payment from Mr Sullivan and that his initial consultation is confirmed for September fourth at our clinic here in Los Angeles, with his treatment confirmed for September eighth at our resort in the Dominican Republic.'

Treatment?

'And can you just remind me what treatment that is for again?' I asked.

'Well . . . for the stem-cell therapy,' replied The Accent.

The *what* therapy?

'We're just so pleased we've had the cancellation and can fit Mr Sullivan in,' he continued. 'Usually the wait's about six months at least, it's so popular.'

'Thank you,' I replied. 'I'll be sure to pass on the message.'

'I'd be most grateful,' replied The Accent.

What the hell was Vincent up to? I wondered. Stem-cell therapy? Wasn't that something to do with trying to conceive a child? He had three already whom he hardly saw.

But as I discovered approximately three minutes later, as I sat in his study and googled *stem-cell therapy*, it appeared that he wasn't about to undergo treatment to conceive a child. Instead he was going to have the cells of six- to twelve-week-old aborted foetuses injected into his thighs, buttocks and stomach, all in the name of anti-ageing.

'God above!' I cried, aware that I was guilty of blaspheming but deciding that the situation warranted it. *Surely not?* This time he really had gone too far. Way, way too far!

I opened up several links, plunging even further into despair as I read what appeared on the screen

> *Foetal tissue has been shown to be highly rich in regenerative stem cells which, when injected into adults, helps the body fight the ageing process . . .*
>
> *More than fifty clinics have sprung up in Moscow over the past three years to meet the demands of wealthy Russians and Westerners alike who flock to the global capital of cosmetic stem-cell therapy . . .*
>
> *Evidence gathered by Moscow police has shown a growing black market in aborted foetuses, which are smuggled into Russia from Ukraine and Georgia . . .*
>
> *Here, poverty-stricken young women are paid two hundred US dollars to carry babies up to the optimum eight- to twelve-week period, thought to be best for harvesting stem cells . . .*
>
> *They are then sold to cosmetic clinics . . .*

And then I opened the Lifespan Clinic homepage.

> *Treatments start at twenty thousand dollars.*

Twenty thousand dollars! Jesus and God and Mary and Joseph, what the hell was he up to?

Still in shock, I printed out several pages. I'll highlight the appalling bits (of which there were many) and jam them under his nose when he gets home, I decided. And demand an explanation.

But he has paid for it already, I remembered. Twenty thousand US dollars! That was . . . I grabbed the calculator and tapped in some numbers . . . that was . . . over thirty thousand dollars! Thirty thousand dollars! We didn't have thirty thousand dollars! Where on earth had he got the money from?

I looked at my watch. He would be home shortly.

My body ached to confront him. I couldn't be sure that it wasn't aching to stab him to death as well, judging by the way my knuckles were turning white as my hand gripped the arm of the chair.

I decided that, in light of this, I couldn't stay in the house. I needed to get outside in the fresh air. I needed a drink.

'I'm just nipping out for a walk, love,' I called out to Davey, as calmly as I could, popping my head into the living room. 'Can you mind the girls? I won't be long.'

'OK, Mum,' he replied. His eyes remained locked on whatever reality-TV rubbish he was watching.

I walked as fast as I could to the nearest drinking hole, three streets away, which happened to be a crowded RSA. I ordered a vodka and tonic (a wine wasn't going to cut it in the present circumstances) and sat down at a small table in the corner, one of the only ones left.

It was bingo night, which meant that all the old people who lived within a ten-mile radius were currently sitting inside, clutching their bingo cards and pens.

'Lucky number three!' called out the grey-haired

man with matching grey moustache, standing beside the bar, microphone in hand.

There was a flurry of hands, pens and paper as all the oldies checked their cards.

I was glad for the distraction as I drank my vodka. I ordered another.

'Lucky number eleven!'

'Bingo!' came a cry from a tiny purple-haired woman at a table to my left. She stood up and waved her card about her head, just in case the man hadn't heard her.

'We have a bingo!'

Within minutes, she was up the front collecting her winnings and meat pack as the rest of the gamblers gave her a round of applause.

I found myself smiling. They might be gambling — which was, according to Vincent, a 'mortal sin' — but they were having a thoroughly good time doing it.

'You in for the next round, love?' asked the grey moustache, as he approached my table.

'Sure,' I replied, taking a card from him and handing over two dollars. 'Why not?'

If Vincent could spend thirty thousand dollars having the cells of aborted foetuses injected into his buttocks, then surely I could blow two dollars on a round of bingo?

I ordered myself another vodka and a pint of lager for the old boy at the table next to me.

'Thanks, luvvie, you're a real sweetie. Give my card a wee kiss for me, will you?' he asked, passing me his bingo card. I obliged and planted my lips against the card.

'I know I'll be winning now,' he winked at me.

And he did. Collecting a cool hundred-and-twenty-two dollars. And a meat pack.

'I don't bloody believe it!' he cried. 'I've never won anything in me whole life.'

He tried to give me half his winnings, but I was having none of it.

'Well, I'm buying your drinks then!' he said, coming back with two more vodka and tonics and placing them on my table.

'Another round?' asked the grey moustache.

'Abo-bloody-lutely,' said the old boy, whose name was Reg, buying two cards for each of us.

I think he meant to say absolutely, but it seemed the pints of lager were taking effect. Not that I could talk; I was on my fourth vodka and feeling a little blurry around the edges, which felt strangely lovely.

I kissed his cards again. And then I made him kiss mine.

'Lucky number twenty-six!' called the moustache.

'Lucky number nine!'

I glanced across at Reg's pen, furiously circling numbers on his card. His hand movements were making me dizzy.

A few more lucky numbers later, we had a winner.

'Bingo!' shouted Reg, standing up from my table, where he was now sitting, and waving his card about.

Again? Surely not?

I looked down at my cards, on which I'd only managed to circle two numbers each.

'Un-bloody-leivable!' he cried, giving me a kiss on the cheek.

He walked to the front of the bar to collect his winnings of one-hundred-and-sixty-four dollars, and another meat pack, smiling like a banshee. The round of applause from the bar was somewhat lacklustre this time, as everyone considered just how bloody lucky he was and why couldn't they win a round for once?

The kids! I suddenly thought, looking at my watch and realizing I'd been gone for an hour and a half.

Vincent will be home by now, I reminded myself. They'll be fine.

'I've got to go,' I said to Reg, standing up from the table. 'I've left my kids at home.'

'You can't!' he cried, grabbing my arm and sitting me back down. 'You're my lucky charm, you can't leave! There's only two more rounds to go!'

He jumped up to the bar, bringing back two more vodkas and placing them down on the table in front of me to prove his point.

Of course Vincent will be home, I consoled myself, taking another gulp of vodka.

Reg didn't win the remaining two rounds, which was just as well because I'd a feeling he'd have been lynched by the rest of the oldies if he had. Winning one round was lucky, winning two in a row was unheard of, winning three would have had them crying *rigged!*, demanding their gold coins back and storming the bar.

Two and a half hours after leaving for my walk, I arrived back home, drunk and clutching a meat pack which Reg had insisted I take, after making me promise to come back the following Tuesday night.

'Where have you been?' asked Vincent, as I stumbled into the kitchen and plonked the meat pack down on the bench. It looked as though the children were in bed.

'Out,' I replied.

'What's that?'

'A meat pack.'

'You left the kids alone, Sally,' he said, giving me a very serious you-are-the-most-irresponsible-mother look. I hated it when he looked at me like that.

'I didn't know I was going to be gone this long. Anyway, Davey is thirteen, Vincent. It's legal.'

'Fourteen is legal, Sally.'

'Well, he'll be fourteen in two months,' I sighed. 'Close enough.'

'Have you been drinking?' he asked, his look evolving from grave to disapproving.

'Yes,' I replied. 'And playing bingo. At the pub.'

I had nothing to hide; I wasn't about to be injected with human foetuses.

'Sally, this is very frightening behaviour. What on earth has come over you?'

'No, Vincent,' I replied, pulling the sheets of paper from my handbag and slamming them down on the table in front of him. 'What's come over *you?* Frightening behaviour is paying thirty thousand dollars to have your bottom injected with the foetuses of human babies, which some poor girl in Russia has been paid to abort for two hundred dollars. All so you can look ten years younger.'

He looked back at me, stunned.

'The clinic phoned, Vincent. The clinic in Los Angeles where you're going in two weeks? Before you fly to the resort in the Dominican Republic? To say they've received your payment and it's all hunky-dory. Foetuses good to go.'

'Sally—'

'Don't pretend you don't know what I'm talking about! Or that it was another Vincent Sullivan they were after! Just tell me,' I spat, 'how the hell you paid for it. And don't lie,' I added.

He took a moment to collect himself, and in that moment I could see his brain churning through the pros and cons of being honest, tossing them around his head like Lotto balls. The pro balls were drawn, but only just.

The treatment was costing thirty-two thousand dollars. Half of that was being paid for from the church fund under the guise of 'professional development'. The other half he had paid for by cashing in a good portion of our superannuation scheme.

'You *what?*' I cried.

'Hang on a minute, Sally,' he soothed. 'Don't blow this out of proportion. I've only borrowed the money. I'll pay it back.'

'*Borrowed?* How will you pay it back? By taking more money from the pockets of the congregation? By cashing in the children's life-insurance policies? What the hell is wrong with you, Vincent?'

'Sally, it's a proven breakthrough in cosmetic treatment,' he replied, as though this revelation was going to make me fine and dandy with the fact he'd just spent thirty thousand dollars on cosmetic surgery, and wish him a happy holiday.

'A *breakthrough?* It's a complete disgrace against humanity, Vincent! That's what it is! And do you honestly think the congregation would be so supportive if they knew what you were spending their money on?'

'They won't know.'

I stared back at him, completely speechless. At exactly what point had he become so completely selfish and self-obsessed?

'Does it bother you, Vincent, that you are going about blatantly ripping off innocent people?' I asked.

'Sally, I'm not ripping them off. They want to give to the church. They need to give to the church. Everyone needs to give, it makes them feel like a better person.'

'And how much do you give?' I asked.

'A lot, Sally. I give my time and guidance, lots of it.

103

And I give the word of Jesus.'

It suddenly occurred to me that he didn't just see himself as a messenger of God. There was a part of him that thought he actually *was* God. A rather large part.

I felt a guttural groan escape my lips as I leaned on the table and stared at him. The vodka pulsing through my body gave me the confidence to stare at him for a full minute before saying anything.

'Vincent,' I said, still looking him directly in the eyes, 'you are full of shit. I am going to bed.'

'You'd better drink some water, Sally,' he called after me. 'To get that Devil's juice out of your system.'

I briefly contemplated turning around and giving him the finger, but I kept walking. My head was pounding and I had a strong urge to get my body horizontal.

He slept in the lounge on the sofa-bed that night. I'd hoped it was because he felt remorseful for what he'd done, but something told me it was probably more to do with the fact I'd been drinking and playing bingo.

Kat

Two months had passed since The Incident and I had no choice but to meet with him. I'd been avoiding his numerous telephone calls and messages, but I couldn't avoid talking to him for the rest of my life. He was my husband, after all. So on Thursday night, after work, I arranged to meet him at home. Our home. As I didn't go out anymore, it was a convenient place to meet.

I was sitting on the sofa when I heard him walk up the couple of steps to the front door and then pause. It appeared he didn't know whether to knock or use his key. He opted for knocking. I opened the front door and there he was. He looked like the same old Gus, my husband, only terrified. The last time I'd seen him he'd been completely naked and . . . *oh God* . . . there goes that bloody image again.

I took one look at him and walked back into the living room.

'Kat . . . I . . .' he said, walking behind me.

I stopped in my tracks, turned and stared at him. If he thought I was going to make this easy for him he was severely mistaken.

'. . . I'm so sorry,' he finished.

'Sorry you were fucking Dan, our friend? Or sorry that I caught you?' I asked. I had quickly decided to make this as difficult for him as possible. It was the very least I could do.

105

'Both,' he replied, meekly.

'That should make me feel better, Gus, but it just doesn't,' I spat, two months' worth of anger firing from my lips. 'Not one fucking bit! How the hell could you *do* this to me?'

'I'm sorry, Kat,' he said again, shaking his head. 'I'm so . . . sorry.' It seemed to be the only word he was capable of saying.

'*Sorry*, Gus, is finding your husband *fucking* another man in your bed. *That* is *sorry.*'

He hung his head. I felt a burning urge to take it and smash it repeatedly against the mantelpiece.

'Why?' I asked. 'Just tell me *why?*'

It was the one question I knew there was no simple answer to. The one question I had to ask.

'Oh, Kat . . .' he sighed, sitting down on the other sofa, either not realizing or not caring that it was now in an entirely different position in the room. 'I don't know.'

Well, fuck it, I wanted to know. He was my husband and I wanted to know what the hell was going on with him. What was happening to *Us*. As furious as I was, I still hoped the whole thing had been a oncer, as Izzy had said. A one-off terrible mistake for which he was about to beg my forgiveness, and with a bit of therapy and lots of talking we'd be able to get over eventually and carry on as normal.

'Dan wants to see you,' said Gus, changing the subject.

'Good for him,' I replied. 'But I don't think that'll be happening any time soon.'

'He's so sorry,' said Gus. 'He feels terrible.'

'What are you?' I asked. 'His spokesperson?'

He looked back at me, an odd look on his face, but said nothing.

'Hang on . . .' I said, stalling as my brain caught up with my mouth. 'Wait a minute . . . you're seeing him, aren't you? You're *seeing* Dan!'

As soon as the words escaped my mouth, I prayed to God they weren't true. Gus shrank so far back into the sofa he all but disappeared.

'You are!' I cried. 'You bloody well are!'

'Yes,' he finally replied, ever so softly. So softly I could barely make out the word.

'Mother of God!' I exclaimed, throwing my hands to my forehead. And then, 'What the *hell* have I done to deserve this?'

'It's not your fault, Kat,' beseeched Gus, standing up and walking towards me, his hands resting on my shoulders. 'It's my fault, not yours.'

'Damn straight it is!' I spat in his face.

I had no desire to know the answer, none whatsoever, but still as tears ran down my cheeks my traitor of a mouth asked the question. 'Do you . . . *love* . . . him?'

There was a silence that could have filled ten wine barrels, ten times over, as I watched his eyes plead with me to ask him anything else. Anything but that.

'Yes,' he replied, his voice a whisper. 'I do . . . I'm so sorry.'

Fuck me days. There it was, ladies and gentlemen. The final bombshell. The crowd pleaser. My husband was in love with a man. A *man*. My *husband*. Just as sure as there are no locks on public-toilet doors.

He was *leaving* me for *a man*. The fact I'd kicked him out was irrelevant. As I said, I still held out a fair whack of hope that he'd simply been *experimenting* and we could work through it. That one day it would simply be *that thing in the past* that we did our very best never to bring up ever again.

The sex was one thing, but here they were, in love. *In love.*

How had it all gone so terribly wrong?

'I love you Kat . . . more than anyone,' continued Gus, uttering the only sensible words to have come out of his mouth all night. 'I always will. But I'm in love with Dan,' he continued, smashing any remaining glimmer of hope to smithereens. 'I can't help it.'

He looked truly pathetic, almost as though he wanted me to feel sorry for him being in love with Dan. Well he could get fucked. I was far, far too busy feeling sorry for myself. It was a full-time job, with overtime.

There were so many questions I didn't want to hear the answers to, but I just had to ask. I sat back down on the sofa to prepare myself.

'How long have you been sleeping with him?' I asked.

I didn't catch his answer, due to the fact he had coughed at the same time.

'Pardon?'

He repeated himself, eventually.

'A *year!*' I shouted. 'How could I not have known?' I asked, more to myself than to him.

'It wasn't your job to work it out, Kat,' he answered.

'How could you not have told me?' I glared at him. '*How?*'

'I don't know,' he replied, hanging his head again. 'I thought it was just a fling. That it would go away . . . that I could make it go away. I honestly didn't mean for this to happen, Kat, really I didn't.'

He raked his hands through his hair. He was crying now.

I looked away.

'I feel like an idiot,' I said to no one in particular. 'All

108

this time I was thinking we would be together forever. That we'd be having a baby soon.'

'Oh, Kat,' he sighed. 'I wanted that, too, *please* believe me. More than *anything*. I wish to God I didn't feel this way. I wish that things could stay the same.'

'Has there been anyone else?' I asked.

Please God, let the answer be no, I prayed. There really was only so much a girl could take.

'No,' he replied, although I wasn't sure I believed him.

'Where are you going to live?' I asked. If he thought I was going to move after what he'd put me through, he was dreaming.

I watched as his eyes darted to the floor.

'You're going to move in with *him*, aren't you?' I hissed.

'I'm going to stay with him for a few weeks, Kat. Just a few weeks, until I find a place of my own.'

I thought he'd been staying with his sister for the past couple of months, but I bet he bloody well hadn't. I bet he'd been staying with *him*. Straight from the marital home into the gay love-nest. It was a wonder he hadn't left skid marks on the front doormat.

Oh no, I thought in horror. It had happened. They were going to be the gay couple who everyone wanted to have at their dinner party. I was going to be the single woman who was invited along only if they needed to make up numbers.

One minute I was happily married, or so I thought, with a baby on the horizon. The next I was single and husbandless. And, let's not forget, childless. My clock had been ticking for the past couple of years, loudly, and now it was lying in tiny, broken pieces on the floor. The fury was all-encompassing.

How dare he? I thought. How dare he ruin my life like this?

The bastard.

Gus gathered a few of his personal belongings together and said goodbye. There were other things we needed to discuss, practical things, like finances and possessions, so many things which entwined us. But now wasn't the time.

'Let's speak soon,' he said, trying to pull me into a hug.

There was a strange unexplainable part of me that wished I didn't know. That wished I hadn't walked in on the two of them and could go on naïvely believing everything was fine. What I didn't know wouldn't have hurt me, right?

Why couldn't he have come out five years earlier? I wondered. Hell, even two years?

I was thirty-five years old. What chance did I have of finding another man I wanted to breed with now? No fucking chance, that's what sort of chance I had. I was going to be a childless spinster rattling around in her large, renovated family home until the end of her days.

I hated him. I hated him for making me believe we would be together forever. For making me believe we would have a family. I hated him for ruining my life.

I was so busy hating Gus that it took a while for my hate towards Dan to settle in. But when it did, it engulfed me like a blizzard. In some ways it was worse. It wasn't uncommon for husbands to cheat (cheating with another man the exception here, obviously), but Dan had been one of my closest friends for nearly fifteen years. Dan who I'd given dating advice to; Dan who I'd vainly tried to match with every attractive single woman I'd ever met; Dan who came around for dinner once a week; Dan who spent every holiday with us. Dan who was like a brother to me. What kind of brother does this to his sister? It hurt. Badly. It was a new, fresh hurt, different from the hurt of being betrayed, lied to and deserted by my husband. And instead of the two combining to make one hideous feeling, they sort of piled on top of each other, each causing me as much grief as the other. I would have done anything for Dan. How foolish I had been.

My life had been trucking along so perfectly, so according to plan. But really I'd just been standing on a rug which had been cruelly whipped out from under my feet, leaving me lying in a heap on the cold wooden floorboards — badly polished ones at that.

Jools

The first week of my new job was horrific. I spent more time in the bathroom or running for the bathroom than I did sitting at my desk.

'Food poisoning,' I said, to my very understanding, slightly alarmed and very naïve new boss. There was no need for her to know I was up the duff. Not yet.

'Poor thing,' she said, passing me glasses of water.

'Anything to eat?' she'd ask as she headed out for lunch.

'No thanks,' I'd reply. 'Not today.'

The only things I could stomach, still, were dry, un-buttered toast and potatoes.

Thankfully, by the beginning of the following week, the constant sickness began to subside. I was twelve weeks pregnant. I felt as though the boat had finally docked and I was standing on dry land for the first time in months.

But just as I began to feel normal and healthy once again, I received a peace-shattering phone call.

'Jools,' said a man's voice, a fairly familiar one.

I cringed in my chocolate-suede knee-high boots.

It was Him. *Him.* What the hell did *he* want?

I'd been hoping he'd been stabbed to death by a pink tutu-wearing frothy-mouthed intruder. Unfortunately, it appeared he hadn't.

'How are you?' he asked.

'Fine,' I replied. If he thought he was going to get more than one syllable out of me, he was sadly mistaken.

'I've heard you're pregnant.'

'You heard right.'

Three syllables. I was slipping.

'Why didn't you tell me?'

Unfortunately this was going to require a few more syllables.

'Two reasons. Firstly, in case you hadn't noticed, I don't actually speak to you any more. And secondly, because it's not yours.'

'C'mon, Jools . . . I know this must be a shock for you and you're probably incredibly tired . . . but we both know this baby is mine.'

'Gary,' I replied, somehow managing to turn my teeth into a set of sharp Arctic icicles. 'I know you have *assumed* the baby is yours, and that it would be *impossible* for you to comprehend the fact that another man's penis had come within ten metres of my vagina. But it did and the baby is his. *Not* yours.'

For the first time in his life, he was speechless.

'B-b-but . . .'

'No buts, Gary,' I cut him off. 'End of story. Goodbye.'

I slammed down the phone.

Yes, I was still a little bitter. I probably should have been over it by now, but I wasn't. Not quite. It's not that I'd thought he was going to leave his wife and family and we'd live happily ever after in a tastefully renovated villa in a nice leafy street in suburbia. I'm not delusional. But I did expect him to treat me with a little more respect. A little less like a plastic poncho he'd bought at a rugby match only to throw into the bin on the way out. I hated him. And it felt good.

'Why don't you let him think it's his?' suggested Francie, later that evening.

'Because it's not.'

'But think about the child support you'd receive!' she pointed out.

She had a valid point. No doubt Gary would throw wads of cash at the baby and me throughout our entire lives. Anything to keep both of us under wraps.

If Gary knew I was pregnant, then it was only a matter of time before my parents caught whiff of the news. I was going to have to break it to them before someone else did.

'What are you going to tell them?' asked Francie.

'God knows,' I replied. 'That one morning I woke up and I was pregnant, just like that . . . not a father in sight. Amazing, isn't it!'

'Hmmm . . . might need some work.'

'Guess so,' I sighed.

'How about telling them you were seeing someone for a while and he's the father, but you don't want him to know about the baby because he's a lazy lout who doesn't want kids and you'd rather raise it by yourself?'

'Sounds better,' I agreed.

At seven o'clock that night I sat in my parents' living room, on a sofa covered in apples and peaches. My parents were both recently retired and still lived in our family home, a large old Tudor-style contraption in a leafy station-wagon-driving suburb. My mother was a huge country-theme fan; there were fruit, floral and animal fabrics everywhere you looked. She was also a *big* Debbie Reynolds fan. In fact, it's probably fair to say she was Debbie's number-one fan. If our country had been lucky enough to be home to a Debbie Reynolds fan club, my mother would have been its president, without a doubt. It was only the fact that my mother appeared to be the only (living) Debbie Reynolds fan in the country that stopped her from forming a fan club.

What did my mother, a girl born and raised in Timaru, have in common with America's golden girl?

Well, for starters, she was the spitting image of Debbie, although this was probably because she'd deliberately modelled herself on her. Right down to the same poofed-up strawberry-blonde hair, the same gold-sequined jacket, the same glittering red trouser-suit, the same pewter heels, and the same dangling diamond earrings and rings. (Only my mother's diamond earrings and rings were substantially smaller than Debbie's.) My mother also liked to sing show tunes; and she was fond of uttering those famous words *I can feel a song comin' on* on an annoyingly regular basis.

But that was where the similarities ended. Unlike Debbie, my mother had been married only once. And Dad was not a Hollywood actor, nor a shoe-store magnate, nor a real-estate developer. He was a retired insurance broker who liked nothing better than to tinker in his shed, play golf, and grow random vegetables in his vegetable patch.

I was nervous, to the point of visibly shaking. In any other circumstances I would have been straight to the liquor cabinet plucking up my Dutch courage. It was hard to say what their reaction was going to be. Although they weren't religious, there was still an underlying assumption in our family that marriage would come before children, and that children would be born with two parents.

At least you're not fifteen years old, I consoled myself. It could be worse.

There was no easy way of delivering the news. No humane way for me to soften the blow.

'I'm having a baby,' I announced, smiling over-enthusiastically, rather like a vaudeville actress wearing far too much blusher. I held the vain hope my over-enthusiasm would send them into fits of joyous rapture.

'A *baby?*' asked Mum.

'A *baby?*' repeated Dad.

'Yes,' I replied. 'A baby.'

'Are you sure?' asked Mum.

'Are you sure, love?' repeated Dad.

It was like being subjected to a private audience with Punch and Judy.

'Yes,' I replied. 'Positive.'

'But *how?*' asked Mum.

'Yes, *how?*' said Dad.

Clearly both my parents had either forgotten what it took to make a baby, or thought I was still a virgin. Or that I was unable to get a shag.

'I think you know how,' I replied, hoping to stir some distant memory of the process of conception without physically having to pull out my notepad and draw them a diagram.

'And here I was thinking you'd just put on a bit of weight,' said Mum.

Bloody great, I despaired. I'm barely three months pregnant and I'm getting fat already.

'I sure as blimey didn't think you'd be the one producing our first grandchild!' exclaimed Dad, who never was one to beat around the bush, or any other garden feature for that matter.

You're not the only one, I thought.

I had only one sibling, my brother, Richie. It's fair to say he was the more likely candidate for first to the breeding post, being that he'd been married for five years. I'd been nowhere near the fence as far as Dad was concerned, let alone the post. Richie was married to Lydia, who was, without a shadow of a doubt, one of the most annoying women in the world. Although she was only thirty-three, she seemed far, far older — about sixty-three. A sixty-three-year-old snob, who not only ironed Richie's shirts but also his underwear. Richie's packaging business had done well, and they were consequently very well-off, which Lydia liked to remind everyone about just as often as she could, especially me. She said things like 'You must go to Françoise, they're having the most fabulous sale!', knowing full well that unless they'd taken ninety-five per cent off everything in store there was no chance in hell I'd be able to afford a handkerchief. Yes, it should have been them breeding first, especially as they were currently undergoing their second round of IVF treatment to try to get pregnant. This is only going to make Lydia hate me more, I thought, although it's hardly my fault I'm so bloody fertile.

'Who's the father?' asked Mum.

'Yes, who's the father?' repeated Dad.

Here we go, I thought. The Bombshell.

'He's someone I was seeing—'

'*Was* seeing?' interrupted Mum.

'—but am no longer seeing,' I continued.

'Oh.'

'How long were you seeing him for?' asked Dad.

'Not long,' I replied.

'How long's "not long"?' asked Mum.

'Three months.'

'You're right,' said Dad. 'That isn't long.'

'How come we never met him?' asked Mum, sounding rather put-out that she hadn't been introduced.

'We weren't that close,' I mumbled.

'And are you going to keep it?' asked Mum, voicing the first sensible question of the night.

'Yes,' I replied. 'I am.'

'Well,' she said.

'Well, then,' said Dad.

'And what does the father think?' asked Mum.

Here we go again, I thought. Horrible Confession Time.

'He doesn't know,' I coughed into my hand.

'Pardon?'

'He doesn't know,' I mumbled again, although a little louder this time.

'She said *he doesn't know*,' repeated Mum; obviously Dad hadn't heard me.

'Don't you think he'd want to know he's having a child?' piped up Dad.

Trust him to take the male's point of view.

'Possibly,' I replied. 'But he's not the most together person in the world and he's told me he doesn't want children.'

'Shouldn't you give him the benefit of the doubt, love?' suggested Dad.

Shouldn't you just shut up? I thought.

'Why don't we leave that up to Julia,' suggested Mum, finally taking some pity on me. 'I'm sure she'll do what's best for the baby.'

'Best for a baby to have a mother and a father, I would've thought,' continued Dad, who clearly hadn't finished.

'Where are you going to live?' asked Mum, tactfully changing the subject.

Live? 'In my apartment,' I replied.

'But it's only got one bedroom,' said Mum

This was a fair point and something I hadn't yet considered. Could I not stay in a one-bedroom apartment with a baby? Was it against baby protocol?

I didn't want to move. I loved the apartment I'd bought only two years before. It was the perfect single girl's den.

Not exactly the perfect family home, though, is it? I asked myself.

'You could always move back here, with us,' said Mum, glancing at a very nervous-looking Dad.

'Oh, I don't think so,' I replied, watching the colour return to Dad's cheeks. 'Thanks anyway.'

Living with my parents was precisely the last place I wanted to be. I hadn't spend the first twenty years of my life desperately plotting how to get the hell out, only to wind up back there at the age of thirty-five, single, and with a baby in tow.

Sally

I found myself sitting in the office of Dr Esther Molloy, clinical psychologist, for the second time, as she smiled her lovely, warm smile at me. There was something calming and comforting about her office, although I couldn't pinpoint exactly what. It was more a collaboration of things: big, soft, comfy armchairs, old photographs on the walls, fresh flowers.

I guess it has to be, though, doesn't it? I thought. Perhaps there was some sort of calming air freshener made especially for shrinks' offices.

'How are you, Sally?' asked Esther.

'OK,' I replied, smiling back at her.

'What have you been up to since I saw you last?'

I filled her in on my job and the children — then told her about Vincent blowing our retirement savings on his 'business trip'.

'Did it upset you that Vincent spent this money without asking you?' Esther asked.

'Of course it did!' I replied. 'It was our money, money both of us had saved, and he's spent it to have aborted foetuses injected into his skin.'

I'd decided there was no point in sparing Esther any sordid details; surely with her credentials she'd know if I wasn't telling her the whole truth, and nothing but.

'It does seem an unusual thing for someone . . .

especially a man . . . to be spending their retirement savings on,' she agreed. 'Have you resolved these feeling with him?'

'No, he sees absolutely nothing wrong with what he's done, which makes it a little tricky to discuss.'

'What's annoyed you the most about Vincent's actions?' asked Esther.

'Aside from the fact that he's blown our savings?' I replied.

'Yes.'

'That he complains about me spending a couple of dollars at the Two Dollar Shop buying things for the old ladies at my home . . . and yet here he is spending thirty thousand dollars on his skin.'

I looked at Esther's face and could tell what she was thinking. It was the same thing I found myself increasingly wondering. What kind of Christian was he?

'Do you buy the residents things often?' asked Esther.

'Every now and then,' I replied. 'Just little things like moisturizer and soaps . . . and feather boas, which they love putting around their necks. And sometimes some music for them to sing along to.'

'That's very sweet of you,' said Esther, smiling.

I shrugged my shoulders. 'Not really. I just like seeing them smile. So many of them don't have any family, or any family who want to visit them . . . it's so sad.'

'They're lucky to have you.'

'Thanks,' I smiled back. 'I wish my husband thought so.'

But Esther didn't want to talk about Vincent any longer. She wanted to talk about me. About my childhood, my family, my dreams.

'When you were a teenager, what did you want to be when you grew up?' she asked.

121

My God, I thought, I've no idea. It's so long ago.

'Try to remember,' prompted Esther.

'A surgeon,' I replied. 'I wanted to be a surgeon.'

That's right. I had wanted to be a surgeon! And here I was a nurse in an old people's home.

'And why didn't you?'

Why didn't I?

'How will you study and look after the kids?' he'd asked me on my twenty-first birthday, the day he proposed.

'Vincent,' I explained. 'He was right, though: there was no way I could have been a full-time student and a mother. Even though I wasn't pregnant and had no desire to be. I dropped the medicine papers I'd been studying at university and started my role as housewife.'

There'd been no suggestion of him giving up his career, I remembered.

'It was only when Hannah started school that he agreed to me studying nursing. I'd already passed half of the papers, so it only took me two years to complete. I loved being a student again, kick-starting my brain after all those years of changing nappies, singing bedtime songs, kindy runs.'

'You say you had no desire to be pregnant,' said Esther. 'Do you mean you didn't want to have children that young?'

'No,' I replied. 'I didn't want to have them at all. Vincent did.'

It was true. I hadn't really liked children, nor had I wanted them.

'Of course I'm glad I did, though. I couldn't imagine my life without the three of them . . . I guess I owe him that.'

Esther smiled at me.

'Tell me about your dreams,' she said. 'What would you most like to do if you could?'

My dreams? Did I have any?

'Take a moment to think,' said Esther.

I took a moment. Several moments in fact.

'I'd like to travel through Italy . . . maybe even hire a house and live there for six months. I want to learn Italian.'

I felt silly talking about my dreams. After all, they were just silly pipe dreams I kept to myself, with no chance of them ever coming true.

'And,' said Esther, 'what else?'

What else?

'I know it sounds silly . . . but I'd like to learn to sail.'

'Sail?'

'I don't know why. It's just always appealed to me for some reason. And I'd like to do a wine appreciation course . . . not that I'd ever be able to.'

'Why not?' asked Esther.

I explained about Vincent's aversion to the 'Devil's juice' and how difficult it was to have one glass of wine in peace.

And then, against my better judgement, I told her about the bottle of vodka in the laundry cupboard.

'Do you think you have a drinking problem, Sally?' asked Esther.

'No. Do you think I have?'

'No, not from what you're telling me. But I do think it's a problem that you feel you have to sneak away and hide in the laundry to have a drink.' She paused. 'These aren't impossible dreams you have, Sally. Not at all. In fact, I'd go so far as to say you could easily achieve every one of these if you wanted to.'

123

Learn to sail? Live in Italy? Was she kidding?

'It's important to have hopes and dreams, whatever they may be, and it's also important to ensure that some of those dreams come true. Being married means we inevitably have to compromise some of our dreams, and create shared dreams together. But it doesn't mean we have to let them *all* go.'

Which is what I've done, I suddenly realized. Pushed my dreams aside to make way for Vincent and his dreams. But why have I?

'There will usually be one person who's the stronger person in a relationship,' said Esther, 'and one who is the peacemaker. That's generally how things work. Sometimes it can be easy for the peacemaker to get, well, sidelined . . . unless they make a stand every now and then.'

She had me. It was as though someone had switched on the light bulb in my head. I was a *peacemaker*. I always had been. In my family, amongst my friends at school. And now in my marriage.

'There is nothing wrong with keeping the peace, Sally,' continued Esther. 'But there's nothing wrong with making your dreams come true either.'

Once again I left her office feeling lighter, relieved.

For the next few days I couldn't stop thinking about what she'd said. About my dreams. Was it really that easy to make them come true?

Kat

Between the furniture-moving, work, comfort-eating and turning down the social invitations which had been pouring my way, I managed to fill the great void that was My Life.

Meg kept asking me out for dinner with her and Joe. I kept declining. I had no desire to sit in a restaurant with a happily married couple, to watch the comfort and ease with which they interacted. To be reminded of the millions of times Gus and I had done just that.

'What the fuck is she thinking?' said Izzy. 'She's got the tact of a three-legged elephant.'

Then there were the messages from all of our married friends, the couples Gus and I used to socialize with on a regular basis. They were always messages, because I recognized their numbers and diverted their calls to answerphone. Invites to dinner parties, cocktail parties, drinks, lunches, birthdays. Not invites for me and Gus, just me. It hadn't taken long for the word to spread. I was confident Meg had had a lot to do with the spreading, but I wasn't angry with her. How could I be? It was great gossip. I was great gossip. Wife deserted by gay husband who runs off with best friend! I doubt you could find a punchier storyline in a Hollywood movie.

Presumably they all thought I needed cheering up. I

didn't. What I needed was to be left in peace, to wallow in my self-pity.

Izzy was the only person who succeeded in getting me out of the house (to the movies twice and dinner once). I didn't mind going to the movies so much; if you timed it so you were running late and went straight into the darkened theatre (which we did), then there was very little chance of bumping into someone you knew.

This was my greatest fear, bumping into an old friend. Or, worse still, a friend of Gus and mine, one who would know what had happened and either shift on their feet in nervous discomfort or embrace me in some sort of gigantic sympathy hug. Even worse! One who had no idea what had happened and who would ask after Gus, blissfully unaware of the dark realms into which their words had fallen. And what would I say? Would I stand there, at the ticket counter, and tell them the whole sorry story? Or would I lie and say he was just fine, giving them a big smile to prove just how fine he was? Then a week later they'd find out about the whole thing and think I was some sort of psychotic weirdo who still thought I was happily married.

I still hadn't told my workmates, but it was only a matter of time. There was only so long I could keep up the charade of the happy wife, and only so many times I could dash off to the toilets for a good bawl in one of the cubicles without being caught. It was a small team, twenty in total, and, although we didn't socialize together on a regular basis, we were still a fairly tight-knit group, most of whom, even the younger ones, had been here for a decent amount of time.

'When's our midwinter dinner?' asked Lee, one of the juniors on my team.

'Not sure,' I replied. It was the second time he'd asked me that week.

I wished he'd just shut the fuck up. He'd really been annoying me lately for some reason, probably due to the fact he was as gay as Christmas tinsel. Openly gay. Openly gay with an openly gay boyfriend. I had homosexual men coming out my ears.

'Hi, Martin,' I said, plucking up the courage and standing in the doorway of my boss's office. Martin was one of the firm's two managing partners. 'Have you got a moment?'

'Hey, Kat. Course. How's things? Gus back yet?'

I'd told him Gus had gone overseas for work, only because I'd got sick of Martin asking after him. Martin and Gus got on like a house on fire. Whenever they met at work dinners, there was no shutting the two of them up, while Martin's wife Anna (a housewife and mother to three young children) and I chatted amiably, pretending we had loads in common when we didn't.

'Actually yes, he is,' I said, sitting down and taking a deep breath. 'But I want you to know that . . . Gus and I have separated, which is why I've probably seemed a bit distracted lately.'

'I hadn't noticed. Shit, Kat, I'm so sorry! Are you OK?'

Don't cry, I willed myself. Not now. Not here.

'I'm OK,' I shrugged, somehow managing to keep the tears at bay. 'I'll be fine.'

'God, you seemed so happy together. I didn't have a clue things weren't good.'

'That makes two of us.' I smiled, wanly.

'Can I ask why?'

Should I tell him why? I wondered, knowing that it wouldn't take long for the news to filter through the office. Oh fuck it, why not?

Plus, there was some sick part of me that wanted to dent the high esteem in which Martin held Gus.

'Gus had an affair . . . with one of our friends.'

I watched as Martin took it in, processing the information and thinking to himself bloody hell, another one.

But I hadn't finished.

'A man,' I said, watching as the penny dropped.

'A *man?*'

'Yes.'

'Holy shit,' he said, shaking his head in disbelief.

I watched as Gus came tumbling off his pedestal. Onto asphalt, I hoped.

'Is there anything I can do?' asked Martin. 'Do you need to take some time off?'

'No, I'll be fine. Thank you, though.'

'OK, Kat,' he said, standing up and giving me a hug. 'Well, you just let me know if there is, OK?'

'OK,' I promised.

As I left Martin's office, I literally bumped into Tom, another of the juniors on my team.

'Sorry, Kat!' he apologized, as I all but flattened him. He really was so sweet; I was clearly the one at fault.

Tom had been working at the firm for only a few months, but if I were to pick a favourite out of the five people on my team it would have to be him. It amazed me that he didn't have a girlfriend (or at least not one he spoke of). He was such a lovely young guy — smart, reliable, motivated, and a real looker, too, with his handsome face, ruddy cheeks, and spiky brown hair. He looked far younger than his thirty-one years.

'I'm going to get some lunch,' he said. 'How about a sandwich?'

'Sure,' I smiled. 'Thanks.'

Five minutes later he returned with a chicken panini and a much-needed latte for me. 'And something sweet for the boss,' he said, placing a slice of chocolate torte on my desk.

'Thanks, Tom,' I smiled. 'You're a gem.'

He really is, I thought. He has the type of personality that could take him anywhere he wants to go. Anywhere at all.

Jools

For the past two weeks I'd been hounded by Gary. Flowers, phone calls, texts, emails. More flowers. More phone calls. More texts. You get the message. I should have promptly thrown each bunch of flowers in the bin, but I couldn't bring myself to. I was a girl, after all, and they really were lovely flowers. Expensive flowers. Instead, my apartment began to resemble a small funeral parlour, as did Francie's.

'If you never forgive him, we might be kept in fresh flowers for life,' she pointed out. 'That'd be lovely.'

Then he showed up at my apartment.

I tried my hardest to pretend I wasn't home but Beyonce was blaring from my stereo and every window in the place was wide open. After listening to him knock persistently, I had no choice but to open the door a crack and tell him to bugger off.

'Bugger off, Gary. I'm not home,' I hissed through the open crack.

'Yes, you are, Jools. I can see you. Please let me in.'

'Why?'

'Because I really want to talk to you.'

I sighed and opened the door. I watched him quickly glance down at my small belly as he stepped through.

I stood with my arms across my chest as he leaned

130

forward, as though to kiss me on the cheek. There were more flowers in his hand.

I leant backwards and watched as he kissed the air.

He handed me the flowers, which I took and shoved carelessly onto the dining table. It was very hard to pretend I didn't want them when we were currently surrounded by about forty bunches. The truth was I'd been brought up in the household of waste-not want-not and so every time I'd held a bunch of flowers over the bin ready to chuck them in disgust I'd heard my mother's voice saying, 'What are you doing, Julia? Those are perfectly good flowers! What would the poor people of the world say if they saw you? I bet they'd love some flowers.' So instead I'd search for yet another vessel which could double as a vase (my four vases having long been in use), bang some water in the bottom and try to find a clear flat surface on which to put them.

I sat down on the sofa and he sat at the other end, without being offered a seat.

If he thought he was getting offered a cuppa, he could go fuck himself.

He looked nervous as all hell, which was lovely to watch. He had always looked so in control, so cool, calm and collected, so sure of himself and his place in the world.

'Talk away,' I instructed, lest he thought this was going to be a lengthy social visit.

'I know that you're angry with me . . .' he started.

He'd hit the nail on the head there, although you'd hardly have to be a shrink to work that one out.

'. . . and you've every right to be.'

Bingo again.

'I know the way I behaved seems unacceptable . . .

131

but I had to protect my image and position, Jools. Surely you of all people can understand that?'

Hang on a minute, it was a dud draw.

I stared at him in pure disbelief.

'Gary,' I snarled. 'I am not some floozy you can cast aside and ignore to save your gold-plated *image*. But it's pointless even discussing this,' I said, waving my hand in the air dismissively, 'when we're not together anyway.'

He looked wounded. Lovely.

'But we can be,' he ventured.

'No. We can't, Gary. Never. I don't know what I was bloody well thinking!'

More wounded eyes.

It was time to spell it out for him. Make it loud and clear.

'Gary, I am not in love with you. Perhaps I could have been if you'd treated me with a little more respect, but you didn't. And it's over. Over. Yes, I am pregnant, but you are *not* the father.'

He stared at me like this was fresh news. That was his problem, I decided. He never really listened to what anyone said.

'Were you seeing someone else while we were together?' he asked.

'You mean was I married to someone else, like you? No. I wasn't. But after Fiji, I did sleep with someone else and this baby is his. Not yours.'

'That was quick,' he snarled. 'I don't believe you.'

Sometimes there was very little difference between him and a five-year-old.

'It's the truth Gary, take it or leave it. Do you think you had exclusive access to me while we were seeing each other? Unfortunately when you're married that's a luxury you're simply not entitled to.'

I was really on fire now!

'You're just hurt, Jools, you're making up stories. Just tell me the baby's mine and we can work it out.'

He really was a conceited bastard.

He appeared to be reaching into his jacket pocket for something. I stared in horror as his hand re-emerged, clutching a chequebook. Surely not? He couldn't be. He was. I didn't believe it!

I watched as he flicked the chequebook open and took a pen out of the same jacket pocket. 'Just say the word, Jools, and it's yours. How much?'

I tore the pen from his hand and threw it across the room. And then I glared at him with all the fury and hatred I could muster, which was a substantial amount given the circumstances.

Finally, I managed to control my anger long enough to form a sentence.

What I really wanted to say was, 'Bend over, you wanker! I'm going shove your chequebook so far up your arse it won't be coming down next Christmas, or any other Christmas after that!' But I felt these were words that possibly shouldn't be uttered by an expectant mother.

'Gary,' I spat, pure disgust dripping from my words, 'I am not some floozy who is after your cash. You cannot buy me, and you most certainly cannot buy my baby! And for the last time,' I continued, 'the baby is *not yours*. So you and your filthy money will be having absolutely nothing to do with it!'

That seemed to stop him in his tracks.

There was a knock at the door as someone opened it and walked through, calling out 'Honey, I'm home!'

It was Francie.

'Oh . . . shit . . . sorry,' she apologized, seeing the two

of us sitting on the couch and the daggers in my eyes. 'I'll pop back later.'

'No need,' I said, standing up as quickly as I could. 'Gary was just leaving.'

If he'd stayed here for much longer, there was a better than average chance that he'd have been stabbed to death with the only thing within reach — the remote control. Being a blunt object, it'd likely have taken a while and wouldn't have looked too pretty.

'You remember Francie, don't you?' I asked Gary, snapping myself back to reality.

'Yes, of course,' he replied, giving a small half-hearted wave in her direction, but obviously hating her for bursting in.

To her credit, Francie beamed back as though she'd just stumbled across Santa Claus in my living room, not Gary the Bastard.

'Guess I'll be off then,' he mumbled, as though he had any choice in the matter.

'Fabulous idea,' I replied, escorting him to the front door.

He looked defeated. Clearly his gallant visit hadn't gone quite according to plan. No doubt he'd assumed that once I saw him in all his physical glory I'd crumble and fall wailing into his arms, blubbering at how stupid I'd been and would he please take me back.

He should be so bloody lucky. I hadn't the energy to wail or blubber these days, the baby was sucking the life out of me.

'I'd like to see you again, Jools,' he whispered. 'Soon. Somewhere private where we can talk properly.'

He was more thick-skinned than I had given him credit for.

Obviously he still didn't believe I'd slept with

someone else. I was going to have to get written proof of the date of conception and wave it in his face. Even then he'd probably put it down to forgery.

'I'll think about it,' I replied. But I already had, and the answer was no.

'Think we'll be getting any more flowers?' asked Francie, once the door had closed behind him.

I told her about the chequebook.

'The absolute wanker!' she exclaimed.

I couldn't have agreed more.

Sally

Vincent headed off on his 'business trip'. 'I've paid for it, Sally. They won't refund the money. It'd be pointless not to go,' he explained.

Aside from the fact he was spending our retirement savings and directly condoning the farming of black-market foetuses, I was looking forward to having him gone for two weeks. It occurred to me how strange it was that someone who regularly preached against pre-marital sex was perfectly happy to have the stem cells of an aborted foetus (more than likely from an unmarried and poor, young Russian woman) flowing through their veins.

The weekend after he left, I flew to Christchurch with the children for a short holiday. They were ecstatic about the plane trip and holiday, even Davey whose prerogative as an almost-fourteen-year-old boy was to be as unimpressed as possible with everything. We couldn't really afford it, in light of how much Vincent's treatment was costing, but bugger it. Just because he's blown our savings there's no reason why the children shouldn't have a holiday — they deserve it. And so do I, I thought, surprising myself.

The girls were so excited they were unable to sleep and ended up hopping into bed with me, where they finally stopped chattering and fell asleep for a few hours.

It was the most enjoyable few days I could remember in a long time. We walked all over the city, went out for brunch, went to the markets and cinema, ate fish and chips on the riverbank, went out for dinner (where I relished a glass or two of wine, without fear of retribution). And we talked and laughed, a lot.

'Are we going to church today?' asked Hannah on Sunday morning.

'How can we if we're in another city, silly?' said Elizabeth.

'Does that mean we don't have to go?' cried Hannah, her little face lighting up.

'Well, we can go to a service here if you'd like to,' I replied.

'Hmm . . .' said Hannah and Elizabeth, as they mulled over my suggestion.

'How about not,' said Davey. 'Just for a change.'

'Yeah,' agreed the girls, giggling. 'Let's not.'

'Well, how about we visit the cathedral instead?' I suggested. 'It's very old and beautiful. I think you'll like it.'

After breakfast we walked from the hotel to the majestic Gothic cathedral in the middle of the city.

'Wow!' said the girls, as we approached its front steps. 'It's huge!'

We walked inside and wandered slowly around its beautiful and impressive interior.

'It's cool,' said Davey. This was high praise.

I sat down in one of the pews and bowed my head in silence. Without prompting, the children sat down beside me and did the same. We sat together like that for a few minutes, shoulder to shoulder, in silence. I prayed to whatever greater power there was to keep the three of them, my beautiful children, safe. And happy.

'Can we light a candle?' asked Davey.

'Of course, love,' I replied, reaching in my handbag for some coins for the donation box. 'Why don't you light one each?'

I watched them walk to the altar and light a candle each, Davey helping Hannah light hers.

They're just so gorgeous, I thought, smiling proudly. My three beautiful children, who are all growing up so fast.

I loved sitting and watching them unobserved; it was my favourite time.

'Can we climb to the top now, Mum?' asked Hannah.

'Let's,' I said, hopping out from the pew.

In single file we traipsed up the lengthy staircase to the cathedral tower, Davey leading the way.

'Insane!' he cried, looking out at the stunning view in front of us, from the city centre below to the Port Hills in the distance.

'Wow, Mum!' agreed Hannah, jumping up and down. 'Look! We're so high!'

We walked around the viewing platform, watching the world below us. Elizabeth somehow managed to spot our hotel and was very pleased with herself.

It occurred to me, as we made our way back down the winding staircase and out the cathedral doors, that they had genuinely enjoyed visiting the church. Such a different experience from the one they endured every Wednesday evening and Sunday. It had been peaceful and calming, with no shouting, clapping or television cameras. No stage for them to reluctantly step onto and no hands to shake.

'What would you like to do now?' I asked, as we turned and took one last look at the beautiful cathedral.

'How about a hot chocolate?' suggested Elizabeth, who was a stickler for routine, bless her.

'OK,' agreed the other two.

'How about you pick us a café, Davey?' I suggested.

So we ambled through the city until we came across a cute little café with a lovely sunny courtyard at the back.

'OK?' asked Davey.

'Perfect,' we agreed.

After our hot chocolates, we moseyed around the city for a while and then made our way to the riverbank with some fish and chips for lunch, sitting on the grass in the sunshine. We all slipped off our shoes, letting the winter sunshine warm our winter feet.

I took a photo of the children sitting on the grass, newspaper and fish and chips in front of them, smiling back at me.

That's definitely a keeper, I thought as I put the digital camera back in my handbag.

'Can we go on holiday again, Mum?' asked Hannah, as we drove home from the airport. 'That was fun.'

I smiled at her in the rear-view mirror.

'Sure, sweetheart. Where would you like to go?' I asked.

'I don't know, anywhere.'

'How about Australia or Fiji?' suggested Davey. 'Somewhere hot?'

'Yeah!' agreed Hannah.

'Sounds like fun,' I replied.

'What about you, sweetie?' I said to Elizabeth.

'Yes,' she smiled. 'That'd be cool.'

'Well, how about we go next winter?' I suggested. 'That'll give me enough time to save the money. Maybe we can go for ten days?'

'Cool!' they all agreed, smiling at me.

I was aware I had just made them a promise. But it was a promise I had every intention of keeping. It would be something for all of us to look forward to.

Kat

Very slowly my furniture-moving fury abated. I'd already rearranged the household furniture into every possible combination; there was nothing left to scrape across the welted floorboards. It was instead replaced by a washing fury, which engulfed me whenever I was home (which was basically every second I wasn't at work). I washed everything, even things which were clean. And then I ironed them; tea towels, T-shirts, knickers, it didn't matter. Izzy was worried I was developing some sort of obsessive-compulsive disorder and that pretty soon I wouldn't be able to leave the house without washing my hands fifteen times in a row.

All day I longed for night-time, when I could lie in bed in the pitch-black and let my mind be carried away by visions of long, painful deaths (not my own) and cold-blooded revenge. It was by far my favourite time of day. I knew the visions I had were psychotic and disturbing enough to constitute a shrink's wet dream, but they somehow made me feel better, more in control of my pitiful life. It's not as though I would *actually* act out the visions. Well, not right now, although I couldn't be sure what the future held. In the process of lying awake having psychotic thoughts, I wasn't getting any sleep. I'd toss and turn, and then toss and turn some more, and finally I'd get up out of bed, resigned to the fact that I wouldn't be getting any sleep at all, and would take to the washing and watch infomercials instead.

'You've got insomnia,' declared Meg. 'Why don't you try meditating?

'Fuck the meditating,' said Izzy. 'You need to go to the doctor and get some sleeping pills.'

I'd never had insomnia in my life. Usually I'm one of those people who falls asleep before their head hits the pillow.

'It's normal,' comforted Izzy. 'You're stressed and in shock.'

She was right. But I didn't want to go to sleep. I was scared of going to sleep, because that meant I would wake up. And when I woke up there would be that lovely fleeting second when I would think that everything was still OK, that Gus was lying beside me. And then my heart would sink when I realized he wasn't. I hated that sinking feeling. I just hated it. I also hated the way time went by so slowly that it appeared to be going backwards. It had been over four months since The Incident, but it felt like a year. No amount of furniture-moving or washing could make time speed up.

Why don't you just sit down on the couch and have a read? I asked myself on Sunday morning, as I put another load of clean washing in the machine. But my body wasn't willing to stop moving, so I decided to take some washing out of the dryer and fold it instead. As I folded the washing and stacked it on my bed, I felt a long protracted sigh escape from my lips.

Oh God, I thought, perching on the bed for a moment. It's happened. I had turned into a *sigher*, just like my mother. She couldn't sit in a chair, cook the dinner, collect the mail, start the car or make a cup of tea without letting out a loud sigh or two. It annoyed the bejesus out of me.

Is this what happened once you hit thirty-five? You turned into your mother? Maybe it had been happening for a while and I just hadn't seen it. Maybe that's what had turned Gus gay — the fact that he'd suddenly found himself married to my mother.

I looked down at the pile of folded washing in my lap. Bloody hell, I even fold washing like her. Knickers neatly in half, bras on top of the knickers, and then hosiery. I looked around the room for other signs of mothermorphosis. And that's when I saw it — the small bowl of potpourri sitting on my dressing table. It screamed *Mother!*

But you didn't buy it, I consoled myself; it was a gift (from my mother).

But you put it on your dressing table, didn't you? myself replied. What the hell were you thinking?

I was still sitting on the bed, washing in lap, staring languidly at the potpourri when Izzy arrived.

'Everything all right?' she asked, poking her head around the bedroom door.

'No.' I explained the potpourri situation and the gripping fear that I'd turned into my mother.

'Come and have a drink,' she suggested. 'And we'll throw *that* in the bin on the way.' She poured two glasses of wine. 'You haven't turned into your mother,' she assured me. 'But you will if you don't start going out every once in a while.'

I stared at her.

My mother's version of excitement was watching the Lotto draw on a Saturday night, poised on the sofa with a pen in hand, scrutinizing her ticket. She lived alone in a little semi-detached townhouse, where she'd moved after my father had died five years before, and she did her very best to avoid any social outings she was invited to, to the point where her friends had stopped inviting her. It was like she'd resigned herself to the fact that my father was the only man she was ever going to love and that she was going to be alone for the rest of her days, just she and her two cats. She claimed she was happy with her 'lot', but I strongly doubted that she was. I think she had just got used to being lonely.

Was I going to turn into her? Was Gus the only man that I would ever love?

'How was your date?' I asked, changing the subject. Izzy had been on yet another internet date the night before.

'Terrible,' replied Izzy. 'He was a lazy kisser.'

I had absolutely no idea what a lazy kisser was, but it was probably not dissimilar to a lazy cuddler. Izzy had broken up with her previous boyfriend, Rob, because he was a lazy cuddler. Until I met Izzy, I'd had no idea that lazy cuddlers existed, or what they were. But they were out there, she assured me, ruining perfectly good relationships. A lazy cuddler (according to Izzy) was someone who didn't put enough effort into cuddling. Someone who lay on their back while you were both in bed and expected you to roll right on top of them if you wanted to have a cuddle, instead of rolling onto their side and meeting you halfway. The Lazy Cuddler was generally no good at spooning (doesn't come in close enough) or hugging (doesn't hug tight enough). Sometimes I wondered whether Izzy wasn't being just a little bit picky.

Jools

Medical science was a wonderful thing. Today I was going to have my sixteen-week scan and be able to see my baby. I'd finally be able to put a face, albeit an alien-looking one, to the nausea and vomiting.

I asked Mum to come along with me. Now that the initial shock at being a grandmother (to a fatherless child with an unemployed, unmarried mother) had abated, she was the most excited I'd seen her in years. She was over-the-moon to be there with me.

I climbed up onto the table, my trousers rolled down to expose my slightly rounded belly. The doctor smeared the gooey stuff all over my belly and then rested the instrument on it.

'Look up there,' he said, gesturing at the television monitor on the opposite wall.

And there on the television screen, in sepia tone, was the beginnings of a little person.

'Bloody hell,' I whispered. 'Look at it!'

I'd no idea I'd be able to see the baby so clearly, or that it would be as well-formed as it was. It had tiny hands and feet! It also sported the oversized head of an alien and a rather prominent hunchback.

I felt a tear slide down my cheek. I had had no idea that I'd find it so emotional to see the little thing. What was happening to me?

'Holy Moses,' said Mum, who until that point had been completely speechless at the advances of medical technology. 'In my day you just took it for granted that there was a baby growing inside you and not just one too many chocolate éclairs.'

I looked back at the little alien-like person on the screen who had woken up and was now waving its little hands about.

'Look at that!' exclaimed Mum. 'It's touching its little ear. And look! Its foot's going, too!'

Anyone would think *she* was pregnant. She was that excited.

'Plenty of room for it to move around,' said the doctor. 'It's making the most of it. Good strong little heart, too,' he added. This was good news. My baby had a strong heart.

'In fact everything's looking just fine and dandy. I'll just take the measurement for the nuchal fold and we're done,' he said, clicking the cursor at the top of the baby's spine.

The doctor gave me a printout to take home with the baby's statistics on it, including the date of conception, which thankfully matched that of the blood test.

'If there's any issue with the nuchal fold, we'll let your obstetrician know straight away,' said the doctor. 'Otherwise assume all is completely fine and enjoy your pregnancy.' He smiled. 'And we'll see you for your twenty-week scan.'

Mum carried the DVD of my baby to the car.

'A DVD,' she marvelled, shaking her head at it. 'I can't wait to show your father.'

That night I played Francie my baby DVD. Five times. She didn't complain; in fact, she was as mesmerized by the image on the screen as I was.

'Bloody hell!' she exclaimed, in awe. 'It's got hands and feet! And ears too!'

When I finally put the DVD back in its case, Francie said quietly, 'Are you going to tell him?'

'Who?'

'Tom.'

'Um . . . you know, I haven't really thought about it.'

And, truthfully, I hadn't. I probably should have by now. I'd been far too busy being happy that the baby wasn't Gary's and feeling queasy for my thoughts to stray that far.

'No need to hurry,' said Francie.

'I suppose I should, though, shouldn't I?' I said. 'Tell him?'

'I guess so.'

'Would you tell?' I asked.

'Geez . . .' said Francie. 'I really dunno. Perhaps you should write a list of the pros and cons? I'll help you.'

She grabbed a piece of paper and a pen and sat back down.

'Start with the pros,' she suggested. 'I'll write them down for you.'

'OK. Well, I guess the pros are . . . that I'd be being honest . . . that Tom would get to have a relationship with his child, if that's what he wanted . . . that the baby would get to know their father and have a relationship with him . . . that . . . I can't think of anything else.'

'The cons?' said Francie.

'That he would think I was using him as a sperm bank . . .'

'But he used a condom,' said Francie. 'Remember?'

147

'OK. That he'd think I was trying to pin someone else's baby on him then . . . that he'd think I was after child support . . . that he'd think I wanted him to be a part of the baby's life . . . or mine . . . that if he has a girlfriend I'm going to ruin his relationship . . . that I don't know him well enough to know what sort of father he'd be.'

'And what about you?' said Francie. 'You haven't mentioned how either option would make you feel. Forget about Tom and the baby for a moment. Could you keep the baby's father a secret? How will it make you feel when the kid asks you where their dad is? Which they will, one day.'

'Terrible,' I replied. 'Like a liar.'

'What's the worse that can happen if you tell Tom?' said Francie. 'That he says you're lying? That he doesn't want to have anything to do with either you or the baby?'

'I guess,' I replied.

'But at least you could say you'd tried, right? You could tell the kid that.'

She was right. I had to tell Tom, for my own sake. Otherwise the secret would just eat me up inside and probably come back to haunt me someday. If he didn't want anything to do with this baby, then it was best to get that out of the way now.

'What do I do?' I asked. 'Turn up on his doorstep, point at my belly and say "Guess what?"'

'Possibly not,' said Francie. 'How about just ringing him? Or maybe writing him a letter?'

A letter? It wasn't a bad idea.

'But I don't have his address,' I replied.

'You could ring him and ask for his address,' said Francie. 'Tell him you have an invite or something to send him.'

'Guess I could,' I replied, marvelling at how Francie always seemed to have an answer for everything. Her talents were wasted as a hand model. She should have worked for the United Nations.

We spent the rest of the evening making up alternative condom advertisements for Sure & Pure.

'Sure & Pure, use our condoms and you're sure to get pregnant,' started Francie.

'Sure & Pure, when you want to get pregnant and keep the element of surprise!' I replied.

'Sure & Pure, when you're not sure if you want a baby.'

'Sure & Pure, when it's pure shock you're after.'

And so we went on for several hours, our creativity only halted by fits of giggles.

Sally

Vincent was arriving back that day. It felt like he'd been gone two days, not two weeks.

'I'll see you at the airport,' he'd said when he'd phoned the night before.

'No, you won't,' I replied. 'I'm working. You'll have to catch a cab.'

It was so much easier to stand up to him when he was on the other side of the world.

He sighed in disappointment. 'I suppose I'll have to then.'

I spent the rest of the day at work trying to keep myself as busy as I could — which was fairly easy in my job — and not think about how lovely the past two weeks had been with just the kids and me. How peaceful, and funny, and normal.

I knocked on Olive's bedroom door, her iron injection in my hand.

There was no reply, but I could hear some strange grunting noises coming from inside.

'Olive?' I called out, but there was still no reply. She was deaf as a doornail. They all were.

I opened the door and peered in.

'Lord above!' I gasped, staring in horror.

There was Fred's saggy white bottom moving up and down on top of the bed, at a painfully slow rate of knots.

A strange howling noise was coming from somewhere beneath him, like the screech of an alley cat. It was Olive, her skinny old white veiny legs spread. And there, above her head, were her enormous pink granny-waisters flung over the bedhead.

The howling noise appeared to be saying, 'Faster! Faster!'

Impossible. He simply couldn't go any faster. She was dreaming.

They are going to kill themselves, I thought, backing out of the room and deciding the iron injection could wait. I should have been used to it by now, it was just another case of RHR (Rest Home Romance). It wasn't the first time I'd caught the two of them in the act. One afternoon, a couple of months before, they'd been sitting in the television room with the others watching reruns of *Coronation Street* when I'd seen Fred's hand disappear up Olive's skirt, not reappearing until the end of the programme. Olive looked as flushed as a thirteen-year-old schoolgirl.

To be honest I was surprised Fred had been able to snare bubbly Olive.

'MORNING, FRED!' I'd yell, as I passed him pushing his walking frame along the corridor every morning.

'Geroff!' he generally spat back.

Fred had a vocabulary of three words or phrases: asshole, geroff (get off) and not on your life. All were uttered in response to a question, query, greeting or any other form of conversation, regardless of the content.

Olive, on the other hand, was our resident escape artist. If any opportunity for escape presented itself, usually via a visiting relative holding the security door open for her, she would hurl herself at it, blue hair and all. It wasn't because she was unhappy at the home, or because she wished she was living somewhere else. She just loved the thrill of the chase. Although there was a clearly visible sign which read *Please, do not let residents through these doors*, it was amazing who did. Olive was such an expert, however, that she could have found her way out of Alcatraz, blindfolded and legless. We often despaired over having let her have the hip replacement.

Just a couple of weeks before I'd had to retrieve her from the women's clothing department of Smith & Caughey's in the city, after tailing the bus she'd boarded on the main road. I'd run out of the rest-home entrance and frantically waved my arms at the driver, who'd glanced across at me briefly, before closing the doors and driving off.

'Oh, hello, dear,' she said to me, when I finally caught up with her in the department store, as though we were two old friends who'd bumped into each other on a Sunday afternoon stroll in the park. 'Lovely day for a shop, isn't it?'

I was glad I'd left the two of them at it, I decided. Due to her penchant for escaping, Olive was leaving the home in a few days, headed for a more secure unit somewhere. I was really going to miss her, although possibly not as much as Fred was. I guessed it would spell the end of their wee romance, the poor things.

It never ceased to amaze me just how promiscuous some of the residents were. The relatives who had deposited them in there would be aghast if they knew that their mother, father or grandparent was spending their final days celebrating free love. Most of the romances had begun after Viagra came onto the market. The men who were 'getting some' could always be relied upon to have a secret stash in their bedside drawer, having somehow convinced the visiting doctor to write them out a prescription and have it delivered. How they managed to afford the stuff on their meagre pensions remained a mystery.

There was even the odd cat-fight over lovers. Men were as scarce as hens' teeth in this place, outnumbered two to one by the women. Olive had 'stolen' Fred off Jean several months before in a scene remembered by staff as The Showdown. Although they didn't exactly trade punches, it was close, with Jean ramming her walking frame into Olive's shins in the television room and pummelling her onto the carpet. The result: bruised shins and a bruised bottom for Olive, and a flattened walking frame for Jean after Olive stole it from her room later that night, hobbled it out to the main road and pushed it into a stream of oncoming traffic.

Thankfully, after being reprimanded by the home manager, they decided to call it quits, with Jean admitting defeat and taking it like a lady (well, a lady scorned, that is). She still blatantly disliked Olive — although she had stopped spitting at her every time they passed one another in the hallway, and she refused to sit beside either her or Fred at dinner, on the bus, in the television room, in the craft area, or anywhere else where sitting was involved. Fred had been delighted at the cat-fight over him, and his street cred among the other men had increased tenfold.

And then there were the women who realized that both statistics and time were against them finding a man and settled for the only other option, requesting to share a twin room for 'the company'. Their relatives thought it was sweet that they wanted to bunk up together like a couple of sorority sisters. Their relatives were usually not nosey enough on their visits to discover the antique vibrators hidden under their beds. Usually their wishes were granted by staff, who thought that if they were fortunate enough to still have a scrap of libido left at their age then they should be entitled to make the most of it, whatever the pairing.

I arrived home from work to find Vincent sitting in the living room, reading the newspaper. At least I thought it was Vincent. He had the same suit pants, silk shirt and shiny loafers as Vincent, but that was where the similarity ended. This man didn't have a head. He had a bandage.

'Hello, Sally,' said the bandage.

It sounded like Vincent.

'Vincent?'

'Yes.'

'What on earth happened?' I asked.

'It's nothing serious,' he replied. 'Please, don't be alarmed.'

I wasn't alarmed, I just wanted to know what he was doing with his entire head wrapped in a bandage.

'I had a little reaction to the treatment,' he explained. 'It's nothing serious.'

'It certainly looks serious.'

'My body rejected the stem cells and I came out in a few blisters.'

'Did they refund the money?' I asked. Surely they must have?

'No . . . not exactly'

'Why on earth not?' I demanded. 'Let me get this straight. You paid thirty thousand dollars, sixteen thousand of which was from our retirement savings, to travel halfway around the world and get a pile of blisters on your face? You are bloody well insane!' I cried.

'Language, Sally!' scolded Vincent. 'The children will be home soon'.

They were home soon, and they enjoyed the heartiest laugh of their lives when they caught sight of the bandage.

'Is that really you, Dad?' asked Hannah, poking at the bandage.

'Yes, love, but please don't poke Daddy, it hurts.'

'You look like a mummy!' cried Davey and Elizabeth.

'Karmen Tutan,' I added, as they rolled around the floor.

He must be hating this, I thought, blisters on the precious face he's spent so much time and money preening. I almost felt sorry for him.

'On the plus side,' said Vincent later, 'the doctor said I'll have layers of youthful fresh new skin once the blisters go.'

Three weeks later, the blisters had gone and I had to admit that, despite what appeared to be some permanent scarring, Vincent did look a little younger, about three or four years. Not the ten years he'd been promised, and hardly worth thirty thousand dollars we couldn't afford and a trip around the world.

I made the mistake of asking Vincent what pearls of wisdom he'd gleaned from his trip. 'Modernization,' he declared. 'We need to bring Divinity Church into the twenty-first century. We need a website.'

He had already employed a hotshot young web designer, Glen, for the job.

'We need to have family pics taken for the website,'

announced Vincent as the five of us sat at the dinner table.

'Why?' asked Davey, which was precisely what I was thinking.

'Because we are the faces of the church,' replied Vincent. 'People need to see me and my family.'

Davey looked crestfallen. It was enough of an embarrassment among his peers that his father was a television evangelist, but to have his face plastered on the website too?

'I don't like getting my picture taken,' said Hannah, which was true.

Elizabeth was the only one who didn't voice a complaint, but then she never complained about anything, that was just her nature. I often wondered where she got it from.

'We might just have to discuss this a bit further, Vincent,' I replied.

'The photographer's already booked, Sally, for five o'clock on Wednesday.'

Kat

Very gradually, and without realizing it, I began to feel more like a human being again, and less like a gaping chasm with limbs. I was even managing to sleep for a few hours at night, without waking up expecting Gus to be beside me. In the process of my return to Planet Normal, it was glaringly evident just how far I'd let things slip in the almost five months since The Incident. Not just physically, in the ten kilos I had gained which was distributed evenly to my breasts, stomach and hips (it hadn't been confirmed as ten kilos because I was too scared to hop on the scales — it was an educated guess based on me feeling as though I'd had at least six number-fourteen chickens attached to various parts of my body); the hair I had let split and grow out of style; the eyebrows I had avoided plucking and which were in the process of creeping towards each other across my forehead; the multitude of blackheads which clung to and bred on the sides of my nose. No, in every area of my life.

For instance, I had run out of food. Actually I had run out of food weeks ago, having not been to the supermarket since before The Incident. But it's amazing how long stores can last, and then, for some reason, the fact that there was no food left in the house had only begun to bother me recently, the day before. Since the weeks of sympathy food courtesy of Izzy and my mother had petered out, I'd been subsisting on a packet of TimTams a day and a multitude of Yorkshire puddings, both of which were well-stocked at my local dairy, which was conveniently located on my direct route home from the office.

I was beginning to see just what a mess I'd let things become, and just how many things I had to do. Although the tasks ahead of me were boring and commonplace, so much a part of my normal routine that I had barely noticed them before, they were now somehow larger, requiring all my effort and concentration. After an hour of scouring through every cupboard in the house, I held the result — a five-page shopping list — in my hand. Basically there was nothing I didn't require, no aisle I could safely skip. *NO TIMTAMS OR PUDDS!!* I had written at the bottom, lest my newfound resolve crumble at the sight of them.

The time had come to leave the house. Brave the outside world. Alone. Go to the supermarket.

What on earth had happened to me? How had I reached the point where going to the supermarket required me to summon every ounce of courage and determination? How had such a mundane chore become akin to scaling a mountain?

As I went to walk out the front door, the phone rang. It was Izzy, enquiring after my health and safety as she did at least twice a day.

'I'm going to the supermarket,' I told her.

'The supermarket!' she exclaimed, making it sound as though I was off for a month in the Bahamas.

'Yes,' I replied, my voice ringing with steely resolve.

'Thatta girl!' she encouraged. 'Well done! Call me when you get back.'

With her words of encouragement ringing in my ears, I embarked on my mission.

I took a deep breath, fetched myself a trolley, and walked through the automatic doors.

How the hell was I going to fit everything I needed in one trolley? Just fit what you can, I told myself, one step at a time.

I finished at the fruit and vegetable section and was heading towards aisle one: so far so good. And then all of a sudden it wasn't good. In fact it was very, very un-good.

'Kat!' I heard someone call out, as my trolley very nearly collided head-on with another.

There was nowhere to run, no way of pretending I hadn't seen him. He was standing right in front of me, directly in my path, staring point-blank at me. Gus. My husband.

And he looked great. In fact he looked better than great.

He had a new shirt on. A lovely jade-green, long-sleeved, silk shirt which brought out the green in his eyes and the tan on his skin. It looked expensive. Very expensive.

A new shirt for a new life, I thought bitterly. How fitting.

I lifted my hand and attempted to brush my fringe down, in the hope it would completely cover my face.

'Hi,' I replied. I had no choice.

'How are you?' he asked, sounding all perky and comfortable, as though we were old neighbours who hadn't bumped into each other for years.

'Fine,' I replied, desperately wanting to add *no thanks to you, asshole!* 'You?'

'Good,' he smiled. 'Just doing some . . . ah . . .

159

domestic chores,' he said, gesturing down at the trolley.

Sixteen years together, ten years of marriage, and here we were reduced to small-talk in the aisle of a supermarket.

Just tell him he's a cunt and be done with it, screeched my inner voice. Go on! You've been looking forward to this moment for weeks!

I saw the bok choy (at least I think it was bok choy) in his hand before I saw him.

Bok choy, how very sophisticated. And gay. It was a gay vegetable, for gay men. It couldn't have been a plain old head of broccoli in his hand, could it? Or a bag of carrots?

'Hi, Kat,' said Dan, looking even more uncomfortable than I felt, if that was possible.

I hadn't seen him since he was lying on my bed, stark naked, and well . . . you know the rest of the story. And there he was. Looking fabulous and healthy and also wearing an expensive silk shirt. A black one. And there they were, supermarket shopping like a proper domestic loved-up couple. It was all I could do not to ram my fingers down my throat and projectile vomit all over the both of them.

There we stood, in the soup and condiments aisle of Foodtown. Me, looking dishevelled, fat, unkempt, frumpy and just like I'd been teleported straight from the set of *Rikki Lake* in my Jenny-from-the-block pink-velour tracksuit. And my husband and his boyfriend, my ex-friend, looking incredibly stylish, healthy, radiant and happy in their expensive silk shirts and designer jeans. I could feel their happy, gay, stylish eyes gliding over me, from top to toe, thinking to themselves, Crikey she's really let herself slip, hasn't she? And so quickly!

And what was worse was that I bet that the sight they

saw before them made them feel sorry for me. I bet it made them glad they were gay. Made the right choice, they were both thinking. Boy! Did we ever.

'How are you?' asked Dan.

'Good,' I replied, avoiding his eyes and looking back at Gus.

I hated Dan. I think I hated him even more than I hated Gus. Yes, I do, I decided matter-of-factly, something oddly heart-warming about this revelation. It was comforting to know there was no limit to the feelings of ill will and hatred I could muster.

I hope you choke to death on your bok choy, I thought, realizing as the thought entered my mind just how infantile it was, but letting it see the light of day nonetheless.

'Well, I'd better get on with it,' I said, gesturing towards my trolley and forcing a smile which felt like a thousand razorblades slicing back and forth across my face. 'Somewhere to be.'

Although the only place I had to *be* was at home, unpacking my groceries. I had hoped to stretch that out all afternoon.

'Where are you off to?' asked Gus.

Why was he such a wanker? Wasn't it perfectly obvious I was making my excuses because the situation we were currently standing in was bordering on suicidal?

'A lunch,' I replied.

'Where?'

Oh for fucksake! Make him stop, someone please!

'At Soul . . . with Izzy . . . and some friends,' I replied, through gritted teeth.

'How is she?' he asked. 'Izzy?'

How come you never came to the bloody supermarket with me? I thought. It would have been nice of you to carry the goddamn shopping bags once in a while.

'She's grand,' I replied. 'Just grand.'

And she's just not going to believe my sodding luck at bumping into you two, I thought. I bet she'll kick herself for not coming along with me. Not because she enjoys frequenting the supermarket, but because running into your husband and his boyfriend, your ex-friend, for the first time since you caught them copulating like a couple of horny adolescent rabbits in your bedroom is not a common everyday occurrence. That's why.

'Well . . .' I said again, inching my trolley forward for the big break. 'Nice to see you.'

Obviously this was a lie, but unfortunately social conditioning dictates that in awkward situations such as this one we err towards being polite rather than the vindictive scathing bitch we would far rather be.

Dan stepped aside to let me pass, and I pushed my trolley between them, sporting what was supposed to be a polite smile but must have looked like the grimace of death itself upon my face.

'Bye, Kat,' they both said, smiling simultaneously, just like a proper couple.

But anyone who bumps into someone they know at the supermarket knows they should never say goodbye or use up all their conversation in aisle one. No. You will most definitely bump into them at least ten more times before you vacate the building, and then one more time in the car park for good measure, because you're bound to be parked right next to each other.

And that's exactly what happened to us, save the car park. I should have ditched the trolley, bolted for the car and gone home hungry; Lord knows I could have done with a spot of starvation. But some annoying blip of stubbornness inside me wasn't having a bar of it. It wanted to me to stay, do what I'd come here to do, stand my ground. And be subjected to the most severe dose of uncomfortableness in my living memory.

Bumping into them the second time, in aisle one, was bad enough as we strained smiles at each other and nervously laughed at the oddity of seeing each other again. In aisle two, we also managed a nervous little chuckle and pleasantry. By aisle three, the smiles and nervous chuckles were fading fast. Basically we succeeded in crossing paths in the middle of every single aisle in the supermarket, due to the fact that we were walking in opposite directions. And then twice more at the butcher and bakery sections for good measure. I even tried changing tack and walking in front of them, only to find that they had forgotten something in aisle five and changed direction back on me. It was like a bad panto skit, but without the rouge.

By the time we got to aisle ten, we simply raised eyebrows at each other. By aisle eleven, I stared intently at the lino and pretended I hadn't seen them walk past.

The result of this excessive amount of uncomfortable encounters was evident in what ended up in my trolley. Whenever I saw them coming towards me I'd grab whatever was on the shelf and throw it in so that I could skittle past them as quickly as possible.

What were the bloody odds? I wondered, as I heaved my laden trolley towards the car. I hadn't been to the supermarket in coming up for *five* months; hell, I'd barely been out of the house in that time and I'd managed to bump into them. *Them!* Of all the bloody people I knew in the world.

'You're a prick!' I hissed, jerking my head towards the sky, as a mother pushing her trolley and small child looked at me and then veered in the other direction.

I spent the afternoon unpacking five hundred dollars worth of groceries (consisting of approximately seven useful items) and cursing myself for not hurling vile abuse and stabbing them both while I'd had the chance.

How could I have been so nice? I wondered, as I replayed the encounter inside my head, summoning up all sorts of satisfactory alternative endings. They all involved me escaping with my dignity and pride, while Gus and Dan cowered in my presence, badly dressed and splattered with blood (their own). All of the onlookers cheered and clapped, instead of wrestling me to the lino and calling the police.

The useful items I'd returned with were: butter, bread, eggs, cereal, toilet paper, cling wrap and oranges. The not-so-useful ones were, among other things: a fly swat, dog food, nappies, men's underwear, beer, incontinence pads, kitty litter tray liners, budgie seed, flour, baking soda (and numerous other baking goods). And five packets of peanuts (to which I was violently allergic). Being that there was at least a fifty per cent chance that whatever I blindly threw into the trolley would be useful to me in some way, shape or form, the odds were distinctly *not* in my favour. This was, naturally, Gus and Dan's fault. Bastards. I should send them the bill.

From now on I'm going to do my supermarket shopping online, I decided. There was far less chance of bumping into my husband and his male lover, my ex-friend, or anyone at all, for that matter. In fact, if I planned it well I could do every type of purchase and monetary transaction online — food, clothing, household appliances, wine, DVDs, banking, gift buying, bill payments — and I would never have to leave the house again (except for work and perhaps petrol).

'Unbelievable!' exclaimed Izzy, when she phoned. 'What did you say to them?'

'That I was fine and how were they,' I replied glumly.

'Oh well . . . I guess it's good to be polite,' said Izzy, clearly disappointed. 'Show them you're the bigger person and all that crap.'

'I don't want to be the bigger person. I want to be the nasty, self-satisfied person who scares the bejesus out of people. I'm over being *nice*. Nice gets you nowhere.'

'You've been scaring the bejesus out of me lately, if that's any help,' she replied.

'Not really.'

'Well, I guess it had to happen at some stage, babe,' sighed Izzy, as I bleated on about how unlucky I was.

She had a point, although that it had happened at the supermarket while I was wearing a pink velour tracksuit, was fat and had no make-up on was an unnecessarily cruel twist of fate. Particularly as it was only my second or third daytime outing in five months, aside from my trek to and from work. Why couldn't I have bumped into them at the petrol station? I wondered. Or the bottle store? Or walking down the street? Somewhere where I'd only have to see them once, not twenty times in the space of thirty minutes.

Meg deemed our meeting at the supermarket a 'milestone on your road to healing' and something which would do me 'the world of good'.

It had felt more like a crash course in humiliation than a milestone of healing, and absolutely no good had come of it so far as I could see.

Although, with gut-wrenching dread, I realized I was

probably going to have to see them together at other times in the future. Unless of course they broke up because Gus came home to find Dan shagging another bloke in their bed (a pleasant thought which had crossed my mind, oh, just a couple of times).

Aside from the one he was currently shagging, pretty much all of Gus and my friends were friends with both of us. Friends who had parties, dinners, barbeques, and other regular social gatherings they would want to invite us both to. Was I going to be one of those bitter and twisted women who refused to go to the party because their ex was going? I had always hated women (I can say women because it usually was women who were (a) the ones who were cheated on and (b) were bitter as a result) who took this stand, only because they made situations so difficult for their friends. I had no desire to be in the same room as Gus and Dan, but I also had no desire to be a pain in the arse to our friends. Not in the long term. Plus, I guessed I was going to have to accept one of the invites which had come my way, unless I wanted them to stop coming for good.

I just wasn't sure I was ready to face the monumental shame of it all, not yet. The shame at having turned my seemingly heterosexual husband into a raving bender. Was I really that lousy in the sack?

Jools

I'd been putting off telling Tom he was going to be a father. I still had the crumpled tissue with phone number he'd left me, and the list of pros and cons ringing in my ears. We hadn't spoken to each other since that Sunday morning, over four months before. The morning after we'd slept together. Before the baby news I'd been happy to leave it as a one-night stand, a chance to get Gary out of my head. I guessed he felt the same way, as he hadn't phoned me. But I hadn't given him my number, had I? Well he hadn't bothered to stop by, and he knew where I lived. Perhaps he had a girlfriend.

I knew my parents thought I should tell him, even though they didn't say so. I could feel it. Although they also thought the two of us had been in a relationship, not just a one-night fling between complete strangers. There was no point in giving them all the details. I had already fallen so far from grace, I wasn't sure there was enough rope to haul myself back up.

But it was time, the pros finally outweighing the cons and the feeling of dread which overwhelmed me. Just as Francie had suggested, I sat down and wrote Tom a letter. A letter telling him I was having a baby, a baby I was keeping, and that he was the father. A letter telling him I didn't want or expect anything from him, only that I thought he should know. That I wouldn't think any less of him if he decided not to contact me, and that whatever he did should be what was right for him.

I phoned him that evening to find out his address. I was scared he wasn't going to remember who the hell I was, which was a fair consideration considering how much time had passed. I was nervous as all hell.

'Hi,' I said, when he answered. 'It's Julia here. We met about four months ago at McDougall's . . . and you stayed the night.'

I figured that was enough information to get his memory going — and if it wasn't, then it was probably for the best.

'Julia! Hi,' he said. Either he remembered me or he was very good at acting. 'Geez . . . you keep a guy waiting! Was I *that* bad?'

I laughed. I'd forgotten his sense of humour. Although in all honesty I'd been far too drunk to remember whether he had one at all. I wasn't even sure what he looked like.

'How've you been?' he asked.

'Good,' I replied.

Don't elaborate, I told myself, just get the point and end the conversation. Quickly.

'I just wanted to invite you to a party I'm having in a couple of weeks. If you tell me your address I can send you an invite.'

'Cool,' he replied. 'Sounds good. It's 23 Bradburn Street, Kingsland.'

'OK, then,' I said, jotting it down as quickly as I could. 'Hope you can make it.'

'Same here,' he replied. 'Perhaps we could get together for a drink in the meantime?'

'OK,' I lied. 'Sounds good.'

'This is your number that's come up on my phone?'

'Yeah, that's the one. Give me a call sometime.'

'Will do. Great to hear from you, Julia . . . finally,' he laughed.

'You, too. Take care,' I replied, hanging up the phone.

I sat down on the couch and let out a long sigh.

I could finally breathe easy; it had gone remarkably well, all things considered. He'd seemed, well, genuinely pleased to hear from me.

I was sure he wouldn't be once he got the letter.

The next morning I posted the letter. My hand trembled as I put it into the mailbox. Now all I could do was wait. Wait and see whether he called or not. And if he didn't, well, that would be that, and that would be fine. At least I'd have been honest with him. I had no preference whether he decided to be a part of the baby's life or not. There were good and bad points for both. But the ball was in his court now.

Ten long days went by and I hadn't heard from him. And then he rang.

'Julia?' he said, when I answered the phone.

I knew it was him straightaway.

'I was wondering if it would be OK to come and see you?' he asked.

I could hear something in his voice, but I couldn't place it. Nervousness, perhaps?

'Yes,' I replied. We made arrangements for him to come over to my apartment at seven o'clock the following evening.

It seemed unlikely that he was making the effort to come and see me just so he could tell me he wanted nothing to do with the baby.

'Oh, God,' said Francie. 'What if he wants to make a decent woman of you?'

169

'What?' I was a decent woman, or at least I thought I was. What was she talking about?

'Marry you, Jools.'

'Shit!' I hadn't thought of that. 'Surely people don't do that kind of thing these days?'

'You never know. He might be from some sort of happy-clappy family who'll disown him if he doesn't make you his wife.'

'Do you not think you could have bought this up a little earlier? Say when we were writing the list of pros and cons?' I asked. For someone who was usually so helpful, she was currently being a big pain in the arse.

'I'm sure he won't be,' she comforted. 'I hope.'

And so did I. Not that it wouldn't be lovely to be proposed to one day. Just not when the man, a virtual stranger, had been forced into a corner and was only doing it to save his own skin. I had more romantic visions. Like being in love.

In the build-up to the following evening I was a nervous wreck. 'Good luck,' said Francie, when she rang at six o'clock. 'Be sure to ring me when he's gone — and I was only joking about him wanting to marry you.'

'I bloody hope so,' I replied.

At seven o'clock on the dot he knocked on my door.

I took a deep breath and opened the door, standing aside to let him in.

'Hi,' he said, giving me a kiss on the cheek.

I noticed he was a lot better-looking than I'd remembered, which only proved I still had the ability to be shallow even in a situation as grave as this.

'All fixed?' he asked, pointing at my leg and smiling.

'All fixed,' I replied.

'I never asked you how you did it? Or maybe I did and I just can't remember. I was pretty drunk.'

'Fell off a bike,' I replied. It was hardly a story I wanted to launch into at that point in time.

I retrieved him a beer from the fridge (I kept a few on hand for when Dad came to fix my window/shower/television/light fitting) and we sat down on the sofa.

'You look good,' he said. 'Positively radiant.'

'Thank you,' I replied, blushing slightly.

'I got your letter,' he said, sipping his beer. 'Although I guess you probably know that. No party then?' he smiled.

'No party,' I replied, smiling back.

'Shame,' he said. 'I love a good party.

'It's a bit weird, isn't it?' he said. 'Sitting here making sober small-talk?'

'Sure is.' I replied. He'd hit the nail on the head: I only wished I could down a bottle of wine to calm my nerves.

'So I'll get to the point,' he continued. 'Firstly, thanks for your letter. It was a bit of . . . well, of a shock, I must admit, but I'm glad you told me.'

'Are you really?' I asked. I still wasn't sure I'd done the right thing by telling him.

'Absolutely,' he replied. 'But there are some things I need to know. First-up . . . are you absolutely sure the baby's mine? I have to ask, I'm sorry,' he apologized.

I wasn't angry. In this day and age, it was a fair question.

'Yes,' I replied, handing him the printout from my scan with the date of conception circled on it.

'And you weren't seeing anyone else at the time?' he asked.

'No,' I replied. 'I had been seeing someone for several months who I'd slept with two weeks before. I asked the doctor about this, but he said there's no way the conception date could be that far out.'

'OK,' he replied. 'I just needed to know those two things. I hope you don't mind?'

'No,' I replied, 'of course not.' And I didn't. 'You're welcome to have a paternity test done once it's born if you like? I don't mind.'

'No,' he said, seeming a bit startled at the thought. 'No need for that.'

'Are you sure?' I asked. I wanted him to be sure.

'Yes,' he replied. 'Honestly.'

'Well, if you change your mind, that's OK.'

He nodded. 'What do you think happened?' he asked. 'I mean the condom didn't break, did it?'

'No,' I shrugged. 'I guess we were just one of the unlucky one per cent.'

'I guess I went for the wrong box,' he said, smiling. 'There were just too many to choose from.'

I laughed, remembering how shocked he'd been at the sight of them.

'I'm sorry it's taken me so long to come and see you,' said Tom. 'It's been a tough week or so thinking about it . . . thinking about everything you said. Thinking about what's best for you . . . for the baby . . . for me.'

I nodded my head. I didn't envy him this decision.

'And I didn't want to come and see you until I was sure what I wanted to say.'

'Fair enough,' I said.

'I've thought about not having anything at all to do with the baby, but the thing is, I don't think I could handle that. I'd always wonder whether it was a boy or a girl, what they were up to, what kind of kid they'd turned into.'

I nodded my head again. I could completely empathize with what he was saying.

172

'So, I guess, what I'm trying to say is that I do want to be a part of the baby's life, be a father of sorts. Do whatever I can to help.'

'OK,' I replied.

'Although at the same time I respect that you'll be the main parent, the one raising it. So I'll only come over or take it out when it suits you. I'm not asking for joint custody or anything like that,' he continued. 'Just to be able to visit and spend time when it suits us both.'

I was glad. A small part of me had been scared he'd want too much to do with the baby. I couldn't help thinking that that wouldn't have worked. Plus, some small selfish part of me didn't want to share my baby. Now that I'd decided to keep it, I was excited at the prospect of raising it myself.

'I know it'll be a slightly odd arrangement,' continued Tom. 'But I guess we'll just have to make it up as we go along.'

I agreed. It was going to be odd, but I also had a feeling we were going to make it work.

'Are you going to tell your family?' I asked.

'Yeah.'

'How do you think they'll take it?'

'OK, I think. There's not much they can do about it, is there?'

'Guess not.'

'How about yours?'

I gave him the rundown on Mum and Dad's reaction, and the fact I'd told them an ex-boyfriend was the father.

'Don't worry,' I told him. 'I'll correct my story before it's born.'

'Good,' he smiled. 'I'm worried enough about your dad lunging at me with a pitchfork as it is. Would it be

OK if I popped back in a month or so to see how much you're growing?'

'Sure,' I agreed. 'I'd like that.'

'I could bring some baby photos of myself so you know what to expect if it's a boy.'

I laughed. 'OK.'

'Do you need anything?' he asked, as I walked him to the door. 'Um, money to help pay for anything . . . scans? Baby clothes? I'm not sure what.' He smiled.

'No,' I replied. 'Thank you.' I needed the money all right, but I wasn't after any handouts. I'd made the decision to have the baby by myself and that was exactly what I would do.

'Will you let me know if you do . . . please?'

'OK,' I agreed. It was very sweet of him to offer.

Sally

He opened the webpage and there at the top, in a horrible fluoro-pink colour, was the church logo and mission statement: *Divinity Church: Bringing the Lord Home!*

Below that was a head-and-shoulders shot of Vincent, arms folded across his chest and looking up at the camera, just like Mr November on the firefighters' Christmas calendar. All eyelashes and half-closed eyes. Except Vincent was clothed in his open-necked aqua silk shirt and steel-grey suit jacket. Another new silk shirt, I noted.

Below that was a picture of Vincent and a woman standing together, hand in hand. The woman had my good cream frock and pearls on. I took a closer look at her.

'Is that supposed to be *me*?' I cried.

'It is you, Sally,' said Vincent, laughing. 'Don't you recognize yourself with make-up on and your hair done?'

'But it doesn't look like me!' I protested. 'My teeth aren't that white! Or that big! And as much as I'd like to be I'm not that skinny!'

'Just a small touch-up here and there,' replied Vincent. 'Glen says it's important that we project a desirable image.'

'That we lie?' I hissed back. 'That we tell people if

they believe in Jesus Christ then their teeth will be whiter and they'll be skinnier too?'

The only saving grace, I thought to myself when I'd calmed down, is that if anyone I know sees it they'll just think Vincent's got a new wife.

I looked at the picture again. We looked just like a happily married couple. Who said the camera doesn't lie? I thought.

Vincent scrolled down the page to the next picture. A family shot: Vincent standing in the middle, flanked by Davey and me, and the girls standing in front of us, our hands resting on their shoulders.

'My hair's blond!' cried Davey.

'It's a little lighter,' admitted Vincent.

'Dad, it's a different colour!'

I looked at the picture. It was, too. Davey's hair was sort of milk-chocolate brown, and here it was blond.

'Why on earth?' I asked.

'Because it's important for the children to look the same,' muttered Vincent, shuffling from one foot to the other. 'Like they have the same parents.'

The children stared at me, wide-eyed and waiting for some sort of clarification.

'But they do have the same parents!' I cried.

'I know that, Sally,' said Vincent. 'But we need to show the world that.'

Exactly how many people did he think would visit this website?

'Oh, bloody hell,' I muttered, just low enough for him not to hear, on the off-chance he'd actually been listening to me.

'Don't worry, sweetheart,' I said, putting my arm around Davey. 'Your brown hair looks lovely and handsome and we'll have them change it back.'

But they didn't.

Apparently the children all needed to have blond hair in order for the website to succeed and the future of Divinity Church to remain secure.

As if plastering fake pictures of myself and the children on his hideous website weren't bad enough, two nights later he made another announcement.

'I've been asked to write a book,' he said, as we sat in the living room, pride bouncing off each word.

'*You?*'

'Yes, Sally, *me*,' he replied, as though this were the stupidest question in the world and he was in fact a writer. 'Henry Dickson has asked me to write one.'

Henry Dickson was one of the congregation. He was also a senior editor at a large publishing company.

'What about?' I asked.

'Family values,' replied Vincent.

I stared back at him, clutching my jaw in my hand, just so it wouldn't drop to the floor.

What on earth did he know about family values? He hardly even saw his own family.

'About being a good family man in today's tough modern world,' he continued. 'About setting good Christian examples for my children.'

I was speechless. He was completely oblivious to the fact that he hardly spent any quality time with the children at all.

'And are you going to write this yourself?' I asked, somehow finding my voice.

'Yes,' replied Vincent. 'With Henry's help. Exciting, isn't it?'

From this point on, what Vincent was writing was simply referred to as The Book. And in no time at all The Book had taken precedence over me and the children, which was no surprise. But it had even begun to take precedence over preparing his precious sermons. There was no conversation that was exempt from reference to The Book. He even mentioned it in his sermons. Regularly. At which point the congregation would enthusiastically nod their heads and clap their hands in approval. You would have thought he was the first person on the face of the earth to ever write a book (not that he had actually started writing it). Every story and anecdote he told would somehow hark back to The Book. It's amazing how many connections there were between Jesus dying on the cross or Moses being found in a basket and The Book.

Two weeks later we had to endure the launch of the website, which of course warranted an extravagant gathering at the church for the entire congregation, at which Vincent was the guest speaker. What amazed me was that so many people turned up to the launch. Do they really consider the website to be that much of an accomplishment? I wondered. And their hard-earned money well spent?

Naturally the children and I were there, in our church outfits, standing beside Vincent as he whipped a large curtain off the wall behind the altar, on which there was a large projected image of the website. The applause was deafening, with even the odd 'whoop' reaching our ears. Vincent found it in himself to bow. Twice.

You'd think he'd designed the damn website himself.

'Have you had many hits, Dad?' asked Davey, as we sat at the breakfast table a few days later. I think he was referring to people visiting the website.

so she wouldn't have to go along by herself. Some of the 'fun' things she'd dragged me along to in the past were Boot Camp Weekend (a whole weekend filled with painful army-type exercise, disgusting food, and being yelled at, which I had paid five hundred dollars for the pleasure of attending), orienteering (where we got lost in the Woodhill Forest for five hours and were finally rescued by a park ranger and his quad bike) and pole-dancing classes (where I swung myself right off the pole in the second class and concussed myself on the side of the podium).

'It'll just be a nice singalong with a bunch of girls. Nothing fancy,' said Izzy.

'It better not be,' I warned, finally giving in and agreeing to go along with her — just once, mind you, and for no other reason than that *Boston Legal* was about to start and I wanted her to shut up. Singing was OK for Izzy, who actually had a voice, but not for me, whose voice was not dissimilar to nails on a blackboard.

'You've a lovely voice,' assured Izzy. 'Really lovely.'

She was lying.

So on Thursday evening at seven o'clock we headed along to the Eastside Community Centre to join the PINK choir. We walked into the hall to find about thirty others milling around and chatting amongst themselves.

'What are the blokes doing here?' I asked Izzy as we approached the group.

The look she gave me suggested she had no idea what they were doing there either.

They were on the feminine side of blokey, but blokes nonetheless. In fact some of them looked more like women than some of the women did. All of the women had short, cropped hair and wore button-down shirts and jeans. There seemed to be some sort of uniform in operation. I hoped like hell we wouldn't have to change into it. Izzy and I looked remarkably out of place with our long hair and skirts.

'They look like dykes,' I hissed.

This proved to be a fairly accurate description, because five minutes later — when the choir leader (Leo, a tiny Hispanic man wearing what appeared to be women's jeans and a very tight and cropped black T-shirt) greeted us all — he announced, in a very loud and high-pitched voice, 'Welcome along to PINK, the best gay and lesbian choir in town!'

Which would explain three things: why there were blokes present, why the women looked like men, and why the choir was called PINK.

I turned to Izzy and willed daggers to shoot out of my eyes and into the side of her head. Just what the hell had she brought me to? And after the whole Gus thing, what's more!

This was just one more nail in my heterosexual coffin.

'You have to be fucking joking,' I mouthed at her.

'I didn't know,' she mouthed back at me.

Before I could pick up my handbag and do a runner, we were ushered into tiered rows on the stage, Izzy and I separated by the choir leader in accordance with the house rules of mixing up the sexes, though I had to wonder what the point was. I found myself standing in the third row, between Ian and Ali, who were both wearing white jeans and skin-tight T-shirts.

And then the singing began. First up was 'Amazing Grace', a perfect match for the excruciatingly high-pitched wails which flew out of Ian and Ali's mouths. The women in the group provided the bass baritone, except for Izzy and me, who found ourselves stuck somewhere in mid-range limbo.

But it wasn't quite up to scratch for Leo, so we had to sing it three more times.

'A little higher if you can, girls!' he instructed us. We were being out-pitched by blokes. I couldn't go any higher, it was impossible.

Once we got it right, we moved on to 'Downtown', 'Wishin' and Hopin'', 'Melting Pot' and 'Build Me Up, Buttercup'. All of which were accompanied by lots of hip-shaking, finger-snapping and clapping, mostly from the men.

I stared at the lyrics sheet in my hand and concentrated on mouthing the words as best I could.

When will this stop? I wondered, shaking my hips (not because I wanted to, but because Ian and Ali were shaking theirs ferociously, and it was either join in or be bounced down onto the heads in front). I was stranded inside a bad Judy Garland musical.

Forty-five long minutes later we stopped for an intermission break, at which point I grabbed my handbag and made a beeline for the exit. Izzy followed dutifully behind me.

'Sorry 'bout that . . .' she said, once we were safely in the car. 'I had no idea.'

Something in the tone of her voice made me look at her and burst out laughing, which started her off too. Before you knew it we were both sitting there, convulsed with laughter, tears streaming down our faces.

'P-p-people must have thought we were t-t-together,' spluttered Izzy.

'Li-li-li-lipstick lesbians,' I added.

'Sh-sh-should get Gus and Dan along,' I croaked. 'They'd l-l-love it!'

'Could b-b-buy them a year's membership,' added Izzy.

Finally we managed to regain our composure enough to drive home.

Then Izzy said, 'Do you think they had to sq-sq-squeeze their balls to get that high note?' and I had to pull over to the side of the road while we erupted into fits of laughter again for another fifteen minutes.

I couldn't remember laughing that uncontrollably in a long time — or laughing at all, for that matter. I'd forgotten how completely exhilarating and exhausting a good laugh was.

Jools

Overnight my medium-sized white woman's boobs had been abducted and replaced with the boobs of a large African woman. My nipples resembled two giant spotlights, only dark chocolate-brown. I was all nipple. And, Lord, how they itched. Especially at night-time. It was a surprise they were still attached to my breasts come morning.

And, Lordy, the size of them! I'd gone from a B-cup to a D-cup in but a few weeks. This, coupled with the fact my arse had no desire to be left out of the game and had also doubled in size, meant that I had to go underwear shopping. For the first time in my life, bra shopping had become about comfort. Not about which bra would look best flung over the side of my sofa after being frantically discarded in the act of hot lovemaking with some foxy man I'd fortuitously managed to pick up the night before. It was a sad day, and Francie kindly offered to hold my hand through the ordeal.

'It looks nice,' she lied, as we stood in the dressing room of Farmers. 'Y'know . . . really comfy.'

I stood in front of the mirror, looking at the cotton lycra beige sports bra covering my gi-normous boobs and felt a tear slide down my cheek. The chances of me finding the bloke of my dreams whilst wearing this hideous piece of man-repellent were so slim they could have slid out under a closed door. It was OK for all those women out there who already had a loving and trapped man. A man who had seen them in their sexiest lingerie enough times and who knew that the beige bra was an interim eyesore that would be over in mere months and just a distant horrible memory (or so they hoped). Plus, they could always put mind over matter and visualize the sexy lingerie — if they were lucky enough to get a shag at any stage in the next nine months. But it wasn't OK for me.

What the hell are you worrying about? I asked myself. As if the man of your dreams is going to come within three miles of a five-months pregnant woman anyway. A hideous bra is the least of your worries. I felt a tear slide down my other cheek.

'Oh, Jools,' comforted Francie, giving me a hug. 'You look gorgeous. The sexiest pregnant woman I've ever seen!'

I knew for a fact that the only other pregnant woman Francie had seen in her underwear was her sister Jennifer, all twelve stone and five-foot-two of her. Still, I let her shower me with comforting lies as I managed to pull myself together and get dressed.

Not being a fan of prolonging any form of agony, I decided to also purchase several pairs of cotton high-waisted knickers, more commonly known as Nana Knickers, because the only person who should ever be caught dead or half-naked in them is your nana. They had quite the selection in a variety of colours: pale pink, pale blue, pale green, and beige. Always one to co-ordinate my lingerie wherever possible, I decided to buy two beige pairs, supplemented with a pair of each of the other hideous pastel colours. After stoically resisting the Nana Knickers for five months, I could no longer deny the fact that if I kept wearing lacy G-strings I would either be sawn in half or lose one forever to the gaping abyss of cellulite that was my arse.

In the midst of such high excitement as shopping for beige underwear, I overshot my twenty-week scan. How could I?

My twenty-week scan meant two things. One, that I was bang on halfway through my ordeal. (Pregnancy, as I had discovered very recently, is forty weeks in duration, which, if you do the maths, is far closer to ten months than nine. You may think an extra month is neither here nor there, but I can tell you that when you have a wriggling parasite the size of a ten-kilo sack of spuds squatting in your innards, it is very much here.) And two, that I could now find out the sex of my baby.

'What do you want to know for, love?' asked Mum. 'It's going to be one or the other, isn't it?'

Still, I wanted to know which one or the other it was going to be. The whole baby thing was enough of a surprise for me without adding more cheap thrills at the finishing gate.

I asked Francie to come along with me.

'Really?' she squealed. 'I'd love to.'

'Have a look at the screen,' instructed the doctor.

And there, on the screen in front of us was a little black-and-white creature that, on closer inspection, looked remarkably like a baby. A little baby waving its little arms and legs about.

I stared at it, speechless. Amazed that this being was currently inside me. Amazed by how utterly human and un-alien it looked.

'Wow!' exclaimed Francie. 'Look! It's waving its little hand. How cute!'

'Quite an active one,' observed the doctor, as its little hands and feet punched the air. This may have had something to do with the two flat-whites I'd just ingested.

'Look at its little fingers!' said Francie, who was still going on about its hands. 'They're adorable . . . just adorable!'

'I'll just check its measurements and heart,' said the doctor, as we watched the cursor stop and click at various points on the baby.

'All looks perfect,' he concluded. 'Would you like to know the sex?'

I looked at Francie, as though she were in some way responsible for my current state and needed to be consulted. She nodded back at me, encouragingly.

'Yes,' I smiled, never in a million years thinking I would find learning the sex of my baby so exciting that I could barely breathe.

Secretly I hoped it was a girl, for no other reason than I seemed to have great trouble forming a lasting relationship with any male and I stupidly feared this might cross over to my offspring. But perhaps a son would be handy? He could fix my broken doorknobs and mow my lawn.

Who cares — I finally settled on — as long as it's all hunky-dory.

'Notice anything missing?' asked the doctor.

I stared at the wee baby on the screen. It appeared to have two arms and two legs, a head, two ears, eyes, the correct number of fingers and toes.

'Um . . . no,' I replied.

'Look again,' he instructed.

'Where's its . . . penis?' asked Francie, who had also been staring at the screen.

'Bingo,' said the doctor. 'Which means that you are having a little girl.'

'Or a boy with a very small . . . y'know,' said Francie, scaring the bejesus out of me.

'It's definitely a girl,' assured the doctor, shooting Francie a look.

'Wow!' I replied, a little lost for words. 'A girl!'

I was having a baby girl. A daughter.

Suddenly the small image on the screen suddenly seemed so real. It was a little girl. *My little girl.*

I felt a tear slide down my cheek. A happy, relieved tear. I was having a daughter and she was healthy.

I looked at Francie, who also had tears in her eyes.

'Unbelievable,' said Francie, as we left the hospital, beaming at each other, a second DVD of my baby in my hand. 'There's a real live baby in there,' she said, patting my tummy.

Francie was of the same school of thought as me. The school of thought which gave no thought at all to the development of a baby until it was born and was more than happy to think of it as some sort of shapeless blob which made women fat and complain about swollen ankles and then miraculously morphed into a mini human being just before it popped out of their vagina. In other words, we were ill-informed and completely uninterested in baby development, or at least we had been.

'You know what we have to do now?' said Francie, as she started the car

'No,' I replied, still smiling like the village idiot.

'Go shopping . . . for baby clothes.'

'But I've no money,' I replied, which was a sad but undeniably true fact. I was broke.

'*Please,*' pleaded Francie. 'I want to buy her something. Let's just go and have a little peek in Child . . . pretty please.'

Child was a children's clothes shop on Ponsonby Road which was filled with the most unbelievably gorgeous babies' and kids' clothes — at hideously expensive prices. All of the Ponsonby mothers shopped there, but the difference was that most of them had money. Or husbands with money. Or both.

But Francie insisted on taking me there, and also insisted on buying the most gorgeous teeny white sundress, covered in hand-painted poppies, and a beautiful white French shawl. My daughter wasn't born yet and she already knew how to shop beyond her means. Just like her mother.

The following night Tom paid me another visit. I hadn't seen him for a month.

'Hey!' he cried, as I opened the front door. 'You've got a little bump!'

'Not that little!' I replied.

He handed me a beautiful bunch of lilac and white lilies.

'Thank you! They're gorgeous,' I said, giving him a kiss on the cheek.

I poured us both a wine, a big one for him and a small one for me, and we sat on the sofa and chatted. I told him all about my scan.

'Do you want to know what it is?' I asked him.

'You mean what sex? Do you know already?'

'Yes,' I smiled.

'Wow! Yeah, OK then,' he smiled back.

'It's a girl.'

'A girl? Fantastic! A little girl!' He couldn't have been happier. 'And everything's OK?' he asked tentatively.

'Yes,' I replied. 'All her measurements are perfect. And the doctor said she has a strong heart.'

'Fantastic news,' he said, smiling. 'Would you mind if I touched your tummy?'

'Not at all,' I replied. I was getting very used to people planting their hands on my belly.

He gently touched my tummy with his right hand. 'It's so firm,' he noted.

'I know, weird isn't it? I've grown out of all my pants and skirts already. Do you want to see a DVD of it?' I asked.

'You're kidding!' he replied. 'Sure, I'd love to.'

The DVD was already in the machine, due to the fact I'd watched it at least fifty times since the day before. I pressed 'play'.

'Wow!' said Tom, his mouth open wide. 'It's so developed! Look at its little hands and feet! Bloody hell!'

He obviously knew as little about the development of unborn children as I did.

'She's so cute,' I sighed. I couldn't help myself.

'She sure is,' he agreed.

'Have you had any dinner?' I asked, when the DVD had finished.

'Ah, no,' said Tom, glancing at his watch. 'Not yet.'

I looked at the clock. It was 6 p.m.

'Sorry,' I said, smiling, 'but if I don't have dinner by six-thirty I self-combust. Why don't you stay for a bite, if you're hungry? It won't be anything flash, though,' I added. This was an understatement, to say the least.

'Great. I'd love to,' he answered. 'Though I've got a

better idea. Why don't you show me around your kitchen and then sit yourself back on the sofa and I'll make us some dinner instead?'

'But you're a guest!' I replied.

'I don't mind at all,' insisted Tom. 'I love cooking, and, I know it's a cliché, but you must be worn out.'

Truth be told, I was a bit tired and my feet were killing me.

Plus I hate cooking with a violent passion and he'd just claimed to love it.

'OK,' I agreed.

It didn't take long to show him around my kitchen, which was mildly embarrassing to say the least. Not only tiny, my kitchen was also incredibly ill-equipped. It was the kitchen of someone who was not only a terrible cook, but who also loathed cooking. My mother despaired over my handicap. She came from a generation where the ability of women to cook and bake was akin to breathing, and she couldn't comprehend how I was incapable of doing either.

'But if you just put your mind to it, Julia, surely . . .' she'd say.

'Why the hell would I put my mind to doing something I hate?' I'd reply. What was the point? And what would happen to all the takeout restaurants in my neighbourhood if I suddenly learned to cook? They'd go under and several people would be out of jobs. That's what.

As I opened my fridge door I saw the look on Tom's face — that happy-go-lucky expression he wore that indicated he could always see the bright side of anything — waver, just for a moment.

His eyes scanned from the butter to the milk, to the one tomato, to the cheese, to the half-eaten bag of lettuce leaves, to the pottle of yogurt, to the pack of chorizo sausages, back to the butter.

'Told you it was a little bare,' I said, turning to him.

'You weren't wrong,' he smiled. 'But fear not, it's workable.'

So I sat back on the couch, my feet on the footstool, and watched the news while a man I hardly knew (who was also the father of my child) cooked me dinner.

'How about we just eat in here?' suggested Tom, walking back into the lounge thirty minutes later with a fabulous-looking bowl of chorizo-sausage pasta and a pear-and-parmesan green salad in tow.

'Wow!' I cried. 'It looks fantastic!'

'Hopefully it tastes OK,' he replied, setting two plates and cutlery down on the coffee table.

It did. It tasted absolutely divine and I told him so. How he'd managed to whip this little five-star feast up in my kitchen with the few mangy items I had in my fridge and pantry was beyond me.

'Are you sure you didn't nip out the back door while I wasn't looking and borrow someone else's kitchen?' I asked.

'No,' he laughed, 'although I must admit it was a bit of a challenge.'

I ate as much as I could possibly fit, which was by no means as much as I would have liked to have eaten. How little am I going to be able to put away when I am nine months pregnant? I wondered. I'd be down to three pinenuts a sitting.

'So, have you told your parents?' I asked Tom, after he'd insisted on clearing the dishes away and was back sitting on the sofa.

'Yes.'

'And how did it go?'

'Pretty good, considering. I mean they weren't overly pleased at the circumstances, but they came round pretty quickly . . . they're really excited about the prospect of a grandchild. They were wondering if it would be OK for them to visit it . . . sorry, I mean her?'

'Of course!' I replied. If they were as nice as Tom, which I was sure they were, I'd be more than happy for them to have a relationship with my daughter. Plus, I thought, this solo mother's going to need all the babysitters she can find.

By the time he left, Tom had been there three hours. It was the escape of a couple of my uncontrollable yawns which prompted him to say 'better let the mother get some rest'. I wasn't yawning because I was in any way bored; in fact I'd thoroughly enjoyed his company. It was just that I was usually in bed by eight o'clock and it was now nine.

'Sorry,' I apologized. 'Bit of a nana these days.'

'How about we catch up again in a few weeks?' he suggested. 'Just so I can check on the bump. Maybe you can come to dinner at my place?'

'Sounds good,' I agreed. 'Especially now I know you can cook.'

I went to bed, happy in the knowledge that it appeared that my daughter was going to have a wonderful father in her life. Tom was sweet and thoughtful, and a gentleman. I was lucky. Out of all the men in the country I could have had a one-night stand with and who would end up fathering my baby, I'd done pretty well. Although I didn't need or want Tom to play a major parenting role, it was comforting to know he was there, and willing.

194

To top off the decline into sensible-knicker land, I had to admit that, after being in constant pain for the past month, my lower back was killing me. I had thought it was the result of sitting at a computer five days a week, but, no matter how many rest periods or stretches I incorporated into my working day, it didn't seem to get any better.

'You'd better go to the chiropractor, love,' said my mother, giving me the phone number. 'You don't want to have a crook back with a wee baby.'

I thought it was highly likely that the wee baby was responsible for my crook back, considering I'd never had back problems before. Since the wee baby wasn't going anywhere for a good few months yet, I decided to make an appointment.

'Do you usually wear heels?' asked the chiropractor, glancing down at my Costume National cream knee-high boots. My favourite knee-high boots, of the twenty or so pairs in my wardrobe.

I was a shoe whore in the dirtiest sense of the words. I would not only sell my body for a pair of new-season Patrick Cox heels, I would throw my soul in for free. Nothing could lift my spirits more than purchasing a new pair. Nothing. I mean *nothing*. Not even sex. I loved shoes. Don't get me wrong, I loved sex too. But I loved shoes more.

'See how they sparkle!' I'd exclaim to Francie, as she dutifully accompanied me on shoe-buying missions.

'They're talking to you,' she'd reply in a wise voice. 'They want you.'

The wanting was usually mutual.

'Every day,' I told the chiropractor.

'Well, I strongly recommend that you don't,' he said, smiling.

Surely the smile meant he was having me on?

'Don't wear . . . *heels?*' I whimpered.

'Yes.'

I stared back at him, a possum trapped in headlights, paws superglued to the tarseal.

'Your entire pelvis is shifting and tilting forward to make way for the baby,' he explained. 'And wearing heels is putting severe and unnecessary pressure on your lower back. In other words, I'd say it's likely that the heels are causing you back pain in your pregnancy.'

But really it was the baby who was causing my back pain, not the heels. I'd worn heels my entire life, I may have even been born with a pair on, and there'd been no problems. None whatsoever. Heels were a part of Who I Was. As necessary to my physique as my fingernails and thigh bones. Without heels I was positively dwarf-like. A gnome. Without heels I could barely reach the top shelf of my refrigerator. Without heels I was five-foot-*nothing*.

'Let's have a look,' he said.

I took my boots off and lay up on the table, while he gently prodded at my lower back.

'The muscles around your pelvis are very inflamed,' he noted.

This explained why every prod of his finger resulted in fiery pains shooting up my back and down my legs.

Next he put me through a series of stretching exercises, including bending forward and touching my toes while he stood directly behind me with his hands resting on my hips. Not the most comfortable position to find yourself in with a sixty-year-old balding chiropractor. But his verdict was still the heels.

He wanted me to stop wearing them, immediately, and return for another appointment in a week.

With tears in my eyes, I reluctantly agreed.

But not before I asked him what the damage would be if I kept wearing heels for the next few months and whether there was some sort of operation that could reverse it. His answers: *irreversible damage* and *no, there wasn't.*

There were operations for every-bloody-thing these days. Why wasn't there one for short pregnant women who needed to wear heels? It wasn't my fault I was short.

I walked my deflated self back to the car and fished my ringing cellphone from the depths of my handbag. It was Francie.

'How did it go?' she asked.

'Terrible!' I wailed. 'I can't wear heels!'

'Oh *sweet* Jesus!' cried Francie, who knew just how vital they were to my physical being. 'Why on earth not? Can't you get a second opinion?'

'I could, but it'd probably be the same. He seemed certain.'

'What the hell are you going to do?'

'I have no idea,' I despaired. 'I guess I'll have to wear flats.'

'*Flats?* Oh God! Can't you wear even a tincey-wincey heel?' she asked.

'No. Apparently not.'

'Crap.'

'Exactly.'

'Don't worry,' she soothed. 'It'll soon be over and you'll be back in heels before you know it.'

Bless her for being so nice, but she was wrong. It wouldn't be over for four months. Four long heel-less months.

'Plus,' she added. 'I bet you can sneak them on

occasionally and he'll never know. Just so they know you still love them.'

So off to work I went the next day in my flat shoes — after I'd gone and bought a pair that is. Sensible flat black shoes. With those and my sensible knickers on, I felt just like a school matron; there's no denying that with the round hump protruding from my front I had a frighteningly similar physique. It was as though any sex appeal had been sucked out of my body by an industrial vacuum, before being smeared across the railway tracks in the beating sunshine.

I'd heard of pregnant women feeling the sexiest they've felt in their entire lives, sporting an insatiable lust for sex, day and night, all but killing their husbands and boyfriends. All I can say is that they must have spent their pre-pregnancy lives either boarding in a nunnery or locked in a dark cupboard. I felt about as attractive as a plate of overcooked haggis. If a good-looking man had come near me, I wouldn't have touched him with a ten-foot bargepole.

As I drove to the office in my sensible black shoes, I tried not to think about how close my contract was to finishing. In three weeks I would be without a job. Again. I'd been searching but there was nothing around, and unfortunately there wasn't any more work available where I was.

'I wish we had something,' said my boss Sarah. 'I really do. You've been wonderful.'

The truth was I'd never worked so hard in my life. I got to work on time and usually stayed late, a combination of not having been out on the booze the night before and no plans to go out that night, as my social life had ground to a halt. And aside from the many mad dashes to the bathroom when I'd first started, I'd never been so focused, once again the result of not having been out on the booze the night before. Sarah thought I was the bee's knees.

'I'll be sorry to see you go,' she sighed.

If I was lucky, I'd pick up another couple of months' work before the baby was born. If not, I wasn't sure what the hell I'd do.

'Something will come up,' Francie kept saying, trying to make me feel better.

But it didn't. And three weeks later I was unemployed, once again. Unemployed and six months pregnant. I tried to reformat my mortgage again and lighten the burden for the next six months — time for me to have the baby and find another job — but the bank wasn't so keen to lighten my load. Bastards, I thought. Have they no compassion for a pregnant and destitute single woman?

So regretfully I faced the grim facts I could no longer avoid, and made a phone call to a number I knew off-by-heart. And with that, a cruel hand pressed the rewind button on the B-grade video that was My Life.

Sally

'How was your holiday with the children? asked Esther.

'It was great, just lovely,' I replied. 'The best few days we've had together in ages. I really need to take them away more often,' I added.

'I'm glad,' said Esther. 'And you enjoyed yourself, too?'

'I had a ball,' I replied. 'I really did. It was so nice to get away.'

'Did it bother you that Vincent didn't go on holiday with you?' she asked.

'No. I'm not sure it would have been quite as enjoyable if he had.'

We talked a little more about the holiday, until Esther expertly turned the conversation back to me, asking me about my job and whether I enjoyed it.

'Yes,' I replied. 'I do. There's something wonderful about caring for people at the end of their lives . . . they know so much and they've given so much. Some of them are such characters, they're hilarious.'

'Is there anything about yourself that you're unhappy with?' asked Esther.

I thought about it. 'It's an old cliché, but I'd like to be a bit slimmer,' I replied. 'Or at least a little fitter. I just feel a bit frumpy at the moment . . . well, ever since I had Hannah really.'

'Do you like exercising?' asked Esther.

'I don't mind it, if it's something fun, it's just trying to find the time . . . I know that sounds silly.'

'Not at all. Trying to balance work life, home life and three children doesn't leave much you-time. But I think that's what you need, Sally . . . some you-time.'

Some me-time? What on earth was that?

'That can just be sitting down for half an hour reading a magazine,' explained Esther. 'Or going for a walk, or taking a nap, or painting your nails, whatever you wish. It's incredibly important to have this time doing something for yourself each day, but you need to consciously make the effort to ensure you do.'

'I'll try,' I promised. Truth be told, I quite liked the sound of this me-time business.

I told Esther about the exercise video I'd been wanting to buy.

'Sounds great,' she laughed. 'And if you think it's something you'd enjoy doing, then go for it!'

She was right. I would buy the video and whip the pudding that was my body into shape.

'Other aspects of me-time,' continued Esther, 'can be hanging out with your girlfriends, meeting them for a coffee or wine, or going to a movie.'

I thought about the girlfriends I could meet for a coffee or wine after work, or even a movie, and that's when I realized that I didn't really have any. Friends, that is. My 'friends' were all people from church, women who Vincent and I socialized with at mutual dinners and church functions, along with their husbands. I never socialized with them on a one-on-one basis. Would I want to? I wondered. No, I decided. Their straight-laced morals and blatant adoration for Vincent annoyed me. There was no way I could ever confide in them about anything. My sister Claire and Henny were the only two people I could consider real friends.

How sad am I? I thought, and then I said it. 'Thirty-five years old and I've only got two real friends, one of whom is my sister.'

'You're not sad,' said Esther. 'Not at all. You seem like a very social and friendly woman who'd have no trouble at all making friends . . . if she wanted to.'

Suddenly I found myself remembering my teenage years, when I'd had three real friends: Jools, Kat and Greta. I remembered the time we'd gone on school camp and snuck out of the cabins at night to have a cigarette, waiting until our teacher Mrs Murphy had started snoring, only to get lost in the bush and not be found until morning, cold and hungry. Needless to say, after the search had been called off and we'd been checked over by the local doctor, our parents had been asked to come and pick us up immediately. The four of us had gallantly stuck to our alibi (for years after) that Jools (who had been known to sleepwalk on occasion) had sleepwalked right out of the cabin and into the bush. Greta, Kat and I had woken up and run after her. It had sounded like such a foolproof alibi, although the packet of cigarettes sticking out of Jools's pyjama pocket tainted it slightly.

'I used to have friends,' I found myself saying. '*Great* friends.'

'What happened?' asked Esther.

'We lost touch . . . I don't really know why. As soon as school finished, we all went our separate ways.'

'If only there had been email,' said Esther, smiling.

'Exactly.' I smiled back. 'I bumped into one of the girls, Greta, a couple of months ago in the supermarket. I'd gone there to get away from Vincent. I was standing there staring blankly at the shelves when she came up to me. She looked so gorgeous, so happy. Just like she used to. She gave me her number and told me to ring her, so we could catch up properly, but I didn't.'

'Why not?' asked Esther.

'I don't know . . . because she looked so wonderful, and happy . . . because I wasn't. I didn't want to have to talk about my life, about my marriage.'

'It's perfectly understandable to feel a bit unsocial when you're not feeling particularly happy, Sally,' said Esther. 'You can always give your friend Greta a call when you feel like being social again. If she's an old friend I'm sure she'll understand.'

'You're right,' I replied. 'I will. And I do want to be more social — it's just that, well, it's such a performance making time for myself that I usually give up.'

'You mean because you're so busy with work and the children?'

'That and Vincent doesn't seem all that keen to mind them by himself.'

'I see,' said Esther. 'Does he encourage you to make time for yourself?'

'Well . . .' I replied, although I'd no idea why my answer required any thought. 'No, not exactly.'

'I see,' said Esther again. But unlike a lot of people who said *I see* and you just knew they couldn't see a damn thing, I felt like she could actually see what I was saying.

'I'd like to have more friends,' I found myself saying. 'Real friends.'

'There's no reason why you can't,' replied Esther. 'If you can learn to make time for yourself . . . and learn to put yourself first sometimes.'

'I'll try,' I promised.

'Sally, I know we've only had a couple of chats together so far . . . but it seems to me that there's only one thing in your life which is making you, shall we say, unhappy . . . and that is your relationship with your husband.'

I looked back at her, my head beginning to nod of its own accord.

'From what you've told me you're happy with pretty much every other aspect of your life, including your job, and your wonderful relationship with your children.'

I nodded again.

'Does what I'm saying upset you?' she asked.

'Yes, it upsets me, and I wish it wasn't the case . . . but you're right.'

'Do you think Vincent would consider coming and talking with me, by himself?' asked Esther.

'No,' I replied, explaining about 'the profile' and his fears of being exposed.

'How about coming along with you then so we can talk about your relationship together?'

'I doubt it,' I replied. 'But I guess I can ask him.'

'Although,' added Esther, 'there's no point embarking on marriage counselling unless you both want your marriage to work. Unless you feel it's worth saving. I guess that gives you something to think about,' she said, giving me that warm smile.

That afternoon, when I got home, I picked up the phone and placed my order for Carmen Electra's striptease workout video.

'What on earth are you doing?' demanded Vincent, walking into the living room three days later. I looked up at him through my split legs. He was upside-down.

'She's stripping,' answered Elizabeth.

'I'm getting fit,' I replied.

'This is indecent,' he hissed, standing over me. 'And in front of the children!'

'It's just exercise, Vincent,' I replied.

'It's filthy rubbish,' he snapped, picking up the remote from the coffee table and switching the television off.

'If you don't want to watch it, then leave the room,' I replied calmly, as I stood up, took the remote from his hand, switched the television back on, and flipped my head back down towards the floor, shaking my bottom as I did so, just like Carmen.

He looked back at me, lost for words.

'Elizabeth,' he said, regaining his composure and gesturing towards the sofa. 'Come with me.'

'But I'm watching Mum,' she replied. 'I've got to tell her when her bum's slipping.'

He looked back at me, through my split legs. He was still upside-down.

'She's right,' I replied. 'She has to tell me when my bum's slipping. It's important.'

Elizabeth nodded back at him, to indicate how serious her role was.

He passed one final horrified look across my bobbing backside and was gone.

'Bum up, Mum!' called out Elizabeth, snapping me back to the job at hand.

Kat

In my washing frenzy I had managed to break the washing machine.

'I've only had it three years!' I complained to the manufacturer, when I phoned.

'How many times a day do you use it?' she asked.

'I used to use it about twice a week, but, since my husband left me for a man, I don't know, probably about five times a day.'

After what seemed like twenty minutes of silence, she asked, 'When did your husband . . . ah . . . leave you?'

'Six months and three long days ago,' I replied. 'But who's counting?'

'Well, that's a little more than the average household use we recommend . . . so I'm sorry to say we won't be able to cover the repair cost.'

This meant that, aside from now having lots of unwanted spare time, I had to make a trip to the laundromat on Saturday morning, a basket of largely clean clothes in tow.

No point in getting changed, I thought, catching sight of my shabby old leggings, T-shirt and unmade-up face in the hall mirror.

Oh for fucksake, I thought, as I walked through the doors of the laundromat. What were the odds? Twice in two weeks. Really, what were they?

They both looked like they'd stepped straight off the pages of *GQ*. Dan in his Diesel T-shirt, army-print cargo shorts and slip-on sneakers. And Gus in his trendy candy-striped polo shirt, jeans strategically worn and faded in just the right places, and designer sneakers. I'd never laid eyes on any of these clothes before. Exactly how many new clothes had he bought? And why the hell didn't he dress this well when *we* were married?

I glanced down at my highly unfashionable lime-green T-shirt and leggings. Thankfully I'd managed to take my slippers off before I left, but the tatty old runners I had on in their place weren't much better.

Not again, I despaired. Dear God, no.

It was too late to turn and run. Much too late. I was standing a mere three metres in front of them, practically perched on their eyeballs. Even if they were both blind (which unfortunately they weren't), they'd still have known I was there.

I hadn't seen either of them since the comedy of errors that was the supermarket visit. It was difficult to say which was more embarrassing: this memory or the fact I looked like I'd stepped straight off the set of *Coronation Street*. There was no other word for how I must have appeared; I was looking *dowdy*.

What the hell are they doing here? I wondered. Dan had a washing machine; I'd seen it with my own two eyes.

'Hiya, Kat,' called Gus, walking towards me and giving me a kiss on the cheek. Dan followed his cue.

Since when did he say 'hiya'? He used to say good old-fashioned 'hi'. What the hell was wrong with that? Not gay enough?

I walked to the counter, changed a note for some coins, and walked back to the only available washing machine which was, you guessed it, right next to theirs.

I glanced at their pile of washing and realized that, unfortunately, they had at least one more load to go.

'Did your washing machine break, too?' I asked. I couldn't help myself.

'No,' replied Dan. 'I'm getting a new bathroom and kitchen put in . . . no water for a few days.'

A new bathroom and kitchen? Renovations? The big R! They'd been living together for a few months and they were already renovating the apartment? I suddenly felt very queasy. Renovations were something people did when they were deadly serious about each other, weren't they? Something married couples did together. Something Gus and I had done together!

'How's work going?' asked Gus, irritatingly relaxed with the fact that we'd bumped into each other again, with his boyfriend, my ex-friend, standing right there.

Can't you at least feign being a little uncomfortable? I wondered. Or are you already so comfortable living your lives as a couple that I'm a mere blip from the past?

'Fine thanks,' I replied. 'You?'

Fuck it! I thought. Here I go again, being all polite when I should be hurling my demented body at the washing machines and them, crying desertion, and frothing uncontrollably at the mouth.

Instead it was like a game of charades, all of us pretending that hanging out together at the laundromat was the most normal thing in the world, just like the good old days. Only in the good old days I was married to Gus. And Gus wasn't fucking Dan.

I couldn't help glancing at the pile of clothes in their washing basket, which Gus was in the middle of folding, while Dan sat beside him, flicking through a magazine.

It was a label-fest. Ralph Lauren polo shirts, Diesel

jeans, and enough Calvin Klein boxers to sink a ship. I suddenly felt very self-conscious about my pile of washing; throwing my Glassons T-shirts and pastel-coloured undies into the washing machine as though they were on fire.

Folding washing? Why the fuck didn't you do that when we were married?

I found Izzy's words ringing in my ears. 'It'll take time, Kat, just be patient.' It'll take a long time, I thought. A very long time.

Gus was busy being Mr Perky. He asked me so many questions about my family, work, Izzy and Meg that I felt like I was auditioning for *Who Wants To Be A Millionaire?*

I tried my very best to make my life sound action-packed and interesting, and not as though I was prone to great bouts of unyielding depression and laundering clean clothes.

In my desperation to vacate the premises I washed only half of my clothes (so it was lucky they were already clean) and I took them home wet.

Do you do anything without each other? I wondered, as I somehow forced a smile upon my naked and dishevelled face and gave them a little wave goodbye. It's like they're bloody well joined at the hip.

The gift for my internal seething was an enormous wedgie, which I could feel as soon as I lifted my bottom from the plastic chair and walked towards the door. It felt as big as Mars. They would have had to have their eyes jabbed with hot pokers not to see it. Did I put my washing basket back on the floor and attempt to yank my knickers from the dark side? Or did I just pretend I couldn't notice the way my substantial arse was doubling in on itself, taking my leggings with it?

Before I could decide I'd walked out the door, my giant wedgie following close behind.

I never used to get bloody wedgies, I thought bitterly, as I rescued my knickers behind the safety of my parked car. It's probably because my arse cheeks have doubled in size; my poor knickers don't stand a chance.

'Kat?' said an attractive woman about my age, who was in the process of hoisting a little girl out from the car parked next to me.

I looked at her. She looked familiar; tall and olive-skinned with a trim, sporty figure and long, blonde hair. Very familiar.

'Greta?' I replied. Greta Ridley? Surely not?

Greta had been one of my best friends at high school. I hadn't seen her for at least fifteen years. Greta, Sally, Jools and me, we'd been the best of friends after meeting on the very first day of school. We were inseparable, the Fab Four. Greta the adventurer, Sally the sweet one, Jools the trouble-maker, and me — well, I guess I was the responsible, over-achieving one . . . or at least I'd used to be. For some reason we'd lost touch over the years, although I couldn't remember exactly why. It had just happened. Greta had moved to Australia for a few years after school, Sally had moved to another town with her parents when we were still at school, and Jools I hadn't seen each other since we'd finished school, when she went off to work and I'd headed off to university.

'Sure is!' she cried, popping the little girl down on the ground and giving me a big hug. 'How are you?'

How was I? Well, pretty lousy actually, having just bumped into my gay husband and his lover, my ex-friend, at the bloody laundromat.

I decided it was best to lie.

'I'm great,' I replied. 'How about you? You look fantastic.'

And she did. Gorgeous and stylish. And happy.

'I'm really good, thanks, Kat. This is Ella,' she said, introducing me to the very pretty little blonde-haired girl who was standing beside her, holding her hand.

'Hi, Ella,' I said, shaking her little hand. 'How old are you?'

'I'm four. And my brother's six,' she replied. 'And I go to kindy.'

I love the way kids answered questions with tonnes of extra information. It's so cute.

Two children and happily married, I thought, glancing at the large diamond on Greta's finger. Some people have all the luck.

'I bumped into Sally a couple of months back,' said Greta. 'I gave her my number. I'd hoped she'd give me a call so we could go out for dinner, but she hasn't yet . . . maybe she still will. It'd be great to get us together again.'

'It would,' I agreed. Although I couldn't think of anything worse at this point in time. Getting together with Greta and Sally, who was no doubt also happily married with a pile of kids, and listening to how perfect their lives were. What would I say when they asked me? Well, I'd thought my life was perfect, until my husband decided to run off with another man, our best friend. Now it was just a bleak, childless, lonely horizon, dotted with endless piles of laundry. I'd just end up depressing them, and myself.

But I still took Greta's card when she handed it to me and put it in my handbag.

'Call me,' she said, when Ella finally got restless of our reminiscing. 'Please.'

211

As I drove home, I found myself thinking about the four of us: Greta, Sally, Jools and me. And the good old days. And they really were good old days, I remembered, filled with laughter, adventure, catastrophes and undying friendship. I remembered the time Greta stole her mother's car and the four of us wagged school and drove to the beach for the day, where we baked ourselves with baby oil and lay on the sand in the beating sun. I found myself smiling at the memory: our bikinis, our Coca-Cola, our pop magazines, our sunglasses and our gossip.

It was only the few patches of sand on the floor of the car which had given us away. There was no fooling Greta's mother. I think Greta had been grounded for three weeks, which had seemed like a lifetime back then. Thankfully her mum hadn't told the rest of our parents, so we were spared the same punishment; she only warned us that the next time she would. She was lovely, Greta's mother. In fact, Greta's whole family was; so warm and welcoming and happy. It was always a treat to be at her house, to be a part of her family for the day.

In my haste to leave the laundromat, I had left some washing behind in the machine, mainly consisting of my underwear, including several pairs of high-waisted granny knickers which were completely devoid of any sexual appeal, or any appeal at all to be honest. But luckily for me, Dan and Gus were kind enough to drop them off on their way home, my several pairs of granny knickers folded neatly and sitting proudly at the top of the pile.

Shamed, I took the pile of laundry and bid them farewell.

Once again I had missed the opportunity to rain my hatred and anger upon them. To show them just how hurt and humiliated I was, and how deceitful and hideous they were.

Why am I so nice to them? I wondered. Why can't I bring myself to be nasty, when I so want to be?

If only Izzy had been there, no doubt she would have given me an elbow in the ribs to get me started.

That afternoon I purchased a new washing machine, over the phone, lest I bump into them at the appliance store.

'Don't you want to come in and see it?' asked the salesman.

'Is it a washing machine and does it work?' I replied.

'Yes,' he answered, wondering why it was always his bad luck to get the nutters on the phone.

'Then, no, I don't.'

I asked for it to be delivered immediately.

'Monday will be the earliest we can have it delivered,' he replied.

That was two days away. What the hell was I going to do for two days if I couldn't do any washing?

'Can I pay extra and have it delivered today?' I asked.

'I'm afraid not, our delivery team won't be back on until Monday.'

I let out a long sigh.

'I guess you could always go to the laundromat if your washing is urgent?' he suggested.

'Not on your life,' I replied. 'Never *ever* again.'

'O-kay then,' he said, rushing through my credit-card details in a desperate attempt to hang up the phone and get the hell away from me.

Jools

'I've made your bed up for you,' said Mum, pushing open my old bedroom door.

I glanced around the lemon-coloured room, with the white lace-trimmed curtains, my eyes resting on the single bed against the wall.

'I thought it might make you feel at home,' she said, as I gawped in horror at the pink Tinkerbell duvet.

'Thanks, Mum,' I lied.

'I'll go and make us a nice cuppa,' she said, as Dad plonked my suitcases down on the bedroom floor.

'There we go, love,' said Dad. 'Good to have you home.'

Instead of unpacking, I lay down on the Tinkerbell duvet and stared at the lemon ceiling.

How had it come to this? Here I was with no job, no home, no husband, six months pregnant, and living back in my childhood bedroom in my parents' house, lying on a pink Tinkerbell duvet.

At least my leg isn't broken, I thought, in a desperate attempt to cheer myself up.

And at least my apartment had sold quickly. So quickly it had been a blur. One minute I was living in it, the next it was sold and Mum and Dad were frantically helping me to pack everything into boxes and arrange a storage unit. The new owners had wanted to move in straight away as part of the deal. I hadn't been as sad to leave it as I'd thought I would be. I felt like I was leaving my single girl's life behind, but my new adult life was about to begin.

Although you'd be hard-pressed to tell, I thought, staring at my new surroundings.

Absolutely nothing had changed. There was the cream dressing table with pink drawer handles, the ballerina jewellery box Mum had bought me for my twelfth birthday, the picture of the flying fairy, the Duran Duran poster, even my old hairbrush. It was like I had stepped into the tardus only to find myself twelve years old again and living in 1984.

Isn't life supposed to be about continually moving forward? I thought. Progressing? Then how the hell have I managed to take such giant leaps backwards in such a short space of time?

'Here we go, love,' said Mum, walking into the room with a steaming mug of tea and snapping me out of my despair. 'Let's get you unpacked, shall we?'

Aside from the embarrassment at having stepped my life back twenty-odd years, it was rather nice living with my parents. My mother fussed over me all day every day, and I loved it.

'For heaven's sake, get Julia a cup of tea, Barry!' she'd yell at Dad. 'Can't you see she's with child?'

The food was constant and outstanding. The type of food that I would have turned my nose up at in my previous life but was thoroughly enjoying scoffing down now. Casseroles, devilled sausages, Wiener schnitzel, peas and mashed potato. Good old-fashioned comfort food. In fact, aside from sitting on my bum watching telly, all I did was eat. And it was lovely. The sole benefit of being pregnant was that I felt I could eat whatever I wanted and not worry about it in the slightest. I mean I was getting fat anyway, so I might as well enjoy the ride. Plus, it was the only consolation for not being able to get liquored.

My mother even made my bed. I'm ashamed to admit it, but she did. Every morning. I tried to stop her, but she was having none of it. 'You're not fit to make a bed the state you're in,' she'd say, shaking her head. 'You're not to overexert yourself. You have to take care of the baby.'

I hardly thought making a bed was overexerting myself, but she had other ideas. It was pointless to argue. Apparently turning on my electric blanket was also overexerting myself, because she did this for me too. Mind you, she did it for Dad as well, and he wasn't pregnant, although his tummy had been steadily protruding for the past ten years. It was just my mother's way. She was a Professional Mother. The type of mother who made a career out of it.

I wonder if I'll be like her, I thought. I doubted it. I feared that the mothering gene might have skipped a generation. Having children had never been the number-one priority on my Life List. In fact, until very recently I wasn't sure I'd wanted them at all. Although I felt a certain bond with the little person who was growing inside me, I was not what you would term 'maternal'. Instead of crowding around the small baby gracing a room, gushing at its smile/eyes/skin/tiny hands and desperately clamouring for a hold, as a normal woman would, I was more likely to stand very still, ensure both hands were full, and pray no one passed it to me just so it could immediately burst into tears, which it inevitably did.

The truth is: I was terrified. Not terrified of suddenly having a small, totally dependent being whose welfare and safety I was solely responsible for, as I should have been. But terrified of never again being able to grab my handbag and waltz out the front door to meet Francie for far too many vinos in some fabulous, newly opened bar in town. Well not in the foreseeable future anyway. I was terrified of losing my independence. My life. I loved being able to go away for the weekend at the drop of a hat, go to the movies and pop out for dinner, without having to consult the schedule of an infant or lug around a bag the size of an air-raid shelter. Some experts (friends) told me that the baby should simply adjust to my life. I liked the sound of this, but failed to see how it would enjoy being carted around the city's bars on a Friday night. Plus, what were the chances of being bought drinks by handsome strangers when you had a baby under your barstool?

Sally

After three weeks of stripping for thirty minutes every day, I found that I'd lost five kilograms. I felt great. My body was more supple and flexible than it had been in years.

Vincent did his very best to avoid the living room, and me, which suited me fine. I gathered I was shocking him and he didn't quite know how to tackle the situation.

But it wasn't over yet.

Now that I felt trimmer and healthier, I realized just how dated and dowdy all my clothes were. I needed to go shopping. For the first time in years I felt like going shopping. But I needed someone to go shopping with.

I phoned my sister Claire.

'Shopping? *You?*' she asked. 'Are you sure?'

Claire was a funky dresser. Claire was single. Claire realized how out of character this was for me.

'Of course I will!' she replied. 'Let's go out for the whole day this Saturday. It'll be fun!'

'It'll be a you-day,' she added. I had told her what Esther had said about creating me-time.

That evening, as he climbed into bed, I told Vincent I was going out for the day with Claire.

'What about the kids?' he asked.

'What about them?' I replied.

'Don't they have sports and things?'

'Yes,' I replied. 'You'll need to drop them off, and

pick them up afterwards. I'm sure if you talk to them and look at the timetables on the fridge you'll be able to figure it out.'

I rolled over and went to sleep. Clearly he didn't want to know where I might be going with Claire. Or he simply didn't care.

On Saturday morning I got dressed to go shopping, which only highlighted the importance of the mission. I had nothing to wear shopping. Absolutely nothing. Finally I settled on an unfashionable pair of wide-legged white drill pants, a plain navy V-neck T-shirt, and a pair of navy sandals. I looked just like the boring housewife I feared I was.

'We'd best be off,' said Claire, bursting into the house, looking me up and down, kissing the children, and marching me out the front door. 'We've got our work cut out.'

The truth was she couldn't stand to be in the same room as Vincent for more than two minutes. She had always been tactful about her dislike, meaning that she'd never actually told me that she didn't like him. But I would have had to have been blind not to pick up on it.

He, on the other hand, never ceased to voice his criticisms of Claire.

'Is it any wonder she's still single?' he'd say. 'A woman like that? She'd scare any self-respecting man to death.'

The children loved her. And she them. She was constantly buying them gifts, taking them on outings and spoiling them rotten. This only served to rile Vincent more.

'I don't think it's healthy that the children spend so much time with her,' he'd say. 'She's not exactly a good role model for them.'

Although he was always the first to suggest I ring Claire whenever we needed a babysitter. She always obliged if she could.

'Right,' said Claire, as we hopped into her little I'm-a-childless-woman-and-happy-about-it silver sports car. 'First stop Stephen Marr. Newmarket.'

'Stephen Marr?' I replied.

'Yes,' said Claire. 'You're getting that unfashionable mop you call hair cut and styled. I've made you an appointment.'

I ran my hands through my shoulder-length bobbed brown hair, which could best be described as scraggly. Scraggly and flecked with streaks of salt-and-pepper grey.

I walked into the Stephen Marr salon behind Claire, who strutted in as if she was a regular customer.

'Hi, Claire,' said the trendy young specimen behind the counter. Obviously she *was* a regular customer.

I glanced around the interior, which was all concrete and stylish, and at every impeccably dressed and trendy person within. I suddenly felt even more uncomfortable in my housewife clothes. My outfit's probably so unfashionable it's almost fashionable again, I consoled myself. Although I strongly doubted it.

Five minutes later, our café-class coffees in hand, we were joined by Adrian, a twenty-something man sporting a haircut I hadn't seen since the early eighties, all short and spiky on top and long at the back.

'Hi, Sally,' he said. 'How are we today?'

'Fine, thank you.'

'And what are we doing with this lovely head of yours?' he asked.

'Um . . .' I had no idea what was happening with my hair.

'Right,' said Claire, taking over the instructions. 'Here's what we need . . .'

An hour and a half later I walked out with a head of fashionable (but not so fashionable that it would be impossible for me to maintain) lustrous-looking, gleaming, blonde-highlighted head of hair, complete with trendy feathered fringe. How Adrian had managed to create something so wonderful from the dregs he was given was beyond me.

I couldn't stop touching my hair. It was so different, but I loved it.

'It looks fantastic,' said Claire, giving me a smile. She had insisted on paying for it, God only knew how much it had cost. 'It really suits you.'

'Thanks,' I said, raising my hand and touching it again.

'Time to go shopping!' she declared, grabbing me by the hand and leading me towards Broadway.

One hour later I was carrying three bags full of new clothes. I couldn't remember the last time I'd carried one bag full of new clothes, let alone three.

My purchases included two gorgeous summer dresses: one red-and-white candy-striped, and one leaf-green with shoe-string straps. Both were pleated at the bottom and flared out in the current trend, which Claire insisted on me twirling about the shop in to demonstrate.

Initially I had complained that I really couldn't be spending that much on clothes, it was ridiculous, and how was I going to afford it? But then I'd stopped because Claire wasn't having a bar of it.

But we weren't done yet — we were just stopping for a lunch break, at a trendy restaurant Claire knew. We found a table in the courtyard, in the lovely sunshine, and before I could stop her she'd ordered us both a glass of bubbles.

'To you and your fabulous new hair!' she declared, chinking my glass. 'And your new clothes!' She had insisted I stay in the red-and-white candy-striped dress.

It was the most delicious and relaxing lunch, washed down by another glass of bubbles each.

'OK, sis,' said Claire, looking at her watch and standing up. 'We've still got work to do.'

She dragged me into at least half a dozen more shops where she ensconced me in the changing rooms and flung item after item of clothing at me, until my body could take no more and I needed to sit down again.

Then she dragged me and my stylish new trousers and jeans and blouses to the nail salon for a manicure and pedicure.

'Because you deserve it,' she said, waving away my protests that I'd probably done enough damage for one day.

By the time she dropped me home I was exhausted. But I was also exhilarated and over the moon with my new hair and new clothes. It had been the most enjoyable day I'd had in years.

'Thanks, Claire,' I said, kissing her goodbye. 'That was so much fun.'

'It was a blast,' she replied. 'Let's do it again soon.'

'What in the Lord's name have you done to your hair?' cried Vincent, when I walked in the door.

'Gone blonde,' I replied. As if it weren't perfectly obvious. 'Just like the website.'

'But your hair is brown.'

'Was brown,' I corrected, flicking back my new perfectly styled, shiny, blonde do.

I had thought with all the image treatments he

regularly indulged in he'd be a bit more supportive of any beauty steps I took.

But he wasn't.

'How much did it cost?' he asked.

'Not as much as your stem cells,' I replied, opening a bottle of wine I'd brought home with me and pouring myself a large glass.

He glared at the glass of wine, but he wasn't going to be diverted.

'Your hair looks expensive, Sally. And the new clothes,' he said, gesturing towards my new dress and the several shopping bags I'd dumped on the kitchen table. 'You know that we can't appear to be too flashy in front of the congregation.'

Too flashy?

'Vincent, you wear three-hundred-dollar silk shirts, you have a wardrobe full of them! You constantly look like you've just returned from a month in the Bahamas! If that's not *flashy*, then I don't know what is.'

'I have to look good, Sally, you know that. The people need to have something to aspire to.'

'And I shouldn't look good? Is that what you're saying?'

'Well, no, but you shouldn't go overboard. I think more subtle steps are required.'

'Vincent. You are so orange that when you stand next to anything more than a sixty-watt bulb you look like you're radioactive. You've had so much botox injected into your forehead that it will never move again. And you dress like a pimp. What in God's name is subtle about that?'

'Sally, do *not* take the Lord's name in vain,' he replied sternly.

'Better than *being* vain,' I muttered.

'Pardon?'

'Nothing Vincent. *Nothing*.'

'I just think we need to be more careful,' he continued. 'Not to look too flashy. Plus, we can't exactly afford all of these luxuries, can we?' he added.

'Luxuries? All I did was have my hair done, Vincent, for the first time in six months, and buy a few new clothes which I desperately needed. Let it go! And if we don't have any money, it's because you spend most of it on yourself!'

How dare he ruin what had been such a wonderful day!

'Nice hair, Mum,' said Davey, sitting down beside me on the sofa.

'Do you like it?'

'Yeah, you look good,' he smiled.

'Thanks, sweetheart,' I said, giving him a kiss on the cheek.

He didn't flinch. Thankfully he hadn't quite reached that age where your mother kissing you on the cheek is akin to being caught stark naked on the side of the motorway. Or if he had, he didn't show it.

'I like it, too,' said Elizabeth, sitting down beside us. 'You look pretty.'

'Bless you,' I said, smiling at her.

Why couldn't Vincent be more like his children? I wondered. And less like himself?

Kat

For the past few weeks, Izzy had been trying to convince me to have a squiz at an internet-dating site she frequented.

'It's perfect for you!' she cried. 'You don't have to leave the house! And it will do wonders for your confidence.'

'I'd rather die,' I argued back.

But one night, after also convincing me to have four gin and tonics, she managed to succeed.

'You don't have to go on any dates,' she promised, clocking my stiffening body. 'We can just have a little look and see if there's anyone who tickles your fancy.'

Before I knew it, she was saying 'Right then', logging onto the Love Match website and typing in the stats of who she thought I should be looking for. Male, thirty to forty, living in Auckland, five-foot-eleven or above, single, professional, gsoh.

'What's that?' I asked.

'Good sense of humour,' she replied, looking at me as though I'd only recently arrived on earth. 'There's a few things you need to watch out for,' she warned, as she scrolled down the pages, looking at the many photos.

'Like what?'

'Like when he says *five-foot-ten* he really means he's five-foot-eight, *tops*. When he says *single* there's only a fifty per cent chance he actually is. When he says *fun-loving* what he really means is *fucking boring*.'

'Anything else?' I asked.

'Yes. When he says *successful* it means he used to be, once upon a time, now he's actually unemployed . . . reminds me of Coupon Man,' she sighed.

Izzy had been on an internet date about six months before where it had all gone swimmingly until they went to pay and he had whipped a coupon out of his wallet. He'd suggested the restaurant, which obviously made Izzy think he'd only done so because he had a coupon for the place.

'The worst thing,' Izzy had said at the time, 'is that it had expired. So we had to hang around at the counter, while other people queued up behind us, waiting for the maître d' (who was virtually waving the coupon above his head) to go out the back and check its validity, only to come back to the counter and yell at the top of his lungs, making love to every syllable, 'I'm afraid it's expired!'

Izzy had been too scared to go out with him again, because she thought he might have one of those restaurant-coupon books which he was planning on working his way through.

'When he says *never had children* it means he probably just doesn't know about them,' continued Izzy. 'And when he says he *loves good conversation* it means he either loves to talk about himself, non-stop, or he loves to sit there, silently, while you do all the talking.'

'Can you believe *anything* they say?' I asked, bewildered.

'No, not really. But you can bombard them with questions prior to meeting them, in an attempt to weed out the scum.'

'There's so many!' I cried, watching in amazement

as Izzy continued to scroll down the pages, stalling occasionally when she thought someone was worth a closer look.

'Well, hel-lo,' she said, stopping on the photo of a very good-looking man, even by my standards (which, since being deserted by my gay husband and never wanting to enter another relationship as long as I lived, were, it's fair to say, a little high).

Izzy clicked on his profile and up popped a page with the same photo, only larger, and his details. His name was Steve and he was incredibly good-looking.

'Can't believe I haven't seen his profile before,' said Izzy, shaking her head in dismay.

'You already have a date this week,' I reminded her.

Izzy scrolled down through his stats.

'Tall, tick. Non-smoker, tick. Thirty-eight, tick. Professional, tick. Auckland, tick. Single, tick.'

'What's the hell's he single for?' I said, ever the pessimist.

'Must be a reason,' she agreed.

'Probably gay,' I said.

Izzy chose to ignore me. 'We need to interrogate him,' she stated. 'In a nice way.'

'What do you mean?' I asked.

'Well, we need to find out what the catches are. How many illegitimate children does he have? How many times has he been married? Is he still married . . . which is more than likely,' she added. 'That sort of thing.'

'Right.'

'Here we go, then,' she said.

Hi Steve, she typed. 'It's probably not his real name,' she added. *How are you? I've just seen your profile and it caught my eye, so I thought I'd drop you a line . . . in the hope of finding out a little more about you. But first I should probably tell you a little bit about me. My name's Katherine, I'm thirty-five, I live in the city, I'm an accountant (don't hold it against me!)*

'What did you type that for?' I asked. 'What's wrong with being an accountant?'

'Well, y'know . . .' said Izzy. 'It's a bit geeky, and if he's a graphic designer or something it might scare the bejesus out of him.'

If it's not too cheeky, continued Izzy, *I'd love to know what you do for a living. What your interests are. If you've been married before.*

K x

'What did you put the kiss for?' I asked.

'It's friendly,' answered Izzy.

'Bit more than friendly! You know I don't put kisses on emails, particularly to someone I've never met.'

Izzy deleted the kiss.

Suddenly we were done and I hadn't had to type a single word.

How does she know exactly what to type? I wondered. She's got it down to a fine art.

'Now we have to attach your picture,' said Izzy.

'What?'

'Well, he's not going to respond unless he likes the look of you, is he?'

'You mean we've got to take a photo now?'

'No,' said Izzy, clocking the state of me. 'You must have one on your computer which will do, or one we can scan?'

We had a rifle through the photo library on my computer and found a picture of me on holiday in Thailand, looking lovely, tanned and healthy. And skinny. The only problem was that Gus was standing right beside me, also looking all lovely and tanned and healthy.

'Don't worry,' said Izzy. 'We'll crop him.'

Opening Photoshop, that's exactly what she did. Suddenly my gay husband had disappeared and it was just me on holiday in Thailand, by myself, looking lovely, tanned, healthy and skinny.

I wished she could have cropped me, too. It was depressing to see how good I used to look. In my Old Life. My married life. I certainly didn't look lovely and tanned and healthy and skinny now. I looked frumpy and fat, or at least I thought I did.

Wasn't it supposed to work the other way around: you got married and then you got frumpy and fat? Because as soon as he slipped that ring on your finger all self-preservation flew out the window? I'd gone to the gym, I'd kept myself in shape my whole married life — and where had it got me? With a gay husband, that's where. I really should have let myself go a lot earlier.

'You don't look frumpy and fat,' argued Izzy. 'You just need a bit of . . . maintenance.

'Probably won't hear back from him,' she muttered, attaching the cropped photo and hitting 'send'.

But she was wrong. No more than fifteen minutes later we had a reply. I had to remind myself that it was me he was corresponding with, not me and Izzy. And if, for some reason, I did end up going on a date with him, then it was probably for the best if Izzy didn't come along too.

Izzy read his reply out loud, even though I was quite capable of reading, and had been for several years now.

Hi, Katherine,

Nice to hear from you! And no, you're not being too cheeky! I'm an engineer, with my own small firm, I'm forty and, yes, I have been married before. I was married for five years and divorced four years ago . . .

my ex-wife and I remain great friends.

He's doing a damn sight better than me, I thought. Bet she didn't leave him for another woman, though.

I'd love to know more about you . . . what do you do for laughs? (When you're not being an accountant.) What do you love/hate most about this city? Red or white? And have you been married before?

'Like the questions!' said Izzy, impressed with his response.

'Should we reply?' I ventured.

'Yes, but we need to think very carefully about what we say.'

'Do you think I could have a go at typing?' I asked.

Izzy looked at me as though I'd just asked her to jump ship in the middle of the Atlantic.

'S'pose so,' she reluctantly agreed, wheeling her chair back. 'Go on, then.'

OK . . . I typed. *Here we go.*

Definitely red. And, yes, I have been married before, for ten years, we separated just over six months ago . . . not divorced yet.

'What are you telling him that for?' demanded Izzy.

'What do you mean?' I asked. 'That I've been married?'

'No. That you've only been separated for six months. He'll think you're on the rebound and out looking for another husband.'

'Well, what should I do? *Lie?*'

'Yes,' answered Izzy.

'Well, I don't want to. If he thinks me being separated for six months is a problem, then I don't want to go on a bloody date with him anyway.'

Izzy decided it was in her best interests to let it go.

'What do I do for a laugh?' I repeated. 'Well . . . I

like to spend as much time as possible inside my house and avoid all social contact if possible . . . I love to wash dishes and clothes, several times a day . . . and I love to go to work because for five days it takes my mind off the fact that my husband has deserted me for another man, our best friend . . . and the only social outing I've had in recent weeks was to sing with a gay choir.'

'Um . . . ' said Izzy. 'You may need to change a couple of things.'

'OK, what the hell did I *used* to do for a laugh, then?' I replied.

I tried desperately to remember.

'Go on holidays?' suggested Izzy.

Yes, I had gone on loads of holidays with Gus. And Dan.

'Go out to dinner?'

Yes, that's right, at least twice a week with Gus. And usually Dan.

'Play tennis?'

Yes, every Monday after work . . . ditto.

'The theatre, movies, concerts?'

Yes, at least once a week with either Izzy, Gus or you-know-who.

'Book club?'

Once a month . . . God, I hadn't seen those girls for ages, and nor had I returned their many phone calls. They probably thought I'd gone and topped myself.

'How about writing those things then?' suggested Izzy.

So I did.

'And we need to ask him one more question,' she added.

'What?' I replied. I really thought we'd interrogated him enough.

'Kids.'

'But it said in his profile that he doesn't have children,' I replied, suddenly confused.

'That doesn't mean he doesn't have them,' laughed Izzy.

'Well what the hell does it mean, then?'

'That he doesn't have children *living* with him.'

'But even if they're not living with him, he's still got them,' I replied, very confused now.

'Exactly!' cried Izzy, even though I had absolutely no idea what she thought was exact.

'Just type this,' she instructed. 'Any little Steves out there anywhere?'

'But I don't actually care if he's got kids or not,' I protested.

'Yes, you do.'

'No, I don't'

'Well you should.'

'Why?'

'Because that means he's been lying to you.'

'But what if he *doesn't* have kids?'

'Then it's all hunky-dory, isn't it?'

I typed in Izzy's question and hit 'send'.

Exactly three minutes later we received Steve's reply.

No little Steves out there . . . that I know of anyway! Although I'd like there to be someday in the not too distant future.

This might be a bit forward, but . . . what do you think about me giving you my phone number and you calling me for a chat if and when you feel like it?

'Yes,' said Izzy. 'Say *Yes*.'

OK, I typed back. What did I have to lose?

Interrogate him as we might, that night we couldn't find any faults, unless of course he was lying. Which, said Izzy, was still a very real possibility.

God, I thought, there were so many rules and traps to this internet-dating business. When I'd started dating Gus, about a million years ago, there was none of this cryptic mind-reading business. You simply asked the person on a date, with any luck they said yes, and off you went. If the first date went well, you'd probably shag them on the third or fourth and marry them a few years later.

Two days later, with shaking hands, I mustered up the courage to phone him.

As the ringing resounded in my ear I prayed for the wrong number, or an answerphone message, or an earthquake, or anything that meant I could safely backtrack from talking to a complete stranger who'd given me his number on an internet-dating site. Before I could come to my senses and hang up, he answered.

'Hi,' I said, somehow finding my voice. 'It's Katherine here.'

'Hi, Katherine!' he replied. 'Lovely to hear from you! How are you?'

He sounded all enthusiastic and warm and, well, genuinely pleased to hear from me.

Although, I thought — Izzy's warnings ringing in my ears — this could just be his 'first-contact good-impression voice'.

But if it was then he was a fantastic actor, because he kept it up for our entire conversation, all fifty minutes of it. (I only knew this because I could have sworn we'd only been talking for fifteen minutes and got a huge fright when I glanced at the clock.) We had lots in common, I mean *lots*. He'd studied at the same university as me, he'd grown up in the same suburb as me, he played tennis, he was a closet country-music fan, and he hated bok choy with a passion.

As our conversation drew to a close (only because he had an early flight to catch the next morning), he asked me out to dinner. I hadn't been asked on a date for exactly sixteen years. I was speechless.

'Can I take your deathly silence to mean yes?' asked Steve.

'Oh, sorry,' I replied, finally realizing I hadn't uttered a word. 'Yes . . . yes, I'd like that.'

We arranged to meet at Dine at eight o'clock the following Friday.

'A date!' cried Izzy. 'A real live date! Well done!'

She was clearly surprised that I'd managed to snag a date in my current state. Especially with someone who appeared to be, to all intents and purposes, very normal. And saucy.

'Right,' said Izzy, serious now. 'You'll be needing a makeover.'

It was true, I was looking a little shabby around the edges . . . or at least I had been when I'd last looked in the mirror about, oh, two weeks before. But did I really need a makeover?

'It's a pity Dan and Gus aren't here to help,' added Izzy. 'We could use some queer eye.'

Instead of shooting her a dirty look, as I would have happily done up until very recently, I found myself laughing at the thought of Dan and Gus fussing over me; preening my face, criticizing the state of my nails, dissecting my wardrobe.

At my protestations that all I really needed to do was wash my hair, give myself a manicure and find an outfit,

Izzy frog-marched me to the bathroom mirror.

'Look,' she commanded, pointing first at my split and shapeless hair.

I'd been wondering what had been tickling my nose and making me sneeze. It appeared it was my fringe.

'Re-growth,' said Izzy, pointing at the very visible ring about two inches from my scalp where sun-kissed blonde turned into mousey brown.

She moved her finger down and pointed at my eyebrows. Or, rather, eyebrow.

Jesus Christ! I reeled back in horror. What had been two perfectly shaped brows had now become one enormous shaggy monobrow. Thankfully my overgrown fringe had been shielding this monstrosity from public view. It wouldn't so much need a plucking as a mowing.

Izzy continued on her downward spiral, pointing out the state of my skin, which once, not so long ago, had been healthy, clear and glowing; one of my finer points. But now it was riddled with blackheads, cloggy pores, dry patches and the odd spot. Not too mention the circles under my eyes, which were so dark it looked as though I'd drawn them on myself with a black marker. The insomnia had certainly taken its toll.

'I haven't had a pimple for fifteen years!' I cried.

Izzy didn't need to say anything. My reflection said it all.

Finally, she broke the silence. 'Deep-tissue facial and vitamin peel, eyebrow shape, eyelash tint, upper lip bleach, manicure, pedicure, plus hairstyle and cut of course. That oughta do it.

'You're taking Monday off work and you're coming to see me,' she commanded. 'And then you're going for a haircut.

'Mental health day,' went on Izzy, when I protested

that I was far too busy at work to take a day off. 'Lord knows you need it.'

Monday rolled around and I headed off to Izzy's clinic. She didn't usually work Mondays, but came in specifically to 'work on me' (her words).

As reluctant as I initially was to co-operate, I couldn't remember the last time I'd experienced a day of such selfish luxury. It was bliss. Unbeknown to me, Izzy had also organized me a full-body massage with her colleague Sam (a professional masseuse) which balanced out the leg, armpit and bikini wax Izzy had given me earlier on. Along with the deep-tissue facial and vitamin peel, eyebrow shape, eyelash tint, upper lip bleach, manicure and pedicure, of course

At six o'clock on Friday evening, exactly two hours before my date, Izzy came to my house to assess the outfits I had laid out on my bed.

'Hmm . . .' she said, running an eye over the first outfit: simple black shoe-string dress to the knee (to be worn with wide fishnets stockings and red sling-back stilettos). Her expression was unreadable as she moved on to outfit number two: cream stovepipe trousers, black silk blouse and cream heels (open-toed). And then outfit number three: a red pleated skirt, with a halter-neck black singlet and knee-high black boots.

'Not bad, not bad,' she finally said. 'We can work with this.'

It had taken me approximately two hours of manic searching and cursing and an hour of resurrecting my wardrobe to come up with these three outfits, so I bloody well hoped we could work with them.

Izzy made me try on every outfit and pose in front of her for at least five minutes. Her silent gaze made me feel as though I was auditioning for *Top Model*. Will I make it through to the next cut? I wondered. Or will I be packing my bags and heading back to Kansas?

'The cream pants and black blouse,' she finally concluded, having made me change back into this outfit again. 'But not the cream shoes. Try the red ones.'

I took off the cream heels and put on the red sling-back stilettos.

'Stand up.'

I stood up.

'Perfect!' she declared.

'Thank God,' I sighed. I was exhausted.

'Well, almost,' she said, undoing the buttons on my blouse halfway to my navel.

'What are you doing?' I demanded.

'You need to show a bit of cleavage,' said Izzy. 'You've a lovely cleavage.'

'No, I bloody don't,' I replied, doing them back up.

'Yes, you do,' she said, undoing them again.

Eventually we came to a compromise with the top three buttons left undone, and strict instructions from Izzy not to do them back up again, under any circumstances. Leaving me with a plunging neckline, a clear peek of the top of my black lace bra, and an overabundance of cleavage.

Izzy left me alone to do my make-up and hair, returning to check on me at five-minute intervals.

Finally I was ready, with enough time to spare for a pre-date glass of wine to settle my raging nerves.

'You look stunning!' declared Izzy. 'Absolutely stunning!'

I looked in the mirror, and for the first time in months what I saw didn't make me want to smash the glass and rub the broken shards back and forth across my wrists. In fact I would even go so far as to say that I was happy with my reflection. Yes, I was happy. I'd finally had the much-needed Break-up Haircut, with a couple of inches taken off and several soft layers now framing the side of my face and neck, as well as the plethora of beauty treatments, none of which had gone astray. I felt as though I had finally regained some composure, at long last.

I was still a few pounds heavier than I had been pre-gay-husband-shock-news, but I was confident this would come off in time. I'd finally stopped eating TimTams and Yorkshire puddings on a daily basis, which had to help. With any luck there was some new pain-free fad diet on the market where I'd simply have to swap an apple a day for a large steak or the like.

'Totally hot!' continued Izzy.

The odd thing was, I actually felt a wee bit hot, too. Something I hadn't felt for a very, very long time.

I arrived at the swanky restaurant and was ushered through to the lounge area, where numerous people were sitting on the dark leather couches, waiting for their tables.

'Katherine!' called a man's voice, as an attractive man in his late fifties, with steel-grey hair, walked towards me.

He looked vaguely familiar. Must be someone I've worked with before, I decided. Or perhaps a friend of my mother's.

But as he got closer I recognized him as the father, or at least the way older brother, of the man I'd seen in the website photo. He might have grown up in the same suburb as me, but it was more likely my parents he'd been to school with.

'Steve,' he said, leaning in to give me a kiss, the warm and enthusiastic voice confirming my heart-sinking suspicions.

At least he knows how to dress, I thought, looking on the bright side. He was wearing a well-cut and expensive-looking chocolate brown pin-striped suit, and a beautifully made open-neck white shirt, both of which complemented his tanned skin. And he had beautiful, well-groomed hands, I noted as I glanced down, presumably scanning for a wedding ring (none present), though Lord knew why I was bothering.

It appeared he wasn't alone.

'This is Alyssa,' he said, gesturing towards the high-class hooker who had appeared beside him, wearing skin-tight red-leather trousers and a matching jacket. And matching shoes, too, I noticed, glancing down.

'Hey-low,' said Alyssa in a thick Russian accent, extending her hand. 'Playzed stew meet chew.'

I think she'd said she was pleased to meet me. Either that or she wanted to stew me.

'And you,' I said, shaking her hand.

I presumed Steve had bumped into Alyssa while he was waiting for me.

'What would you like to drink?' asked Steve. 'We've got time for another while we're waiting for our table.'

'Bubbles, please,' I replied.

In fact we had time for two drinks before our table was ready, Alyssa staying to join us for another one. I wasn't sure who she was waiting for or which table she was sitting at. But this became clear once Steve and I were ushered to our lovely table in the corner by the maître d', because Alyssa walked with us, and then she sat right on down at our table. It appeared she was dining with us.

'You don't mind, do you?' smiled Steve, smiling at the look of confusion on my face. 'If Alyssa joins us?'

Mind? Did I mind? It was hard to say if I minded or

not, having never been on a date where the man invited another woman along too.

'No. Of course not,' I replied. *What choice did I have?*

'It's Alyssa's birthday,' announced Steve, as a bottle of champagne was delivered to the table in an ice bucket.

'Happy birthday,' I said, as we raised our glasses to her.

It's a sad, sad state of affairs, I thought, having to tag along on someone else's date on your birthday. I was pleased I hadn't yet sunk that low. I was guessing Steve felt sorry for her, which explained why he'd asked her to join us.

By the time our mains were served, it was plain to see that Steve and Alyssa knew each other fairly well, judging by the way her hand snaked across his thigh. By dessert it was glaringly obvious, as Steve made another announcement.

'Alyssa is my wife,' he said, which probably explained why she was now chewing on his neck, all the while looking up at me to make sure I was watching. It was hard not to. I was pretty confident everyone else in the restaurant was, too.

Why the hell did he want to go on a date if he already had a wife?

'Do you watch *Big Love*?' asked Steve.

Wasn't that the television programme about the bigamist? With three wives? Oh, Jesus.

I endured another thirty minutes of what was bordering on a live soft-porn show, for ten minutes of which Alyssa's head had disappeared under the table. Steve and I carried on chatting, me pretending that it was the most normal thing in the world for her head to disappear under the table like that, doing God knows what while it was down there. The next thing she was sitting back up and Steve had his arm draped across her shoulder, his hand slipping inside her skin-tight and plunging red-leather jacket and blatantly beginning to fondle her left breast. Once again we continued talking (about dogs) while his fingers rhythmically pinched her left nipple and I tried my very hardest to stare at his forehead. The little squeals of delight coming from Alyssa's mouth made this a difficult task. I was sitting in fear that given another twenty minutes they'd be naked and shagging on the dining table in front of me, like a couple of extras from *Boogie Nights*.

'Why don't you come back to our house for a nightcap?' suggested Steve, while we were waiting for the bill.

'Yesh,' smiled Alyssa. 'Playze.'

'I think I'll just go home,' I replied. 'Thanks anyway. I'm a little tired.'

They looked extremely disappointed. Alyssa stopped squealing for long enough to start pouting, just like a five-year-old who's had their party pooped on.

Oh, dear God, I thought, as someone switched on the lights. I had ruined her party. I was supposed to be her birthday present! Call me a prude, but heading home with two people I'd only just met — a man who was old enough to be my father and his Russian bride — for a birthday threesome wasn't exactly what I'd had in mind for my first date in sixteen years.

I gave the date rundown to Izzy as she sat on the sofa nodding her head. Apparently (according to Izzy) it wasn't uncommon for women to go on an internet date, only to find the man had brought along his wife or girlfriend.

'How was yours?' I asked, when I'd finished. Izzy had

also been on a date the night before, with a guy from the same website.

'Terrible,' she replied.

'What did you do?'

'Went to Soho.'

It didn't sound so terrible to me. Soho was divine, gorgeous food and setting.

'What was he like?'

'Oh . . . tall, fit, short brown hair, green eyes, tanned.'

'And?'

'And he was polite, and interesting, I guess, and a reasonably good dresser.'

'So what was so terrible?'

'The shoes.'

'The *shoes?*'

'They were dusty.'

'*Dusty?*'

'Yes, dusty. We met at the bar, he bought me a bubbles. We were chatting away, it was all going fabulously . . . until I caught sight of the bloody shoes.'

'What sort of shoes were they?' I asked, hoping this might have been to his benefit.

'I don't know,' sighed Izzy. 'Dusty ones. And not just a couple of spots either. They were covered in the stuff. How could he not have given them a polish before he left the house?' she continued. 'Or at the very least a wipe?'

'Maybe he didn't notice they were dusty?' I suggested.

'How could you *not* notice?' replied Izzy. 'It's like they were his *one* good pair of dating shoes that hadn't seen the light of day for at least ten years.'

'Then you had dinner?' I asked, hoping this would take her mind off the shoes. 'What did you order?'

'I can't remember. All I could think about was the bloody shoes.'

'What did you talk about?'

'God knows, I couldn't concentrate on anything he said. It probably would have been interesting and intelligent conversation under normal polished-shoes circumstances.'

'You don't think you might be overreacting just a wee bit?' I ventured. Surely a pair of dusty shoes was nothing compared with bringing your wife along on the date?

'Nope,' replied Izzy, defiantly. 'You should have seen them. It was embarrassing. Plus, I couldn't take him seriously. If he was the type of person who could go around wearing a dusty pair of shoes on a first date, then we clearly had nothing in common and there was no point in pretending we did. Even if we went on another date and he wore a pair of shiny, clean shoes I'd still be thinking about the dusty ones he had on last time.

'It was as bad as looking down and finding a pair of boat shoes staring back at you,' she continued.

This was a serious claim. We both knew the only viable excuse for wearing a pair of boat shoes was being on a gin palace (so long as he owned it), and even then their presence was debatable.

Jools

'How about Assisi? Or Calypso?' suggested Francie, as we sat on the apples and peaches.

If I didn't know better, I'd have assumed she'd started dating an oil tycoon.

'I don't think so,' I replied. 'A little too out there.'

'Dido?'

'Ditto.'

'How about Elizabeth? Or Sarah? Or Camilla?' yelled Mum, popping her head around the kitchen door. She was a big fan of old-fashioned English names and the royal family. Lord knows where she'd got Julia from.

How about you both shut up, I thought to myself. They'd been hurling names at me for the past few weeks and it was starting to wear thin. Francie with her names which would probably sound perfectly normal on an olive-skinned baby from Makenos, but not on a pasty, ruddy-cheeked baby from New Zealand. And Mum with her boring straight-laced names which all but put me to sleep as soon as she said them. I wanted something easily spellable and sayable, which was also memorable and not too common. No small ask, I know, but I was sure I'd come up with something, by myself.

'I know you wanted to be my bridesmaid,' I said to Francie, changing the subject, 'but since that's no longer looking like a likely scenario . . . will you be my birthing partner instead?'

'Oh, Jools,' said Francie, giving me a hug. 'I thought you'd never ask. I'd love to!'

'You know what this means?' I said.

'Being at the birth?'

'Yes. *And* coming to antenatal classes with me.'

'Of course,' said Francie, patting my arm.

'For eight weeks,' I added.

'*Eight weeks?*'

'One night a week,' I clarified.

'Oh. That's fine then.'

'You know what they'll think, though, don't you?'

'That you haven't got a husband?' replied Francie. 'Or a boyfriend?'

'No,' I said. It was best she was fully prepared. 'They'll think we're Les-Bi-Ans.'

'Really?'

'Yes. Really. Two women going to an antenatal class together, without a man in sight. So,' I continued, 'when we introduce ourselves, just make sure you say that you're my friend. *Friend*. You got it?'

'Got it,' replied Francie.

The following Monday night we trotted along to the first class. We arrived ten minutes late to find fifteen other pregnant ladies there, all with their husbands or partners, all of whom were male.

'One of these things is not like the other . . .', the famous *Sesame Street* words rang in my ears.

Don't be nervous, I told myself. It doesn't matter what anyone else thinks.

I looked at Francie, who gave me a smile which managed to be both encouraging and nervous at the same time.

'Welcome,' said the teacher, Carol, giving us an extra warm it's-just-lovely-to-finally-have-some-lesbians-in-the-class smile.

Everyone was sitting with their chairs in a circle. We made our way to the only two remaining chairs, right beside Carol. Everyone in the class stared at us thinking just one thing. *Lesbians.*

We were just in time for the introductions, which thankfully began on the other side of Carol. We were instructed to say our name, occupation, how many weeks pregnant we were, how much we were looking forward to having our baby, and how much time we'd be taking off work once the baby was born. The women, who were all between six and eight months pregnant, were all enthusiastic and glowing, and all called Jenny, Lisa or Susan. Most of their husbands and partners looked as though they'd been dragged along by their ears under threat of no sex again. Ever. They looked bored out of their skulls already, and half of them appeared to be asleep, getting nudged awake (rather violently) when it was their turn to introduce themselves. Jenny/Lisa/Susan all planned to take an average of ten years off work after the birth of their baby, at which their husbands suddenly jolted awake and stared at them as though this was the first they'd bloody well heard of it.

Suddenly it was my turn to speak and I was nervous as hell. Something to do with getting pregnant on a one-night stand, not initially knowing who the father was, the father not knowing he was having a baby, and the fact that I was back living with my parents. But somehow I got through it.

'My name's Julia. I'm twenty-eight weeks pregnant. I'm really looking forward to having this baby. I'm a brand manager and I'm planning on going back to work a couple of months after the baby is born.'

At this last bit, Jenny/Lisa/Susan all but sucked the air right out of the room with their united gasp.

Unlike you spoilt bitches I have to go back to work, I thought. Because I don't have a dutiful hubby to pay the bills.

Their husbands opened their eyes and looked at me with the utmost respect. Then they stared at their wives, then back at me. Wives, back at me.

'Do you have someone lined up to look after the baby?' asked Carol, sweetly.

'Yes,' I replied. 'My mother.'

This was a lie. I hadn't actually asked her yet, or even thought about who would look after the baby. But I was confident she'd jump at the idea, particularly if the only other option was a crèche.

Then it was Francie's turn.

'My name is Francie and I'm Jools's birthing partner. I'm not planning on taking any time off after the baby's born. But I'm really looking forward to it.'

More collective staring.

Could you not have just said *friend?* I thought as I looked sideways at her.

To begin the class we all hopped down onto the floor and Carol guided us through some breathing exercises.

There was a multitude of groans as sixteen pregnant women attempted to lever themselves onto the carpet.

'Excuse me?' said Lisa somethingorother, waving her hand in the air. 'Should we be sitting with our legs crossed?'

Even though Carol had just answered this question by

saying 'sit whichever way is most comfortable for you', she kindly answered it again without flinching.

'Excuse me?' said Lisa, approximately thirty seconds later. 'How many breaths should we be taking a minute?'

Everyone in the class looked at Lisa, including her husband. Once again, this was a question Carol had already answered before we started.

'Ten to fifteen, although this is only a guideline,' she said again, smiling sweetly.

There always has to be one, I thought, as Francie and I glanced across at each other, smiling. A question-asker. It didn't matter what the class was — French, cooking, tantric sex — there was always one person in the class who felt it was their duty to ask far too many stupid questions.

After the breathing, Carol treated us to the sight of a plastic baby being born from a pelvis. One minute the doll's head was engaged and the next minute it just slid right out. No problems.

'Looks like a piece of cake,' I whispered to Francie.

'Don't think it's quite that fast, babe,' she replied. 'Or quite that small.'

Francie was an 'experienced' birthing partner. She'd been at the birth of her sister's first child. I remembered her saying at the time that if anyone else asked her to come to the birth of their child, family or otherwise, she'd tell them to jump off a fucking bridge.

'This is obviously not the size of a real baby,' said Carol, waving the doll about. 'Or how long a real birth will take.'

'Oh,' I sighed. Francie was right. Every other woman in the class looked as deflated as I felt.

Next we were divided into groups with the purpose

of coming up with a series of questions for Carol about labour and birth. Carol obviously hoped that by putting us into groups some of the questions would be answered by know-it-alls before they got to her. But she was shit out of luck with our group.

I did manage to answer a question from Jenny, who was wondering what a placenta was, as Francie and everyone else in our group stared back at her like she was barking. Even her husband could have answered this one for her. It was comforting to know there was someone else who knew even less than I did about this baby thing.

We spent more time chatting about who'd been the most ill throughout their pregnancy and who was missing the booze the most (it appeared I was).

'So, do you mind me asking,' said Jeff, husband of Susan, one of the only husbands who'd managed to stay awake, 'how you two, um . . . y'know . . .'

His wife, aware of what he was about to ask, attempted to silence him with a death-stare. But she was too late.

'. . . got pregnant,' he finished, ignoring her.

'I'm not pregnant,' replied Francie, adding to his confusion. 'Just Jools.'

'We're NOT TO-GE-THER,' I replied, very loudly. Just loud enough for everyone inside the church, and the neighbouring houses, to hear. 'We're JUST FRIENDS.'

'So how did you . . . um . . . get pregnant then?' he asked me, refusing to give up, as Susan fired daggers through the side of his head.

'The old-fashioned way,' I replied. 'My ex-boyfriend.'

'Oh,' he replied, nodding his head, the confusion finally fading from his face. 'I see.'

'Ouch!' he cried, as Susan's elbow collided against his ribs.

Sally

'You're looking great! And I love the hair!' said Esther, sitting down in the armchair opposite me and crossing her right leg over her left.

'Thanks,' I replied, smiling at her. 'Me, too.'

'How's the exercise video going?' she asked.

'Great!' I replied. 'I'm loving it! I had absolutely no idea there was a stripper inside me waiting to get out . . . but it appears there was.'

She laughed. 'Why do you think it makes you feel good?'

'I don't know…' I replied. 'I guess I like the way it makes me feel uninhibited, if that doesn't sound weird?'

'Not at all.'

'Plus, I like the fact I'm finally doing something good for my body.'

I told Esther about my shopping day with Claire, and how much fun I'd had. I even gave her a rundown of all the new clothes I'd bought.

'I haven't been on a shopping spree like that in years,' I admitted. 'It was fantastic.'

'It's invigorating, shopping your heart out every once in a while, isn't it?' she agreed. 'It sounds like a lovely day. What did Vincent think about your new hairstyle and clothes?'

'He thinks I'm being flashy.'

'Flashy?'

'Yes. Ironic, I know.'

I watched her scribble a little note on her pad.

'Do you mind if I ask you a very personal question?' said Esther.

'No,' I replied.

'About your and Vincent's sex life? Is it what you would consider healthy?'

'We don't have sex,' I replied. 'Vincent would far rather have sex with himself.'

'With himself?'

'Sorry, what I mean is that he's so busy preening himself all day and looking at himself in the mirror that making love to someone else is not really, well, something he's interested in.'

'Do you find his lack of sex drive slightly unusual?' she asked.

'Not really. He's never had an exceptionally high sex drive, not even when we were young, although we used to have sex of course.'

'How often would you have sex now?'

'I don't know . . . about once every three months, or something like that . . . I guess.'

'And are you happy with having sex every three months?' asked Esther.

'In some ways. I don't . . . well . . . I don't find Vincent all that attractive any more, now that he dresses like a used-car salesman. But in other ways, yes, I miss it . . . I miss the intimacy.'

'So, I gather Vincent's physical appearance has changed somewhat?' asked Esther.

I explained his metamorphosis from normal bloke to pimp / car salesman.

251

'That is quite a transition,' she agreed. 'So, he wasn't always this obsessed with his appearance?'

'Well, he always checked himself out in mirrors, but he certainly wasn't so concerned with his clothes, or hair, until he started on the stage.'

'On the stage?'

'Sorry . . . I mean since he started preaching.'

'Is that how you see it?' asked Esther. 'As a stage?'

'Well,' I replied, shifting in my seat, 'he seems to be acting most of the time . . . to me anyway.'

'You mean his personality changes?'

'Not exactly. But he does things he wouldn't normally do.'

'Like what?'

'Like put his hands on people's foreheads and tell them he can feel the Lord in them. Or take small children by the hand and walk them onto the stage and embrace them.'

'Is he affectionate with his own children?'

'He barely knows they exist,' I replied. Once the words had fled my lips I realized just how scathing my remark was — and just how true it was. Vincent ignored our children.

Out of nowhere I felt a tear slide down my cheek. And then another.

'I don't know why I'm c-c-crying,' I stammered.

'It's OK,' comforted Esther, passing me a tissue.

To her credit she didn't say *just let it out.*

In fact for a couple of minutes she didn't say anything at all. She just sat there, smiling her warm and concerned smile at me, and handing me tissues.

Then she said, 'It's good to cry, to let our bodies release. It's healthy. Sometimes we don't even know why we're crying . . . and we don't have to either. It can be something small, or a number of things that have been building up inside us, but when the urge takes us we should just go with it.

'Feel better?' she asked, as I finally stopped sobbing, the last tear sliding down my cheek.

'Yes,' I replied. 'Much better.'

And I did. God knows why, I wasn't prone to sitting on couches blubbing. In fact, I couldn't for the life of me remember the last time I'd cried. Not for a long, long time.

'I'm guessing that's the first time you've cried in a long time,' said Esther, reading my mind.

'Yes,' I replied, dabbing my eyes.

I felt a long sigh escape my lips, followed by a small smile.

Kat

Despite my many fierce protestations, one week later Izzy somehow managed to convince me to log on to the dating site again.

Meg's voice rang in my ears: 'It's full of psychopaths and rapists. Why don't I organize you a date with one of Joe's friends instead?'

To which Izzy had said, 'She's the only psychopath I know. You're not going out with one of Joe's boring old-codger sexist mates!'

'Just give it one more go,' encouraged Izzy. 'You're getting near a successful date, I can tell. You can't give up after just one!'

I was more than happy to give up after just one date, particularly in light of a date like the one I'd had, but she somehow managed to convince me otherwise. I really should have put up more of a fight.

'Plus, you need to give the washing machine a break,' she continued. 'Just for a couple of hours.'

So once again we sat down in front of my laptop and logged onto Love Match.

'How was your date?' I asked Izzy as she once again scrolled down the pages and pages of smiling faces. She had been on a daytime date the previous day with another bloke from the internet.

'Not so good.'

'Why not?' What they had planned to do had sounded lovely. He was picking her up and they were driving up to Omaha for a walk along the beach and a picnic. And yesterday had been a gorgeous, sunny spring day.

'He was a whistler,' replied Izzy.

'What do you mean?'

'I mean he whistled. Non bloody stop.

'It took us an hour to drive to the beach and every time he stopped at the lights he'd start bloody whistling, just like he was a boiling kettle. It was hideous. At first I thought he was whistling along to the music, but then the CD stopped and he just kept going.'

'Maybe he was nervous?' I suggested. 'How was the beach?'

'Gorgeous. Perfect white sand and sunshine. And there would only have been about five other people on it.'

Sounds lovely, I thought to myself. And just what I was in need of: a good walk in the fresh sea air to clear the cobwebs from my head. Gus and I had frequently gone for walks together on the beach, taking our shoes off as soon as our feet touched the sand.

'For a while we just walked along in silence,' continued Izzy. 'Which was lovely. Just the sound of the waves breaking and the seagulls squawking . . . but then I glanced across at him, and his lips were all puckered up and he'd started again! What the hell was he whistling to?' she cried. 'The sound of silence?'

'Did you have a picnic?' I asked, changing the subject.

'Yes,' replied Izzy. 'That was the only relaxing part — he couldn't whistle while he had his mouth full. I kept trying to get him to eat more so he'd keep quiet, but it was short-lived. He whistled all the bloody way home too. It did my head in.'

'You're getting warm,' I encouraged. 'He was single, good-looking, a nice guy . . .'

'But he whistled,' replied Izzy. 'And you know I can't stand whistlers.'

'At least he didn't bring his Russian wife on the date,' I pointed out.

'Hey, he's a bit of all right!' said Izzy, clicking on the photo of a rather ruggedly handsome, tanned face with short black hair and a gorgeous warm smile.

'Looks promising,' she said, scrolling down his details. He was single (or so he said), a professional, thirty-eight-years-old, living in Auckland, childless.

'Shall we send him a message?' suggested Izzy.

'OK,' I replied. What did I have to lose? If he really was all of the above, he probably wouldn't want to go on a date with me anyway.

So Izzy sent him a message:

Hi Nathan,
How are you? I've just seen your profile and it caught my eye, so I thought I'd drop you a line in the hope of finding out a little more about you. But first I should probably tell you a little bit about me. My name's Katherine, I'm thirty-five, I live in the city, I'm an accountant (don't hold it against me!). If it's not too cheeky, I'd love to know a little more about you. What your interests are.
K x

This was obviously Izzy's standard interrogation come-on. I let her get away with the accoutant quip, but not the kiss. She attached the pic of me on holiday in Thailand, *sans* Gus, and hit send.

Nathan was a little slower off the mark than Steve, and I assumed he didn't like the pic of me on holiday in Thailand. But the next evening he replied:

> Hi Katherine,
> Great to hear from you. I won't hold your job against you . . . but I probably should!
> I'm into a little bit of everything — wine, theatre, film, travel, tennis, skiing. I live in Mt Eden. I'm a trader for a living. I'd love to know what you do for fun. Any chance I could give you a bell for a chat?
> Nathan

'Very forward,' deduced Izzy. 'Kinda nice for a change, though. Usually they're so scared to make a move that you end up wearing off your fingertips before you make it on a date.'

'Perhaps a bit too forward,' I replied. I still had no idea what the rules were, so this was just a guess.

'Well,' said Izzy. 'It's not like you have to go on a date with him, he just wants to ring with a chat. If you don't like the sound of him then you can just hang up, can't you?'

'I guess.'

'Worth a shot then, I'd say.'

'I wonder what he trades. Should I ask him?'

'No,' answered Izzy. 'It'll be money or shares or power or something. He'll think you're a thicko if you ask.'

But, oh, how I wish I had asked.

Izzy was kind enough to type my reply for me:

> Sure, give me a bell. My number is 021 600 543. — K

That sounded nonchalant and disinterested enough. But not enough to put him off, because at ten o'clock the following morning, while I was sitting in my office, he rang. Not recognizing the number I very nearly didn't answer it.

I almost couldn't make his voice out over the racket in the background. Lots of yelling and shouting, and a fair bit of banging.

'Sorry,' apologized Nathan. 'Bit noisy here.'

I guessed he was at work. He must be a share trader, I decided.

'Busy place,' I said.

'Sure is,' he replied, laughing. 'Very hard to get away from the noise.'

Surely you could step outside for a minute? I thought. But, then again, maybe share-trading was one of those jobs you couldn't leave, not even for a few moments. It always looked incredibly busy and stressful in the movies.

We chatted for a few minutes. He had a lovely-sounding voice, all warm and bubbly.

He explained that he'd be tied up for the next few days but would really like to meet me for a drink later in the week.

Why not? I thought. He sounded lovely, and normal. And, as Izzy said, if I get to the bar and realize I'm going on a date with a knee-high sixty-year-old I can always turn and do a runner before it's too late. It's not as though he'd be able to catch me.

We arranged to meet at a new lounge bar downtown on Thursday night. After much deliberation, although not nearly as much deliberation as for my previous date because I was sceptical that it would be worth the effort, I settled on a low-cut and clinging navy halter-neck dress and cream open-toed heels. All without Izzy's help.

I arrived at the bar and spotted him sitting at a table in the corner. I gave him a little wave, and made my way over. He looked exactly as he did in his photo, very handsome, although possibly a little broader, which wasn't a bad thing. He also appeared to be alone, with no red-leather-clad wife hanging off his arm.

He stood up, gave me a brilliant smile and kissed me on the cheek. He even appeared to be telling the truth about his height.

He immediately went to fetch me a glass of bubbles.

'How's your day been?' I asked, once he had returned with my drink.

'I like your outfit,' he said, ignoring my question. 'It matches mine.'

I was confused and not entirely sure this was a compliment, being that he was wearing jeans and a blue shirt. The only similarity was that we were both wearing something blue, although in entirely different shades.

'How's you day been?' I asked, attempting to steer the conversation away from our matching outfits.

'Great!' he replied. 'I got out today.'

Got out? Was this not something he did often?

'Where did you go?' I asked.

'Home,' he replied, looking at me as though this was the most stupid question I could possibly have asked.

'Right,' I said, taking a large gulp of wine. 'And what did you do?'

'Y'know, unpacked, aired out the house, opened my mail . . . pretty busy day really.'

'Have you been away?' I asked.

'Yeah, sort of.'

'Where have you been?' I asked, though for some

259

strange reason a little voice told me that I really, really shouldn't.

'In the slammer,' he replied. 'Three months.' As though being in jail was the most normal thing in the world and wasn't it perfectly obvious where he'd been?

At this point I inhaled the olive I was chewing, rather than swallowing it, resulting a fit of unsightly coughing and choking to death.

'Water?' said the waiter, placing a glass of water on the table in front of me.

'Please,' I managed, knocking it back and finally regaining some composure.

That'll explain the racket in the background when we talked on the phone, I thought. I guessed that whatever he was trading wasn't entirely legal. And as for living in Mt Eden, there was a fair chance it was Mt Eden prison he was referring to.

'You OK?' asked Nathan. 'Would you like another drink?'

The waiter was on standby, waiting to take our order.

A drink? I'd like ten. Dear God, I thought, I've somehow managed to hook up a date with a prisoner. Surely this was one for the internet-dating books? I'd no idea how he managed to get his share of wine, theatre, film and travel inside the slammer. Clearly our country's remand system had a lot to answer for. Or how the hell he'd managed to email me from inside. Is that what our country's prisoners did all day: sat at the computer logging onto the internet?

'That's amazing,' said Nathan, as I ordered a vodka and tonic. 'That's my favourite drink too! We must be connected in some way.'

I chuckled back at him, nervously, very much hoping he was kidding.

But by the time we were seated at our table, it was apparent that he probably wasn't kidding. He was busy planning camping trips, visits to amusement parks, and overnight excursions. For the two of us. His enthusiasm was frightening. It was almost as though he was peeing on me and staking his claim.

'My ex-girlfriend didn't like camping,' he continued. 'She didn't like me much either.'

Somehow this didn't surprise me. I didn't like camping either, but I didn't feel the timing was entirely right to disclose this.

I excused myself to the bathroom, and, while I was there, I plucked up my courage. I simply had to ask him, I decided.

'Can I ask what you were in jail for?' I said, as I sat back down at the table.

'My bitch of an ex-girlfriend sent me,' he replied.

This was not good. Not good at all.

'She took out a restraining order and I broke it,' he explained.

A restraining order? Dear God.

'Wasn't my fault, though,' he continued. 'We broke up and she didn't want me coming around anymore. Then she started seeing this jerk of a guy. Complete asshole. Anyway, I went around one night and smacked him over, and, well, that's how I ended up in the slammer. They didn't charge me with assault, though, only breaking the restraining gig.'

Apparently he thought this was good news.

'Can I ask you how you managed to email me from prison?' I asked.

'I got one hour's access a week,' he replied. 'Part of the reintegration into the community crap. Bloody wardens standing around staring over your shoulder.'

Not staring hard enough, I thought. Surely dating sites were considered out of bounds? Especially for someone who was in jail for breaking a restraining order against their ex-girlfriend.

As we finished our drinks, and I naïvely thought things couldn't possibly get any worse and at least the end was in sight and I might make it home alive, he asked me the age-old question: is the glass half full or half empty?

'Half empty,' I replied, a little pessimistic at that point in the evening.

'*What?*' he said, sounding less than pleased with my reply. In fact, he sounded rather pissed off with it. '*How* can you think *that?*'

He then refused to talk to me for fifteen minutes and we finished our drinks in complete silence.

For God's sake just get up, grab your coat, and walk out, I told myself. But for some unexplainable reason I was rooted to the spot. It's like I was witnessing a train wreck I was powerless to stop, but I just couldn't turn my eyes away.

Eventually he broke the silence.

'My ex-girlfriend was a pessimist,' he said.

I guess that's why he wasn't too pleased with my reply.

'It's OK,' he said, when I didn't answer. 'I forgive you. I'm sure you didn't mean it.'

Forgive me? It was definitely time to go, I decided. The trains were about to crash, blood was going to be spilt. Probably mine.

'I'm going to head home now, I'm a little tired,' I said, standing up and smiling, lest he lunge for a steak knife and stab me repeatedly in the chest.

Then I'd have to take out a restraining order on him, too. If I was still alive.

Thankfully he let me put some money on the table and leave, without doing anything more than staring at me psychotically, without blinking.

On the way home I phoned Izzy and officially fired her as my internet-dating adviser.

Jools

I sat down at the dinner table to chicken casserole, green beans and mashed spuds. Yum.

It was now or never, I decided.

'Tom wants to meet you both,' I said.

'Who's Tom?' asked Mum.

'Yes, who's Tom?' said Dad, bringing up the rear.

'He's the baby's father.'

'You mean your ex-boyfriend?' said Mum.

'Not exactly.'

'You mean he's still your boyfriend? That's great news, love!'

'No, um, wrong again. Tom . . . was never my boyfriend . . .'

Tread carefully, I thought. Remember the generation gap and step over it, tactfully if you can.

'We were never together, as such . . . we only slept together once and . . . although we used protection . . . a condom . . . I got pregnant. I guess the condom failed.'

'Well, then,' said Mum, 'I see.' Her tone suggested that she was trying her very hardest to understand how her daughter had a one-night stand with a stranger and came away pregnant, but that she'd probably never be able to get the swing of it entirely.

No response from Dad as yet. He had gone unusually quiet. I wasn't sure if it was due to the mention of sex, his daughter having it, or the failed condom. Or all three. He silently spooned his mashed spuds into his mouth.

'What's he like?' asked Mum.

'He's lovely,' I replied. 'He's been very good to me and he wants to be a part of the baby's life.'

'Really?' asked Mum, her tone sporting undeniable and hopeful traces of wedding bells.

'We've become good friends,' I continued, nipping her unfounded stray thoughts in the bud. 'And I hope we remain friends.'

'He doesn't have a . . . girlfriend, does he?' asked Mum.

'No,' I replied, very matter-of-factly. I had no idea whether Tom was currently seeing anyone, and it was none of my business, but the last thing I wanted was my mother giving him the third degree when he came over.

'And what does this Tom do?' asked Dad, finally, as though Tom were some sort of eligible suitor who had his eye on me, and not some bloke I'd met at the pub and shagged once.

'He's an accountant,' I replied.

'Well, I'd love to meet him,' said Mum. 'And so would your father.'

Dad glanced sideways at her as though he hadn't quite made up his mind, but then quickly resigned himself to the fact that it really didn't matter at all whether he'd made his mind up or not, as she had spoken for him. In fact, there was very little use in him bothering to think for himself at all.

I woke up and for some reason I felt a little nervous. Tom

was coming around to visit my parents after work that night. I don't know why I felt nervous about his visit, it was not as though it was imperative that he and my parents hit it off, although part of me hoped they would.

I found Mum fussing around in the kitchen at five o'clock, as though it was the Queen herself who was paying us a visit, and not a man I'd met at the pub and had a one-night stand with.

'What does he like to drink?' she asked.

'Who?'

'Tom, of course!'

'God, I don't know, Mum.'

She threw me a look that suggested I should bloody well know what the father of my unborn child wanted to drink.

'He'll have a beer,' said Dad, who was sitting at the kitchen table in his golfing fit-out, having returned from the club early for The Visit. 'Or a whisky.' His tone implied that Tom had no choice but to have a whisky or a beer, and if he selected anything else then he'd automatically plummet a couple of notches in Dad's books.

'Are you going out tonight?' I asked, noticing that Mum was prancing round in her Debbie Reynolds get-up.

'No, love.'

'You mean you got dolled up for Tom?' I asked.

'Well,' replied Mum, 'there's nothing wrong with presenting a good face. Time to go and get changed, Barry,' she added, pointedly.

'I'm staying like this,' replied Dad.

'You can't stay like that!'

'Yep. I can.'

Dad was standing his ground. He obviously thought that by staying in his golf gear it'd be obvious to Tom that he was a golf player, and that if Tom thought Dad's attire was a bit strange then he clearly wasn't a golf player and Dad probably wouldn't bother talking to him because they'd have absolutely nothing in common.

'Get changed,' said Mum, trying one last time. 'You'll embarrass poor Julia.'

I really couldn't have cared less what Dad was wearing.

'No,' said Dad.

It wasn't often Dad stood his ground, so Mum wisely decided to call it quits.

'Why don't you run and get changed then, love?' said Mum, turning to me.

'Why?' I replied, glancing down at my well-worn pregnancy jeans, T-shirt and pink jandals. 'I'm comfy.'

'How about just changing your top then . . . and shoes,' said Mum. 'And popping on a bit of lipstick.'

'For God's sake, Mum, I'm not trying to impress him.'

'Nothing wrong with a bit of lipstick every now and then.'

I put on some lip-gloss to shut her up, and brushed my hair. That was as far as I was prepared to go.

I noticed that Mum had whipped up a plate of hors d'œuvres for the occasion; smoked salmon and cream cheese on crackers, some carrot and cucumber sticks and dip, and a bowl of nuts. Tom was obviously worthy of a plate of her 'flash snacks'. The only people who usually qualified for these were the ladies from the golf club, the Neighbourhood Watch group, Bob and Elaine from down the road, and Father Peter. And no doubt Debbie Reynolds if she ever happened to drop by.

I helped myself to a salmon cracker, only to find my hand being slapped away.

'Out!' cried Mum. 'They're for Tom!'

Unbelievable. Here I was pregnant and starving and my mother was saving the salmon crackers for a bloke she'd never even met.

I whipped a cracker away when she wasn't looking and sat down beside Dad.

'Now you're not to pick on him,' I said to Dad.

'What do you mean, love?' he replied.

'I mean you're not to interrogate him about his job, or what sports he plays, or his views on the government.'

'Doesn't leave much to talk about then does it?' said Dad.

'Be nice,' I warned. 'He's nervous enough about meeting the two of you.'

'Hi,' I smiled, opening the front door.

'Hey there,' said Tom, stepping through and giving me a kiss on the cheek. 'And hey to you, too,' he added, giving me a wee pat on the belly.

'Hello, Tom. Lovely to meet you,' swooned Mum, who had decided the occasion called for her very best royal manners.

I watched nervously as Dad lunged for him with The Handshake. Dad was famous for his handshake. It was so firm that he'd been known to crush a few bones over the years. Nothing pleased him more than giving another man The Shake, particularly any man who had turned up on the doorstep over the years to take me out.

To his credit, Tom showed no signs of flinching; instead he looked into Dad's eyes and returned his shake with what appeared to be a rather firm grip. It was like watching some sort of territorial ritual.

Swap the living room for the insides of a cave, I thought, pop them in a couple of animal skins, and man hasn't really evolved all that far.

'What would you like to drink, Tom?' asked Mum, as she ushered to him to the apples and peaches.

'I'll have a beer, please,' replied Tom.

Dad flicked me a conspiratorial nod of his head.

'What club do you play at?' asked Tom, noting Dad's get-up.

'Helensville,' replied Dad. 'Do you know it?'

'I've played there a couple of times,' replied Tom. 'Not for a few years, though. It's a good course from memory, well-kept greens.'

I watched as Dad visibly thawed before our eyes. He was like a cat that just needed to be stroked in the right spot, under the chin, and he'd melt in your arms. Tom had definitely found his G-spot. Golf.

'Do you play often?' asked Dad.

'Not as often as I'd like,' said Tom. 'Probably only about once a month these days.'

Dad and Tom continued to talk golf for a few more minutes before Mum butted in, much to Dad's annoyance.

'Where do you live, Tom?' asked Mum. She already knew the answer to this question, because I'd told her each of the three times she'd already asked me. Why did all mothers feel it necessary to ask the same question, not only several times, but also to different people? Did they think the answer was going to keep changing? Did she think Tom was now going to be living some-where else?

'Kingsland,' replied Tom.

'Are you flatting?' asked Mum. Another question

she already knew the bloody answer to. I flicked her the sideways daggers.

'No,' answered Tom. 'I live by myself. I'm just renting a small place while I keep saving. I'm planning on buying somewhere in a few months.'

'Buying?' said Mum. 'How lovely.'

My parents were from the generation that consider owning property as a sign of maturity and achievement, regardless of the amount of debt one accrues in doing so. For them, owning a piece of land is a sign of stability and grown-up commitment, a place to build a nest and raise a family. Not that I didn't also want to have a nest again, now more than ever, but I didn't consider it a major achievement. Instead I was prone to regularly breaking out in cold sweats and grinding my teeth in my sleep at the very thought of a mortgage.

'Another cracker, Tom?' said Mum, holding the platter in front of him.

'Lovely,' he replied. 'They're really good.'

'Thank you,' said Mum, who appeared to be blushing. She really needed to get out more often.

'I'll have a cracker, too,' I said, as she moved the platter away.

Mum and Dad continued to take turns interrogating Tom: Dad about his golf handicap, preferred sports, career prospects and political alliances; Mum about his family and family friends. Tom took it all in his stride, expertly firing off replies that both charmed and amused them, and also asking questions of them in return, which they were more than happy to answer. They were getting on so well I could have snuck off to my room for a cuppa and a lie-down. I doubt they would have noticed.

Mum offered Tom another cracker, before she

suggested that I show him around the house.

Show him around? What were we? Twelve years old and playing at my house after school?

'Sounds good,' said Tom, ever polite.

I walked him through the kitchen and dining room, out to the courtyard and garden, and then upstairs to the bedrooms.

'So your parents have lived here for a long time, have they?' said Tom, as we climbed the stairs.

'Too long.'

'I dunno. It's kinda nice that they've stayed in the same place. We moved around so much that it's hard to think of one place as our family home.'

'Yeah . . . I guess it's nice never having had to shift all my stuff out.'

I showed him Mum and Dad's room, the spare bedroom, the office. And then my bedroom.

'And this . . . is my room,' I said, opening my bedroom door.

'Nice . . . um . . . room,' said Tom, running his eyes across the lemon wallpaper, white lace-trimmed curtains, finally resting them on the single bed against the wall and the Tinkerbell duvet.

'And nice duvet.'

'Thanks,' I replied. 'Mum put it on especially for me when I moved in. Lovely, isn't it?'

Tom was far too busy laughing to reply. I gave him a friendly elbow in the ribs.

I really will have to do something about the single-bed situation and duvet, I decided. But the truth was I was quite enjoying sleeping in a single bed (duvet cover aside). I felt snug and cosy, and, aside from the couple of times I'd misjudged its narrow width and ended up on the carpet, I liked the feeling. There was no fear of sleepily reaching out for that imaginary partner when you were ensconced in a single bed.

We went back downstairs, whereupon Mum and Dad continued to interrogate Tom for another thirty minutes before he very politely excused himself. Mum gave him a farewell kiss on the cheek and Dad gave him another firm handshake to send him on his way.

'I know this is a bit weird,' he said, as I walked him to the door, 'but my parents would really like to meet you, too, if that's OK?'

'Of course,' I replied, although the prospect made me more than a little nervous.

What will his parents think of me? I wondered. The slapper who had a one-night stand with their son? It was one thing having parents suspect you'd been shagging their son, but it was quite another having a huge protruding belly which practically screamed Yes! We had dirty old sexual intercourse! It was me!

Mind you, their son is also a slapper who'd had a one-night stand, I reminded myself.

'What a charming young man!' said Mum, as I walked back into the living room.

'Nice firm shake,' said Dad, which was the highest praise he could possibly have bestowed.

But I needn't have worried about meeting Tom's parents, because when we did meet, two weeks later at Tom's house, they were unbelievably lovely and didn't make me feel like a dirty slapper at all. In fact, I was strangely relaxed in their company. They were both as easygoing as Tom, and as friendly. Tom had obviously filled them in on my current state of unemployment and living arrangements and, much to my relief, they avoided asking me questions about either.

Tom cooked us a lovely dinner and we talked about all sorts of things: films, travel, their family, what Tom was like as a baby and child (which I found strangely intriguing; thankfully he was a placid baby, although a slightly cheeky child). And when I was leaving, both his mother and father gave me a kiss on the cheek and said they hoped to see me again soon. So, clearly they didn't think I was too much of a dirty slapper, which was nice.

Tom seemed to be a complete mix of both his parents. He had the relaxed and self-assured personality of his father, mixed with the energy and enthusiasm of his mother.

His mother, having three sons, couldn't hide her delight that I was having a girl.

'Such a nice change,' she whispered to me, conspiratorially.

'Thanks for a lovely dinner,' I said to Tom, when I phoned him the next day.

'You're most welcome, mother-to-be,' he replied, having taken to calling me this lately. 'They loved you,' he added.

'So they didn't think I was a dirty slapper?'

'Not a chance!' he laughed. 'In fact they were wondering if you'd like to come to their house for dinner sometime soon.'

Kat

'Guess what?' I said, when Izzy answered the phone. 'Gus and Dan are having a dinner party and they've invited us.'

'You and me?'

'That's right.'

'Holy shit!'

'No kidding . . . what the hell do I say?'

'That's a tricky one,' said Izzy, mulling it over. 'If you don't go, then you'll look like a scaredy-cat. And if you do go, it could well be one of the worst nights of your life.'

'So many glorious options,' I sighed.

'I think we should go,' said Izzy. 'It'll be painful, but they're obviously trying to extend an olive branch.'

'I'd like to shove the branch up their arses,' I replied. 'But they'd probably enjoy that, wouldn't they?'

'You know, the more times you see them together the easier it will become,' said Izzy, ignoring me.

'S'pose so,' I agreed.

It had been over eight months since The Incident, but the very thought of that night still sent waves of paralysis through my system. Although, on the upside, the tears were few and far between these days and my desire to turn myself into a psychotic Sadie the Cleaning Lady was finally abating.

'Who else will be there?' asked Izzy.

'Scott and Maggie and Liz and Harry.'

'Wow, I haven't seen those guys for ages,' said Izzy.

'Neither,' I replied.

Scott was Gus's workmate and friend, and Maggie was his wife — a couple Gus and I used to do coupley things with from time to time. Liz was Gus's cousin, an absolute hoot whom I adored but whose calls and requests for a catch-up I'd been avoiding, along with everyone else's. Harry was her incredibly young and good-looking boyfriend.

'Has Harry finished school yet?' asked Izzy, who liked to tease Liz whenever she got the opportunity.

'Not only finished school but they're getting married.'

'Jesus! Is that legal?'

'You're just jealous,' I laughed.

'Of course I am. He's gorgeous.'

On Saturday night Izzy and I headed off to Dan's apartment (where Gus was *still* living) but only after I'd thrown two shots of straight vodka down my throat.

'A stabilizer,' I assured Izzy, as she stared worriedly at me.

As the eight of us sat at the exquisitely laid-out dinner table in Dan's stylish and roomy art-clad warehouse apartment, with its sparkling new kitchen and bathroom, drinking hundred-year-old bottles of wine, at long last I knew why I had been so sickly sweet to Gus and Dan at our supermarket and laundromat encounters. It appeared that I *could* be nasty, it's just that I required the false confidence that can only stem from having had two shots of straight vodka and five too many glasses of wine. With that in my system, there really was no stopping the amount of venomous anger that could avalanche from my lips.

I wasn't sure if it was the way Gus called Dan *honey* (which is what he used to call me) or the way Dan talked about their upcoming holiday to Rome and Florence (two cities Gus and I had wanted to visit together and had been making plans for prior to The Incident), or how ridiculously happy and in love they both looked, but something finally sent me over the edge. *Well* over.

'You know what?' I screamed at both of them, slamming my cutlery down on the expensive bone-china plate and promptly bringing the conversation to a screaming halt. 'You're a couple of fuckwits!

'You were supposed to be my friend too!' I screamed at Dan, before I stood up and hurled my full wine glass across the table at him (he ducked but there really was no need, it ended up hitting the wall and smashing into tiny crystal pieces a good metre to his right). 'How *could* you?'

To say what ensued was a hushed silence would be an understatement. It was the type of silence that could only be heard in a graveyard after the stroke of midnight.

'Hear, hear to that!' said Liz, raising her glass and proposing a toast 'To the fuckwits!'

I glared at Gus and Dan as their frozen eyes looked past me towards the black horizon, beyond the floor-to-ceiling glass windows, as if searching for a rescue ship.

'Kat,' said Gus calmly, standing up and urging me to sit back down. 'You've every right to be angry.'

'*Every right?*' I replied. 'Damn straight I do! And then some! How the fuck could you have done this to me, Gus? Cheated on me for a year? A fucking *year?*'

In my peripheral vision I saw eyes dart about the table; this was obviously news to some people.

'All the while making me think we'd be having a baby soon and that everything was fine. But you knew it wasn't and you were just going to rip my life and plans to shreds and leave me sitting on the shelf like an old spinster.'

Strangely enough, no one was tackling me to the floor or making a move to silence me, not even Izzy.

'Then you invite me around to your love-nest for dinner and expect everything to be hunky-dory? Good as old cheese? Well I fucking hate cheese, Gus, especially old cheese!' (This was definitely the booze talking.)

'And don't think you're any less of an asshole!' I yelled, pointing at Dan. 'Do you have any idea how hard this has been for me, *honey?* Losing my husband *and* my friend? Bumping into you at the supermarket and the laundromat? Like a thousand fucking needles being stabbed into me on a daily basis . . . that's how hard! If I had another glass, I'd throw it at your bloody head and make sure I hit it this time.' Everyone had promptly moved their glasses down the table and out of my reach after I'd hurled mine.

The amazing thing was that I wasn't crying; I hadn't shed one tear. I was *far* too angry and deranged to cry.

'And you know what else?' I said, sitting back down at the table and pouring myself another glass of wine, having wrangled Izzy's glass from her. 'You dress like you're in a boy band. Both of you. It's bloody ridiculous, you look like twins.'

An audible chuckle rippled around the table.

'Anyway,' I said, draining the glass of wine in one long gulp and standing up again. 'Thanks for a lovely dinner, I'll be off now. It was lovely to see you all.'

Everyone seemed at a loss for words, but gave me a series of friendly little waves and smiles instead.

Izzy took her cue and trailed behind me, muttering 'Cheers, thanksalot' as she did.

'Best bloody dinner party I've ever been to,' said Liz, running after me and hugging me goodbye.

'Do you think I got them back?' I asked Izzy, as we slumped in the back of a taxi.

'Oh yes,' she replied, laughing. 'Without a doubt.'

That night I slept like a baby. It could well have been the booze, and to a certain extent it probably was. But I was sure it was also because I had finally unloaded all of the anger and hurt I'd been holding inside for so long. It was the best sleep I'd had in over eight months.

Izzy was there in the morning when I woke, with the sole purpose of assuring me that, although I had created one of the more memorable dinner party scenes ever, my tirade of abuse was well overdue and they deserved every word of it, especially the boy-band comment. Plus, she admitted, she was sick of me being so nice to them.

Surprisingly, I didn't wish a gaping great hole to come along and swallow me up, as I'd presumed I would. Instead I was remarkably unashamed about my performance. I had lost it, that was indisputable, and the setting possibly wasn't the most appropriate, but there was nothing I could do about that now. I was a little embarrassed at having had several witnesses to the act (namely Scott, Maggie, Liz and Harry), but I was fairly confident all four would wave it away if I rang them to apologize. The only thing I was truly sorry about was having waited eight long months to let the two of them have it, and causing myself even further anguish in the process.

That aside, I guessed I should be phoning Gus and Dan to apologize (at least for smashing the glass). But before I could, Gus phoned me.

'Kat,' he said, before I had a chance to say a word, 'I just want to let you know there's no hard feelings about last night, none whatsoever . . . We deserved every bloody word of it. I feel like such a pillock for not realizing how hard this whole thing's been for you. You just seemed like you were coping with everything so well.'

'Pride is a strange thing,' I replied. 'But if it's any consolation, I should have blown my top a long time ago . . . it's made me feel much better.'

'I'm glad,' said Gus. 'You just need to work on your aim.'

I laughed.

'Will you be OK?' he asked. 'Is there anything I can do?'

'I'll be OK,' I replied, realizing that eventually I *would* be OK, possibly even better than OK. 'I just need time. And space.'

'Of course. Do you think we'll be able to be friends again one day?' he asked, hope in his voice. 'I really miss you.'

'I think so,' I replied. 'So long as you promise not to sleep with my boyfriends.'

Jools

I had been staying in the five-star service of Hotel Familial for nearly two months when things took an unexpected turn for the worse.

'It looks as though we might have a visitor for a while, love,' said Mum, as my fat belly and I lay on the apples and peaches.

'Who?' I asked. Truth be told I was getting a bit bored and could do with some new blood around the place.

'Nan.'

Oh. God. No!

'Nan?'

She wasn't exactly new blood. More like incredibly mad, batty, old blood.

'Why?'

'Because the rest home's asked us to remove her.'

'They're kicking her out?' I cried.

'Well,' said Mum, 'I wouldn't put it quite like that but, yes, I guess so.'

'Why?'

'Because they think she needs a more secure place.'

'Is she still doing the runners?'

'Yes, it appears so.'

Nan was a professional escape artist. She was forever trying to bust her way out of the rest home, which would have been fine if she'd been able to remember for one moment where she lived. It wasn't because she didn't like it there (according to her, she did), it's just that she loved the thrill of the chase.

Last time I'd been to visit her, she'd even tried to sneak out the door past me.

'Nan,' I said, grabbing her arm as she whizzed past. 'It's Jools, where are you going?'

'To get my hair done, love,' she'd replied, without hesitation. This was a lie as the hairdresser came to the home, but it was good to know she was still quick off the mark with her fibs.

The home had helped to arrange for a hip replacement the year before, which had only enhanced her ability to leg it. I was pretty sure they regretted this now. A few months back, one of the nurses had had to haul her back from Smith & Caughey's where she'd taken up residence in one of the changing rooms.

'How long will she be staying here for?' I asked Mum, dread hanging from my words.

'Just until we can get her into another place . . . a couple of months I guess.'

'A couple of *months!* Can't she stay with anyone else?'

'Unfortunately not. You know that Linda works. And Nan won't cope with the trip up to Ian's.'

Linda and Ian were my mother's equally useless sister and brother. They had somehow managed to absolve themselves of all responsibility towards their aged and widowed mother: Linda by working well beyond her use-by date, and Ian by moving to another city six hours away. So it was my mother who was left to organize a rest home for Nan, to which she dutifully traipsed along several times a week to see her and take her on outings.

I may have seemed less than thrilled at the prospect

of squatting with Nan, but she was hard work. *Very* hard work. She was batty, completely and certifiably batty. She had severe dementia, which had progressively worsened over the past ten years. She'd come out of her bedroom wearing her knickers on her head every morning if she was left to her own devices. And she never stopped talking. I mean *never*. And the worse thing was she kept saying the same things, over and over again. Although generally no one had a clue in hell what she was talking about.

'When?' I asked, fear and desperation in my voice.

'Next week,' replied Mum.

I frantically scoured my head for other hotel options, but my options were limited. There was Francie's, but the downside was she couldn't cook nearly as well as Mum, and she probably wouldn't make my bed. There was Richie and Lydia's. On the plus side, Lydia was a good cook and she probably would make my bed. But the price would be high: I'd have to listen to her bleat on about why her hairdresser was a 'must see' and why you should always buy fresh herbs from the greengrocer, not the supermarket. It was all about the quality, apparently. I would be continually biting my tongue from replying, 'Shut up, you complete and utter snob!'

Dad was even less thrilled at the prospect of Nan's imminent stay.

'For the love of God!' he wailed to Mum. 'Tell me you're having me on, Brenda?'

And then he frantically got on the blower and summoned every golfing partner he'd ever met to play with him every single day for the next two months. The desperation dripped from his words like perspiration. I'd never seen him be so intimate with the phone for such an extended period of time in my entire life.

True to Mum's word, the following week rolled around and, no matter how much Dad and I prayed otherwise, Nan arrived to stay.

'Hello, luvvie,' she said to me, as Mum lugged Nan and her bags into the house. 'Where's that husband of yours?'

To be honest I was surprised she remembered who I was. I hadn't been to visit for a couple of months, not wanting to explain my belly situation. Although I don't know what I'd been concerned about, as she was clearly completely oblivious to it.

'I don't have one,' I replied. She looked at me strangely, but thankfully stopped the questions. For a couple of minutes anyway.

'Where's that husband of yours?' she asked again, as she, Mum and I sat down to lunch.

'Julia doesn't have a husband,' answered Mum. 'But she's having a baby. Isn't that lovely?'

Yes, that is lovely, agreed Nan. But where is her husband?

It was one thing to be single and facing the prospect of raising a baby all by yourself, but having your eighty-six-year-old batty-as-a-meataxe grandmother rub it in your face was another thing entirely.

I raised my eyes at Mum and openly sighed. It was going to be a long, *long* few months.

'Where's that man?' asked Nan. I wasn't sure if she was referring to Dad or my imaginary husband.

'Barry's playing golf,' said Mum. 'Remember?' But she was pushing shit uphill, because the chances of Nan remembering that were slim to none.

But Nan nodded her head at Mum as though, yes, of course, she remembered, there was no need to say it twice.

'Where's that man?' asked Nan again, approximately thirty seconds later.

'Golf,' I replied, saving Mum the trouble.

She nodded her head at me, although I could have said, 'He's standing over there in the corner with the leopard-print miniskirt on. Can't you see him?' and she still would have nodded her head at me.

Sweet Jesus, I thought, she's way worse than I remembered. Way worse.

I looked across at Mum. It must be hard for her to see her own mother like this. It was hard enough for me to see. Nan used to be a force to be reckoned with. Fiery, bubbly and full of life and sharp wit. She was a *man's woman*, and back in her day she'd certainly had a few, or so legend went. A few more than Grandad knew about anyway.

Mum was great with her. So patient and attentive. Not once did she lose her cool and scream, 'For the love of God, he's playing golf! Stop asking me the same fucking questions, you batty old cow! You're doing my head in!'

'Where's that man?' she asked twice more, before we'd finished lunch.

'Golf,' replied Mum and I in unison. Nan nodded knowingly at us.

She was like a goldfish. But surely goldfish had better memories?

I hope it's not genetic, I thought to myself, glancing across at Mum. There was no way in hell I was cut out to play Florence Nightingale if she came down with it.

Oh God! What if it skips a generation and I get it? I

looked down at my belly and felt heartfelt sympathy for the wee baby inside.

That night I bumped into Nan in the kitchen, at 3 a.m., as I got myself a glass of water and a TimTam. She was standing inside the pantry, giving me a hell of a fright when I flicked on the light and opened the pantry door.

'Jesus Christ!' I hollered, jumping back. Then, once my heart had found its way back to my chest, 'What are you looking for, Nan?'

'The toilet,' she answered.

'Well, I think you'll find that's the pantry you're in,' I said, escorting her to the bathroom, and then chaperoning her back to her bedroom, lest she think that was the laundry or garage.

'Can't you put a lock on her door?' I pleaded with Dad the next morning, before he headed off to golf.

He mumbled something like 'and if I had my bloody way I'd throw away the key'.

Unfortunately Mum wasn't having a bar of the lock. 'What if she needed to go to the toilet in the middle of the night and we didn't hear her?' she said.

'Get a baby monitor,' I suggested. But Dad was having none of that.

The truth was Nan made me nervous. I knew it was only a matter of time before I woke in the middle of the night to find her sitting on the end of my bed staring at me dementedly, the fright of which would likely kill me, or the baby, or both.

The worse thing about Nan's condition was that she was fit as a fiddle. In fact she was fitter than a fiddle. All of the nutrients that would usually be devoured by her brain were being pumped around her body instead. This meant that she was in a prime position to run off at high speed if anything she fancied caught her eye.

A couple of days later I decided to take her shopping with me to give Mum a wee break. It turned out to be quite a break, because by the time the police delivered Nan back home to us she'd been gone for nearly eight hours. We'd only headed to the local shopping centre, where I had to pick up a few small things for the baby and myself. As soon as we got there, I was, typically, busting to go to the toilet. I found a seat for Nan outside the toilets and told her in no uncertain terms to stay put until I came back. I even waggled my index finger at her so she'd know I was serious. But by the time I came out of the toilets, no more than three minutes later, she was nowhere to be seen. I mean *nowhere*. I frantically asked the girls at the nearby information desk and people in the surrounding shops, with no success.

How could she have disappeared? And so quickly? Even I couldn't leg it that fast, pregnant or not.

I decided to hang around the seats for five minutes in case she had some freak flash of clarity and decided to make her way back. But no clarity was forthcoming, so I went back to the information desk, reported her missing and batty, and then started my own search, shop by shop.

A few people thought they'd seen her, but they couldn't be sure. Little old ladies with permed, blue-rinsed hair, navy cardigans and mid-calf skirts were a dime a dozen in these parts.

Every five minutes I could hear her name announced over the loud speakers, asking her to make her way into a shop and tell them her name.

That's if she can remember it, I thought.

Finally I came upon a shop assistant who was positive she had talked to Nan only five minutes earlier. She pointed me in the direction she'd seen her heading, and I bolted out the door. But, once again, she appeared to have vanished into thin air.

She'd give David Copperfield a run for his money, I thought, cursing the fact I'd wanted to give Mum a break and wishing I'd just left Nan safely at home. My first outing with my grandmother in decades and I'd managed to lose her. How would I explain to the rest of the family that I'd misplaced Nan? Possibly forever?

An hour later, I reluctantly made my way back to the information desk, after scouring every shop in the entire complex.

The ladies at the desk, who were being very sympathetic about my lost nan (probably because I was heavily pregnant), suggested they phone the police, in case she'd wandered out of the shopping centre.

While they did that, I had another call to make. I pulled my mobile out of my handbag and made the dreaded call to Mum. Full credit to her, she didn't hit the roof and start hurling abuse at me. On the contrary, she said, 'You poor thing. She's always bloody well wandering off. Might have to start putting a kiddie leash on her.'

The fact that Mum took the news so well made me calm down a bit. She told me to wait where I was and that she'd be there soon.

'Bring a photo,' I urged her, 'for the police.' I had watched one too many episodes of *Missing Persons* for my own good.

As I sat on a bench seat beside the information desk, an attractive lady with a small blond-haired boy approached me.

Maybe she knows where Nan is, I thought to myself, looking up.

'Jools?' said the lady.

I stared back at the very pretty, recognizable face in front of me.

'Greta?' Was it really her? Greta Ridley? It had to be, she still looked exactly the same. With her tall, trim figure, beautiful olive skin, and long blonde hair.

I hadn't seen her for years. God, it must be nearly twenty! Not since the end of high school when she'd moved to Sydney and I'd started working.

Greta, Kat, Sally and me — we'd been the best of friends.

'Yes!' she cried, as I stood up to give her a hug.

'Wow!' she said, pointing at my belly. 'How exciting! When are you due?'

'End of November,' I replied.

'Not long to go. You look great!'

'Thank you,' I replied. Surely she was lying?

'So, how on earth are you?' she asked, sitting down beside me.

How was I? Hmmm, let's see. Well, aside from being single, unemployed, eight-and-a-half months pregnant and living with my parents, I was a little distressed because I'd somehow managed to misplace my eighty-six-year-old grandmother who, coincidentally, I was also living with.

'I'm good,' I lied. 'But I seem to have lost my grandmother somewhere in this place.'

'Oh God!' cried Greta, when I'd filled her in on the vanishing. 'Is there anything I can do?'

'No,' I replied, telling her I'd already searched everywhere and was now waiting for my mother and the police. 'Thank you, though.'

But she insisted on fetching me a hot chocolate and staying with me until Mum arrived. Her son, Sam, sat beside her, patiently drawing in his colouring book.

We found ourselves chatting away about our old school days, me keeping one eye out for a glimpse of Nan, should she decide to come to her senses and reappear again. I was glad for the conversation to take my mind off the guilt of losing her.

I reminded Greta of the time Sally, Kat and I had dressed her up in my mother's clothes and make-up (because we thought she looked the eldest) and sent her into the liquor store to buy the four of us a bottle of gin, while we waited outside.

'How old were we?'

'Fourteen . . . I think,' said Greta.

She'd come out of the liquor store with a bottle of lemonade and a warning from the man behind the counter not to dress up in her mother's clothes again.

We laughed at the memory.

'We were convinced you looked at least twenty-five!' I said.

'So was I!' cried Greta.

'Have you seen Kat and Sally?' I asked, my memory smiling at the thought of them.

Sally was so sweet, and Kat, the over-achiever, surely she was the head of some multi-national organization by now?

I bet the two of them are happily married to adoring husbands, I thought. And with fantastic careers. I bet anything, they aren't living with their parents.

'It's so weird!' said Greta. 'I hadn't seen either of them since school, and then I bumped into them both a few months back. I don't think any of us managed to stay in touch after school.'

'If only there'd been email,' I replied. 'It might have been a different story.'

'So true,' smiled Greta. 'None of us were ever any good at writing letters.'

My mother arrived, and promptly enveloped Greta in a great big bear hug.

Greta took a look at the photo of Nan and said she would keep an eye out and ask around some more while she was doing her shopping.

'Thanks, dear,' said Mum, who immediately set off on a loop of the shops for herself, ordering me to sit back down and stay put.

'Give me a call and let me know when you find her,' said Greta, who had given me her card, and written down her home number. 'Please.'

'I will,' I promised, hugging her goodbye.

Twenty minutes later, Mum arrived back Nan-less.

This is serious, I thought. Mum could find anything. I mean *anything*. Missing socks, passports, earrings, a contact lens on a shagpile carpet. But she couldn't find Nan.

The police finally arrived, asked us all sorts of questions, took a description of Nan and her photograph. And that was that. She'd been missing for two hours by this stage.

We were told that the best thing for us to do was to go home. And wait. They'd find her, they assured us, she couldn't have gone far. And as it turned out, she hadn't gone far. Only in our description of Nan we'd got one crucial thing wrong. When asked by the police officer if Nan was partial to a drink we'd both replied no, not on your life. But it appeared that Nan *was* partial to a drink. Several drinks in fact. When the police finally found her and dropped her home six hours later, she was as drunk as a skunk. They'd found her in a nearby pub, only two blocks from the shopping centre, a gin and cigarette in hand, and several more gins lined up along the bar top.

'But how?' I asked. 'She didn't have any money!'

Nan had been forbidden from carrying a handbag, a wallet, or even a cashflow card, because they were invariably never to be seen again, and she could never have remembered the pin number anyway.

'Seems she made a few friends,' said the officer, smiling.

Quite a few male friends, as it turned out, all more than happy to buy Nan a gin or two.

Quietly I was extremely proud of her. Eighty-six years old and she could still pull a free night on the booze. No small feat. I put it down to her legs, which were still in good shape and had been known to turn a few heads back in their day.

The officer carried a giggling Nan out of the police car and into the lounge.

'Jesus, Mary and Joseph,' said Dad, when he copped a look at the state of her.

I think he'd secretly been hoping she was gone for good.

'Yoopsie Dayshe,' squealed Nan, as she all but fell onto the sofa.

'Best you get some water and food into her and put her to bed,' said the officer.

I stared at Nan. She was like a fifteen-year-old who'd snuck out of her bedroom window to the local nightclub, only to be escorted back home by the police. I couldn't be angry with her. She looked as though she'd had the time of her life.

Mum gave her some dinner and a bath and tucked her up in bed. And for once she slept like a baby, not found wandering the house in the small hours by anyone.

Sally

'Can you come to church tomorrow afternoon?' asked Vincent.

'Why?'

'There's something I'd like to show you.'

He seemed unwilling to elaborate.

'OK,' I agreed.

What can it be? I wondered. Probably another hair-brained scheme like the website, or something to do with that damn book.

'It'll be exciting,' he promised.

I doubted it. Our ideas of exciting tended to be worlds apart these days.

'Don't forget we've got Elizabeth's school play tomorrow night,' I reminded him.

I arrived at the church office the following afternoon, but Vincent wasn't there. He was in the church itself, which was more like an auditorium than a church, with its theatre-like rows of seats and carpeted floor. A 'new-age church', Vincent called it. I thought it looked more like a conference centre than a place of worship.

I walked in to find Elvin himself sitting in the front row. I hadn't seen him for at least five years.

'Sally!' he cried, enveloping me in an over-the-top embrace.

He looks more greasy and adulterous than ever, I

noted. The smell of his aftershave was overpowering.

'Elvin, hi. Vincent didn't tell me you were back in the country.'

'Just a fleeting visit, honey,' said Elvin, flashing me his blindingly white and uber-large teeth. They were even bigger and whiter than Vincent's.

'That's because it was a surprise,' said Vincent, walking up behind Elvin.

Was Elvin the exciting surprise? Surely not?

What were the camera operators doing here? I wondered, noticing the two men at the front of the church, beside the stage.

'Now, honey,' drawled Elvin, taking my hand and leading me towards the stage. 'Come with us. Have we got a surprise for you!'

How has he managed to cultivate an American accent in such a small amount of time? I wondered.

I glanced at Vincent, who winked at me. What on earth were they on about?

'Elvin's had a great idea!' exclaimed Vincent, leading me to an armchair on the stage and sitting me down. 'How about you tell her, Elvin?'

'Sure thing,' said Elvin, sitting in a chair opposite.

'Well Sal . . .' I really hated it when he called me Sal. 'Here's the thing. Now this is really exciting, honey. What's been happening in the States lately is that some of the preachers with their own shows have been allocating some of their airtime, a segment if you like, to their wives. Great, huh?'

I stared back at him, blankly. What on earth did this have to do with me?

'The wives use their slot to talk about all sorts of things, not just Jesus . . . they talk about their families, their children, their husbands.'

293

I stared around nervously. At Elvin. At the two camera operators. At the sound technician. At Vincent, who nodded his head at me and winked at me again.

'Sooo . . .' drawled Elvin, 'Vincent and I thought what a great idea it would be for you to have your own segment on his show!'

'On TV?' I asked, staring at Vincent for some sort of clarification.

'That's right,' answered Elvin, talking to me as though I were one of the five-year-olds who got hauled onto the stage by Vincent during his sermons. 'Now wouldn't that be great?'

'No, Elvin,' I replied, as calmly as I possibly could, 'I don't think that would be great. In fact, I think that would be less than great. I have no idea what's prompted this *idea* of yours, or why the two of you thought it would be something I would be remotely interested in doing. But I can assure both of you, it's not.'

'C'mon Sally!' cried Vincent. 'Elvin's come all this way for us to try and get this thing off the ground.'

I turned to face Vincent.

'Let me get this straight . . . Elvin has flown all the way here to help you launch my television segment, and yet you haven't once mentioned this idea to me? Given me one hint you wanted me to be on television? Let alone asked me if it is something I'd want to do?'

'Well . . .' stalled Vincent. 'I didn't expect you to have a problem with it.'

'No, Vincent. I don't think that's the way it is. I think you thought that by having Elvin here you'd be able to keep me in the dark and then bully me into doing something that I don't want to do.'

How can he have possibly thought this is something I'd want to do? I wondered. Did he even know me at all?

I'm a reasonably shy person, someone who values their privacy. I found it hard enough having to smile for the cameras at the end of his show.

He knows you all right, I realized. How can he possibly not after all these years? He just doesn't care.

'Y'know,' said Elvin, 'how about you take a moment, Sal, grab a coffee, and then we'll just try running through the little script I've got here, just a small one . . . You never know, honey, you might just love having the cameras on you.'

'I really don't think so, Elvin,' I replied, standing up.

I walked off the stage, saying to the camera operators and sound man as I passed, 'I'm sorry to have wasted your time.'

'Sal, honey!' called Elvin after me.

Vincent followed me to the exit at the back of the church, grabbing my elbow as I opened the door. Firmly.

'Sally, this is *really* important!' he pleaded. 'This could be a big deal for us, a huge deal. Can't you just forget about your pride for a minute?'

'How could you?' I hissed, snatching my elbow back and walking out the door.

At seven o'clock, Davey, Hannah and I waited outside the front of Elizabeth's school hall. Even though I was livid with Vincent, I also knew it was important for all of us to sit together, so that when Elizabeth looked out into the seats in front she'd see the four of us looking back at her, her whole family.

When the last call came to take our seats, we went inside and sat down, without Vincent.

How can he do this to her? I thought, my eyes scanning the back of the hall one last time as the curtains opened. But there were no late arrivals. Perhaps he'll sneak in soon and sit at the back somewhere, I hoped.

The play was *Bad Jelly the Witch*, and Elizabeth had been cast as Rose, one of the two main characters, after auditioning against ten other girls for the part.

She was brilliant, reciting her lines clearly, without stumbling once. Her beautiful young voice projected throughout the hall. Her movements were all completely in character, totally believable. I'd had no idea she was so good at acting. It looked like the drama classes she'd been going to for the past couple of years had really paid off.

This will do wonders for her confidence, I thought. She had always been a slightly shy child, compared with the other two.

I couldn't take my eyes off her. She was truly amazing, my little girl.

I wasn't the only one who thought so, because when the play ended Elizabeth got a standing ovation.

The three of us waited for her outside the front of the hall. I had given up any hope that Vincent had snuck in late; there was still no sign of him.

'You were wonderful, darling,' I said, giving Elizabeth a huge hug. 'Just amazing!'

'Awesome!' said Davey, which was very high praise.

'Yeah!' agreed little Hannah. 'Awesome Lizzy!'

'Thank you,' she smiled. I could tell she was buzzing after her performance, and so she should be.

'Where's Dad?' she asked, looking around, her voice remaining casual but her eyes betraying her.

'He couldn't make it, love,' I lied. 'He got called

back to church, an emergency. He's so sorry to have missed it.'

I could tell she only partially believed me. She was still a child, but she wasn't stupid. I don't know why I felt I had to lie to her, I was only trying to protect her little heart.

I took the kids out for dessert and we dissected the play, all of us heaping much-deserved praise on Elizabeth and her performance.

Vincent didn't arrive home until the children were all in bed, sound asleep. I was waiting for him in the living room.

'Where the hell were you?' I asked, not caring that I'd uttered a sinful word. He deserved it.

'I was entertaining Elvin,' he replied. 'I took him out for dinner.'

'And what about your daughter?' I hissed, trying hard to keep my voice down. 'And her play?'

'Oh, darn . . . I forgot.'

'You forgot? How could you forget, Vincent? I must have reminded you a hundred times!'

'It was a busy day, Sally, and with you not coming to the party with the television slot . . . well, it just threw me.'

'So it's my fault you missed the play, is that it? You are truly unbelievable! I suggest you apologize to her tomorrow,' I said, standing up from the couch. 'And you might want to think of a better excuse than you forgot. This was important to her, Vincent,' I added. 'Really important.'

With that I headed off to the spare room. There was so point in continuing the discussion when he clearly had no concept of what was important in his children's lives.

Kat

With The Great Unloading of Emotions, it appeared the urge to turn myself into a human laundromat was finally exorcized from my body, once and for all. I no longer felt the need to fill every spare moment with a pile of washing, laundry powder or an iron in my hands. Instead I filled my spare time with largely normal things: reading, drinking coffee, watching movies, shopping, and gardening. Things I used to do in my Old Life.

As I sat down at the kitchen table with a fresh cup of coffee, the phone rang. It was Mum.

'I've just been looking in the death notices . . .' she said.

What on earth was she looking at the death notices for? In the hope she spotted someone's funeral she could leg it off to?

'. . . and I've seen the name Greta Ridley,' she continued. 'Aged thirty-five.'

Greta? Surely not? But how many Greta Ridleys aged thirty-five could there possibly be? Oh Jesus. It had to be her.

'You're joking!' I cried, when I finally found my voice.

''Fraid not, love,' replied Mum. 'I'm sorry, dear. She was a good friend of yours, wasn't she?'

One of my best friends.

'But how?' I asked Mum, who didn't know the answer.

'It says she died suddenly,' said Mum. 'The poor thing. When did you see her last?'

I thought back to when I'd bumped into her outside the laundromat, as I was getting into my car, hurrying to escape Gus and Dan. She had given me her card and I'd said I'd call her. Why the hell hadn't I?

Because I was scared, that's why. Scared of meeting with her, and Jools and Sally. Scared of how perfect their lives would be, how they'd all be happily married with lots of kids. With everything I didn't have.

Oh God, she probably thought I was such a bitch, I thought in horror. That I couldn't be bothered picking up the phone and giving her a call.

If only I had. I really could have done with another friend like Greta.

'A couple of months ago,' I replied, a tear sliding down my cheek. 'She looked so well, so happy.'

I remembered how radiant and youthful she had looked, and her beautiful smile. She was so full of life.

'I met her little girl, too.'

'How old?' asked Mum.

'Little. Four I think. Her name's Ella. She was so cute. And she had a son, too, he was six. *Oh God*, the poor kids.'

'Poor little tykes,' agreed Mum. 'Losing their mummy.'

It was just so sad.

'When's the funeral?' I asked.

'Monday at three o'clock,' replied Mum.

As I hung up the phone I really started to cry. Poor Greta. She was far too young to die.

Five minutes later, Mum rang back to tell me how

Greta had died, after phoning the funeral director. I had guessed it was cancer, the cause of so many premature deaths these days. But it wasn't.

'She was hit by a bus,' said Mum.

'Hit by a *bus?*'

'Yes. She was walking across Symonds Street on her way to work. It was the 035.'

I didn't know what to say. I know people were always talking about getting hit by a bus — it was a figure of speech — but I'd no idea people *actually* got hit by them. What a ridiculous and senseless way to die. One minute you're walking to work, minding your own business, and the next you're hit by a bus and dead.

As I hung up the phone from Mum, again, I wondered whether Jools and Sally would be at Greta's funeral too. I toyed with the idea of tracking them down to let them know, in case they hadn't heard, but I had no idea where to start.

I wondered what they were doing now. If Sally had become the doctor she always wanted to be. I assumed so, she had always been so studious at school. And Jools, the cheeky one, she had wanted to have her own company, hadn't she?

No doubt they're both married with loyal, non-cheating, straight husbands, I thought. And a couple of loyal, non-cheating, straight children, too.

I felt the tears begin again, but this time they were for me, not Greta. Just when I'd finally begun to feel like my normal old self.

Jools

I was no longer capable of walking normally; instead I waddled. Just like a gargantuan talking duck. This was due to the fact that my arse was now the size of a tardus. I never used to notice the size of my arse, it was just something that was there, somewhere behind me, thankfully not too big and not too small. But now I felt its girth in every step I took. I was positive it must be the size of a small house, although Francie kindly assured me otherwise. I used to be a fabulous social vixen, a notorious booze hag. And now here I was, a waddler. Oh, how my life had plunged.

No one tells you about the waddling, the hairy trail down your stomach, the pimples on your back, or the enormous lumpy, itchy-as-all-hell nipples, do they? No, they don't. It must be because if you heard about any of the side effects there'd be no more breeding at all; the human race would simply peter out. All I'd ever heard people talk about prior to being up the duff was the 'glow'. Well I was now nine months preggers and I'd yet to get *the glow*. I had the pimples, hairy stomach, itchy nipples and waddling all right. But no bloody glow.

I also appeared to be suffering from emotional diarrhoea. I would burst into tears at absolutely everything and anything, without any warning at all.

301

Television advertisements would really get me going, especially ones that featured a small fluffy animal or, worse, a baby. I would begin to sob uncontrollably, not because I was sad or distressed to see the fluffy animals or babies, but because I thought they were the most beautiful wee creatures I'd ever seen.

'Get her a tissue, for God's sake,' Dad would say to Mum. 'She's going to rot the carpet.'

'It's hormones, Barry,' Mum would reply. 'Leave the poor girl alone.

'You bloody men don't know how lucky you've got it,' she'd add, returning with three boxes of tissues.

When I wasn't bursting into tears, I was busy fighting Dad for the television remote.

'Let her watch what she wants!' Mum would scold him. 'She's with child!' At which point he would reluctantly pass me the remote control and I would smile smugly back at him. Without even trying I had surpassed him in the favouritism stakes, and understandably he wasn't too happy with my promotion.

He was even less happy when he went to watch the golf on telly one Sunday afternoon (I had no idea how anyone could stand watching golf on telly, I was sure there were knitting competitions out there that were more riveting) and someone had stolen the batteries from the remote control.

'It would have to be Julia,' Dad said to Mum. (I was out shopping with Francie at the time, so I've had to rely on Mum's version of events.)

'Why would Julia steal the batteries from the remote?' replied Mum.

'To get back at me,' said Dad.

'Why on earth would she want to get back at you?'

'Because I watched the rugger last night and she

missed *The Apprentice*.' (That was true, and I had been very dark with him at the time. I had a certain empathy for the young female apprentices who gave it their all, dressing as sexily as they could and flirting wildly with The Don, only for him to say 'you're fired' in the next episode. The bastard.)

'I bet she's hidden them somewhere . . .' said Dad. 'In her bedroom!' he cried, running upstairs.

'I've found them,' said Dad, returning back downstairs. 'In this thing here.'

'Are you sure?' said Mum, as she tried to work out what on earth it was that Dad had in his hand.

'God knows what the hell it is,' said Dad, waving the thing about.

Mum took The Thing from him for a closer inspection.

'Damned if I know' was her verdict.

Mum placed The Thing down on the kitchen table. Dad took the batteries out and headed back to the sofa.

A couple of hours later my Aunt Evie, Dad's sister, popped by for a visit.

'Don't suppose you know what the hell this is, do you, Evie?' Dad asked her, pointing at The Thing, which was still sitting in the middle of the kitchen table.

Evie picked up The Thing, cocked her head to one side, placed it back onto the table and replied, 'I think it might be a clitoral stimulator.'

'A what?' said Dad.

'A clitoral stimulator. You strap it on to your thigh, I think, and it, well, rubs against your clitoris until you climax.'

At which point Dad (according to Mum) went as white as a sheet, managing only to mutter 'Christ and Lord above'.

'I can't believe I didn't know what it was!' Mum said to me later that evening. 'I may not be Pamela Anderson but I'm not over the hill either.' I think she was a bit disappointed that Evie had got it first hit.

Dad excused himself and went back to watch the golf. The combination of his pregnant daughter owning a sex toy, which she obviously used, and his younger sister knowing what it was used for, was all too much for him to take.

'But she's pregnant!' Dad had said to Mum, once Evie had gone.

'Just because she's pregnant doesn't mean she doesn't want a bit,' replied Mum.

I came home, The Thing having been placed back in my bedside drawer, batteries included, and I wouldn't have known any different had I not said to Mum, 'Dad's acting bloody weird. He won't look me in the eye.' At which point Mum relayed the story to me.

Oh, dear God, I thought, is there anything worse in the world than your father walking around the house with your clitoral stimulator in his hand?

A couple of days after the missing-batteries incident, my mother came running (literally) into the living room, waving the newspaper in the air.

'Newsflash! Newsflash!' she screeched.

'What?' I said, putting down my book.

'What?' said Dad, who still couldn't quite look me in the eye.

'Debbie's coming! Debbie's coming!'

We gave her a searching look. Who was Debbie and why was she coming?

'Debbie!' screamed my mother again, her smile wider than I'd ever seen it before. 'Reynolds! She'd doing a show here!'

'Debbie Reynolds?' chorused Dad and I in unison.

Both of us were at a loss to comprehend how on earth she was possibly going to fill a theatre. How could there possibly be more than one (living) Debbie Reynolds fan in the city, let alone the country? But I was soon to find out, because my mother was hot off the phone from booking two tickets to her show. Naturally one was for her; the other one was up for grabs.

'If you think I'm going, you're out of your head,' said Dad, getting in first.

Mum looked at me, beseechingly. I tried to look away. But I knew I was done for.

You see, unlike my mother, none of her friends were Debbie Reynolds' fans, at least not the type of fans who would want to sit through an entire concert with just Debbie Reynolds at the helm. My mother knew this.

And with my father being somewhat quicker off the mark than myself, in my current pregnant and several-beats-behind-the-drum state, that left only one candidate for the remaining ticket. Me.

'*Please,*' I begged her. 'There *must* be someone else you can take?'

'You'll love it!' she urged. 'All our old favourites!'

Mum thought that just because she'd regularly performed her Debbie Reynolds repertoire to me when I was an infant and I'd rewarded her with a smile, I was therefore a Debbie fan and would remain so for the rest of my life. The truth was I was a baby, she could have been singing Celine Dion and I still would have smiled back at her.

Dad stretched back on the sofa with his book,

305

confident in the knowledge that he was safely out of the running. Smug bastard.

Stonkeringly pregnant and off to see Debbie Reynolds in concert on a Saturday night. Was there no justice left in the world? No law which said that if you were pregnant and off the sauce for nine months then this was enough punishment and you should be spared from further heartache? There should be, I thought as I wondered what to wear. And then thought better of it. It didn't matter what the hell I wore. For starters I was quite obviously pregnant and therefore highly unlikely to be impressing anyone of the opposite sex with my sultry get-up. And, secondly, it was even more unlikely there would be anyone there of the opposite sex who was under seventy. I pulled on my pregnancy jeans and a long, black, fitted jersey.

'Is that what you're wearing, love?' asked Mum, as I walked down the stairs. Naturally she was wearing her red trouser-suit with the sequined trim, and her patent gold high heels.

'Yes,' I replied. 'And I'm not getting changed either.'

I sounded just like a petulant five-year-old. Snap out of it, I told myself. This was the biggest night on my mother's calendar this year, if not this decade, and I shouldn't be ruining it for her.

We arrived at the Aotea Centre and my predictions were promptly elevated to the status of premonition. Never in my life had I seen such a collection of walking frames; the foyer was a sea of them, so it looked like some sort of low-slung jungle gym. The odds of collecting one as we fought our way through to the ticket desk were a bookie's worst nightmare.

Much to my mother's delight, Debbie was wearing a gold sparkly trouser-suit, not dissimilar to the red one she had on, and identical gold heels. And much to all of the old fellas' delight, Debbie looked pretty amazing for a woman who had to be pushing seventy-five, although clearly having had the odd pinch and nudge along the way.

As soon as she pranced across the stage and uttered those famous words *I can feel a song comin' on*, I resigned myself to the fact it was going to be a very long night and the best thing I could do was attempt to master the art of sleeping with my eyes open. This proved very difficult with Mum elbowing me in the arm every time Debbie launched into another melody (which was far too often).

Francie wasn't nearly as appalled at my Saturday night outing as she should have been. She considered Debbie to be *kitsch*, but this was only because she'd once seen Debbie perform at Caesar's Palace in Las Vegas years ago, whilst under the influence of several champagne cocktails and illegal substances and in the company of several flamboyant and extremely camp friends. I tried to explain that seeing Debbie live at the Aotea Centre, when you were heavily pregnant, stone-cold sober and with your mother in tow was a rather different experience.

Tom was far more sympathetic to my plight, when we caught up for a coffee the next day. Well, sort of.

'Poor you! Isn't she the one from that movie with Meryl Streep?'

'That was Shirley MacLaine. Close. Debbie Reynolds is Princess Leah's mother.'

'Oh, right. Gotcha.'

I found a reference to *Star Wars* (where possible) always seemed to provide clarification for boys.

'And Liz Taylor stole her husband,' I added. Which was superfluous information, but I thought I'd throw it in there anyway, somehow having managed to retain a snippet of the barrage of Debbie Reynolds trivia my mother had rained down upon me my entire life.

The next morning I woke up, and for a lovely fleeting second I forgot. Forgot it was my birthday. But then the realization came flooding in, like a tsunami. I was thirty-five years old. But not only was I thirty-five years old, I was also thirty-five years old and lying in my childhood bed, in my childhood home, living with my sixty-year-old parents and eighty-six-year-old grandmother, single, pregnant, unemployed and, let's not forget, homeless.

I shut my eyes and prayed for a quick, painless killer virus to strike me down. But then I remembered the baby and immediately felt guilty. It was hardly her fault her mother was such a complete failure.

I hope she does better at life than I have, I sighed to myself.

Wouldn't be hard, though, would it?

'Happy birthday, darling,' said Mum, poking her head around the door with a steaming mug and plate of toast in hand. 'Cup of tea?'

'Thanks, Mum,' I said, propping myself up.

I'd drunk more tea in the past two months than it was safe to remember. My parents were solely responsible for keeping Mrs Dilmah in silk kaftans and gold jewellery.

I was dead keen to lie under the covers and mope for

at least the rest of the day. But I was also starving.

'Twenty-one again,' she said, giving me a kiss.

'Think you'll find she's thirty-five, Brenda,' said Dad, walking into the room behind her and giving me a kiss on the cheek too.

'Thanks,' I replied, looking as unamused as someone sitting under a Tinkerbell duvet could.

'A mere spring chicken,' he added hastily, responding to the dual glare.

'Where's the mad old duck?' I asked, changing the subject.

'Asleep, thankfully,' replied Mum. 'Only because she was up half the night. Found her standing in the linen cupboard at 4 a.m.'

'Looking for the toilet?' I guessed.

'No. Looking for Dad.'

Oh well, that was a new one. She hadn't looked for Grandad in years. With good reason, as he'd also been dead for years.

I let out a long sigh and dragged my heavy self out of bed. I didn't want to waste the day after all.

Oh, God, I thought, it's happened. Without trying, without even sitting on the same bus or in the same car park as trying, it had bloody well happened. I had morphed into my mother. *I don't want to waste the day* was one of her favourite quips. And she didn't want to. Ever.

What has happened to me? I despaired, straightening the Tinkerbell duvet. I used to see nothing wrong with wasting the day, several days in fact, often in a row. I used to take great pride in wasting days, lying on the sofa, usually in the possession of a colossal hangover, watching videos and eating takeaways, and I didn't see anything wrong with what I was doing. Did this fear of wasting days mean that I was suddenly afraid of them running out? That I could sense there wasn't a bottomless pit of days so who cared if you dipped your hand in and threw a couple away? Did this mean I was Getting Old?

I waddled into the shower. Francie was taking me out for a birthday lunch and would likely draw the line at pink penguin-covered flannel pyjamas.

'Right, chickadee,' she chirped, as we hopped into her car. 'Have I got plans for us!

'I thought we'd have lunch on the waterfront, followed by a spot of birthday shopping. But first we're going for a massage and pedicure at Heidi's.'

Heidi's was the loveliest beauty salon in the city, complete with a powder room of every girl's childhood dreams, with its fluffy pink walls, gilded mirrors and chandeliers. Clearly Francie was trying to compensate for the fact that I couldn't get disgracefully legless on my birthday, as one was rightly entitled to do. She was doing a good job so far.

'Sounds fabulous!' I replied, perking up no end at hearing the word 'massage'.

So there are fun things to do without alcohol, I thought. You just have to look for them.

It was a wonderful day, and Francie made me feel like a pampered birthday queen. Kind of similar to the way Gary used to make me feel sometimes, when he'd whisk me out of town for the weekend, but without the baggage and conditions that came with it. Or the sex, mind you. *Gary*, I thought. My mind hadn't strayed to him for him for months now, not since I'd found out he wasn't the father. The thought still sent a flood of relief washing through my body. Whatever we'd had, it wasn't love, I realized. Lust perhaps. Well, whatever it had been was gone, I also realized, for good.

After dinner (Weiner schnitzel, mashed potato and peas) my parents said they wanted to have a talk with me. They even put batty Nan by herself in front of *Coronation Street*, so I decided it must be serious. I wondered if they were going to ground me. But I hadn't done anything naughty, had I? I didn't recall sneaking their car out at night and pashing up some Grammar boy in the back seat. At least not recently. I'd snuck the odd glass of wine, but surely I was old enough? And surely it wouldn't be worth grounding me? It's not like I went out anywhere.

I helped Dad clear the table and we sat back down.

'We want to talk to you, love,' said Dad, starting the ball rolling, 'about getting your own place.'

Oh, God! I thought in horror. My parents are kicking me out! Pregnant and all! Next stop'll be the homeless shelter! I bet it's because of the bloody remote-control batteries. Dad still hadn't quite managed to regain the intimate and loving relationship he'd once shared with the remote control. Every time he nervously picked it up to turn the telly on, he'd sigh with relief when it actually worked.

'It's OK,' comforted Mum, reading my mind. 'We don't want you to leave.'

'We just think you should have your own place. If that's what you want,' said Dad.

Of course it was what I wanted, but I couldn't bloody well afford it, could I? Why were they rubbing my face in it?

'What your father's trying to say,' continued Mum, 'is that we'd like to help you buy a house. We've been to the bank and sorted everything out, so it's all ready to go.'

'And we don't want any arguments from you,' said Dad, stopping me in my tracks.

I didn't know what to say.

'It'd be a loan, of sorts,' said Mum. 'But there'd be no hurry to pay it back,' she added. 'Not until you're well and truly back at work.'

'And there'd be no hurrying back to work,' added Dad. 'Not until you're ready to.'

I was speechless.

My parents aren't wealthy people. They're comfortable, but they'd worked bloody hard all their lives for everything they have. And they were finally at the point where they could sit back and enjoy it. The last thing I wanted was to be responsible for them stepping backwards.

'But what would this mean for you?' I asked. 'For this house?'

'Nothing,' said Dad. 'It's money we had tucked away for a rainy day. And money we'll need someday, but not for a wee while yet.

'With what we can lend you and the money you've got in the bank, you should be able to buy a nice little house for you and the baby,' he added. 'With a small mortgage which we can afford to cover until you're ready to go back to work.'

I couldn't believe it. Something, maybe the look in their eyes, told me not to argue with them. To just accept their generosity and be grateful for it.

'Thank you,' I said, getting out of my seat and giving them both a huge hug (or trying to, but really just shoving them with my bump). They were so unbelievably kind to me. I was sure I didn't deserve it.

'That's what parents are for,' said Mum, giving me a kiss. 'You'll do this yourself one day.'

'Settle down, love,' said Dad, who wasn't one for any lengthy or unnecessary displays of emotion, although I did notice a tear in the corner of each of his eyes.

'How about you start looking this weekend?' suggested Mum. 'I'll give you hand. We both will.'

'Sounds great,' I agreed. 'And you know what?' I said, smiling at them both.

'What?' said Mum.

'I can feel a sooong comin' on.'

Sally

Greta was dead. I couldn't believe it! Run over by a bus. Gorgeous, vivacious Greta.

What a hideous and senseless way to die. Claire had phoned me after hearing the news from Emily, an old school friend of hers. Emily was always up to date with gossip about girls we'd been to school with and what they were doing these days.

Poor Greta, I thought. It was just awful. So very tragic. She was so young, far too young to die. Her poor husband. And her poor children, losing their mummy like that; they were so young.

The thought of it brought tears to my eyes. I couldn't imagine leaving my children. Not seeing them grow up, take on the challenges of life, or see them have children of their own one day. Poor Greta, she was going to miss out on so much.

I remembered when I had bumped into her at the supermarket all those months ago, as I was staring blankly at the shelves, like a crazy person. She had looked so gorgeous, so happy. She had given me her card, I remembered. And I'd promised I'd ring her. And that we'd go out for dinner. Oh God, why hadn't I? Why hadn't I phoned her?

How shallow of me, I thought, to have put my own insecurities before our friendship. She would have been a good friend to me. Just what I needed.

I wondered if Kat and Jools would be at her funeral. I wished I had their phone numbers to let them know, they would want to be there for sure. They'd been such good friends with Greta, too. We all had — the best of friends.

Would I even recognize them? I wondered. Would they recognize me?

But then I'd recognized Greta, hadn't I, and she'd recognized me. Maybe we didn't change as much as we thought we did.

I wondered what Kat and Jools were doing with their lives. Probably happily married to normal, non-botox-injecting-and-pimp-dressing men, I thought. Maybe they'd know who Vincent was and judge me based on him?

Oh, God, I couldn't bear that.

I wondered if Kat had become the accountant she'd always wanted to be. Probably, she was so studious and focused at school. And if she'd had that clutch of kids she'd always wanted, one of each I think it was. And Jools — troublemaker Jools — had she ended up being the hard-nosed business woman she'd wanted to be? I presumed she had, with that fierce determination she possessed.

I wondered if the three of us would still have anything in common, our lives no doubt having taken such different paths. Would it be possible to link the tracks?

Life can be so unbelievably cruel, I thought, my mind turning to Greta once again. And so unpredictable. One minute you're minding your own business and walking to work, and the next you're dead.

Gone. No more.

I hope she'd been as content with her life as she'd seemed. That she didn't have too many regrets. That she'd truly been happy.

Can I say the same? I wondered. If I happened to get hit by a bus today?

I wasn't sure I could.

Kat

I brushed my hair and took one last look in the mirror.

Not too many lines around your eyes, I told myself, which immediately made me feel a little better. And then I couldn't help myself from thinking such a pathetic and childish thought: please God, let them have lots of lines. This wouldn't make up for not having a husband or a child, but it would be nice. I still had no idea whether Jools and Sally would be at the funeral, although I hoped they would.

The church in the city was packed and overflowing. I'd never been to a funeral with so many people before. There were hundreds. I arrived in time to squeeze into a spare seat towards the back of the church, but I was one of the lucky last.

I looked around but couldn't see either Jools or Sally, or any other familiar faces. I wondered who these multitudes of people were. Friends of Greta's? Her workmates?

I could just make out her family in the front row: her parents, sister and brother I recognized after all these years, even from the back of their heads. The sight of two small heads bobbing in the front pew made my heart race. There was Ella, her little head of long blonde hair turned, as she looked towards the back of the church. She looked exactly like Greta. And that must be her father sitting beside her, I guessed, Greta's husband. And her brother sitting on the other side of him. God, they are so small, I thought, they're just babies.

I felt a tear slide down my cheek as I watched their little heads. They had lost their mother. How could life be so cruel?

After the heart-wrenching service was over, I watched as Greta's coffin was carried out of the church by the six pallbearers, her husband and children walking behind it.

Then I waited out the front of the church, on the off-chance I would spot either Jools or Sally. But I didn't.

They spotted me.

Firstly Sally, who came running over and pulled me into a huge hug. I hardly recognized her with her blonde hair. She looked fantastic; in fact, she looked better than fantastic. She'd always had a lovely voluptuous and sexy figure, and twenty years hadn't changed it at all.

Then a heavily pregnant woman, who on closer inspection turned out to be Jools, joined us, giving us both a big hug also, as best she could with the large baby bulge protruding from her middle. She looked as pretty and youthful as ever, her petite frame still visible behind her pregnant belly.

'Wow!' we all exclaimed, thrilled beyond words to see each other again.

'I was hoping you'd both be here!' said Sally.

'Me, too,' agreed Jools and I.

'It's been too long.'

'Way, way too long!'

Jools and Sally had also come along by themselves and the three of us edged away from the crowd which had gathered at the front of the church.

'That was just awful,' said Jools. 'Poor Greta.'

'And her poor little kids,' said Sally. 'It's so sad.'

'I can't believe she was hit by a bloody bus . . . what a stupid way to go.'

'I know,' agreed Sally and I. 'So bloody senseless.'

'I cried like a baby,' I confessed.

'Same here,' said Jools. 'I had to flog extra tissues off the woman sitting next to me.'

We watched as the hearse bearing Greta's coffin drove slowly away.

'Bye, Greta,' we murmured, fresh tears running down our cheeks.

'How about we go for a glass of wine somewhere?' suggested Sally. 'If you have time? And have a proper catch-up?'

'Let's,' agreed Jools and I.

It wasn't as though I had any other plans.

'I'll just ring my husband,' said Sally, pulling her mobile phone out of her handbag and taking a few steps away from us.

'I won't be home for a few hours . . .' we overheard her say, '. . . because I'm going out for a drink with Kat and Jools, my old friends from school. Yes, a drink . . . just to a bar, Vincent . . .'

It sounded like she was getting the full interrogation from her husband.

'That means you'll need to get the kids' dinner,' continued Sally, an unusually nervous tone in her voice. Perhaps it was embarrassment at Jools and me overhearing her conversation.

'Well, I'm busy, too, Vincent, and I'd really appreciate it if you could look after them tonight. You haven't seen them all week. Well, maybe you can write your sermon later on.'

It didn't sound as though Vincent was all that willing to get the children's dinner. Or look after them. What kind of archaic chauvinist had she married?

'Sorry,' said Sally, as she hung up the phone. 'Let's go.'

We headed to a wine bar nearby which Jools recommended. 'If it still exists,' she added. 'I haven't exactly been out on the ran-tan in a while.'

It did and it was lovely. Big comfy plush sofas everywhere and perfectly dimmed lighting.

After our second glass of wine (lemonade for Jools) we had relaxed into each other's company and, without even trying, had slipped back into the conversational ease with which we used to be so familiar. There was so much for us to catch up on. Twenty years' worth.

We chatted about Greta, all our memories of her and of each other.

'You know,' said Sally, 'I bumped into her earlier in the year, at the supermarket. She looked amazing. She gave me her card . . . I was supposed to ring her and go out for dinner . . . but I didn't. God, I feel so terrible!'

'I bumped into her, too,' I admitted. 'A couple of months ago.'

'So did I!' said Jools. 'Just a few weeks ago. I'd lost my grandmother at the mall and she was so sweet, waiting with me and helping to look for Nan. She said she'd bumped into you two.'

'How weird!' exclaimed Sally. 'All of us bumping into her within a few months of each other, when we hadn't seen her for nearly twenty years.'

'Where did you see her?' Jools asked me.

'Outside the laundromat. She looked incredible, while I looked completely dowdy. She gave me her card too . . . and I said I'd call. But I didn't either,' I said, patting Sally on the knee. 'I just wasn't feeling all that social. I really wish I had, though.'

'I rang her,' said Jools. 'To tell her we'd found Nan, she wanted to know. But then I was supposed to ring her back the next week, we were going to go to lunch . . . but I didn't. I kept meaning to but, I don't know, she seemed so happy, with her lovely husband and her adorable kids. I wasn't sure I'd be able to stack up. I know that sounds silly.'

'It doesn't,' said Sally. 'That's exactly how I felt.'

'Me, too,' I admitted. 'That and I presumed you two would be living happy ever after as well. I was scared of seeing you, too.'

'I'll be the first to admit my life's not exactly a fairytale,' said Sally.

'Mine neither,' said Jools.

'But you're pregnant,' I said. 'And you look fantastic. Who's the lucky man?'

'Ah, well, that's where the fairytale takes an unexpected turn for the worse,' she smiled. 'You see, there isn't one.'

For some reason, perhaps it was the smile on Jools's face, Sally and I begin to giggle.

'What do you mean?' asked Sally.

'I mean I'm not with a bloke. I just happened to get pregnant, a little unexpectedly . . . and I decided that it was time I became a mummy.'

Jools filled us in on her largely disastrous love life, the baby's father, her ex-boss, and the ex-bosses before him.

'I remember you wanted to own your own company,' said Sally. 'You were adamant you wanted to be the boss.'

'Teenagers are so ambitious,' replied Jools. 'They

have no idea how cruel life can be.'

'No kidding!' agreed Sally and me.

'Oh God!' said Jools. 'It's finally happened! I've finally become an adult!'

It was a sobering moment and one which promptly brought tears to her eyes.

'But it's probably a good thing,' she added, 'being that I'm almost a mother.' The word 'mother' brought more tears to her eyes and she appeared to be having a mild panic attack. 'Sorry . . . bit emotional at the moment,' she choked.

'Don't be sorry,' said Sally. 'It's only natural.'

I passed Jools my glass of wine and she took a gulp.

'You'll be just fine,' I assured her. 'You'll be an amazing mum.'

And she would be too.

'You were so adamant you wanted to get married, Jools,' said Sally. 'Not like me, remember?'

'I did want to get married,' replied Jools. 'I still do, I guess. It's just that all the men I've been out with happened to be married to someone already.'

'And you wanted to have four kids,' I added.

'I've left it a bit late for that,' replied Jools. 'I'll still be having them when I'm sixty.'

'Remember how we said we wouldn't be too strict and we'd let our kids do whatever they wanted?' said Sally.

'Over my dead body!' replied Jools. 'God, we were so young and naïve.'

'And remember how we thought anyone over thirty was old?' I reminded them.

'Oh, God,' they both sighed. 'What little bitches we were.'

Sally told us about her three children and her job, both of which she obviously loved immensely. And then, when prompted, she told us about her husband.

'I'm just not sure I can take much more,' she confessed, giving us the rundown on the metamorphosis that was Vincent. 'He is slowly driving me insane.'

She also confided in us that he'd been sending her to a psychologist.

'What he doesn't get,' said Sally, 'is that I love going to see Esther. It gives me the chance to unload about all the ridiculous things he's been up to.'

She told us all about Vincent's beauty treatments and the stem cells.

'Excuse me for being so blunt,' I said. 'But I can't help thinking he's the one who might be better seeing a shrink.'

'I agree,' said Sally. 'Gosh it feels so good to be able to talk about him to you two; it's not the kind of conversation I can have with anyone from church.'

'You deserve to be happy,' assured Jools.

'And you deserve someone who makes you happy,' I added.

In return, I decided to fill Sally and Jools in on my life, the real version. There was something about their honesty and trust and the realization that their lives were far from the perfect scenarios I had imagined which made me want to open up, made me want to tell them the whole sorry story. And as I did, I felt a sense of incredible relief wash over me. It felt so good to tell others about it, my only real confidante for the past nine months having been Izzy.

And they didn't look sideways at me, as I'd feared they would, thinking I'd either married a raving bender or turned my husband gay. Instead they were nothing but sympathetic and understanding. And supportive.

'Oh, Kat,' said Sally, reaching over and wrapping her arms around me, 'that's just awful. You poor thing!'

'Bloody hell!' agreed Jools. 'What a shock it must have been!'

'It was.' I agreed. 'I felt like I'd been hit by a bus.'

A hefty silence followed my words and it took me a while to realize what I'd just said.

'Oh . . . God,' I sighed. '*Please* tell me I didn't just say that.'

Sally and Jools put their hands over their mouths and then, very slowly, erupted into a fit of uncontrollable giggles, tears rolling down their cheeks.

'Oh, God,' I said again. 'What an idiot!'

'Don't be silly, Kat,' laughed Sally. 'It's just a turn of phrase . . . and if Greta was here you can be sure she'd be laughing too.'

'To be honest, I'm surprised I haven't said it yet tonight,' said Jools. 'I say it all the time!'

When we finally had our laughter under control, I found myself opening up to Jools and Sally even more, telling them how badly I wanted to have a baby. Jools reached across and put her hand on my leg.

'I'm so sorry, Kat,' she said. 'I've been so completely insensitive sitting here bleating on about babies!'

'Don't be silly,' I smiled back, putting my hand on top of hers. 'You weren't to know. And anyway, surely there's no need for us to tread lightly around one another? We never used to.'

'No kidding,' said Jools.

'I think you even stole my boyfriend once!' said Sally to me. 'Mikey McManus.'

'No, I didn't,' I replied. 'That was Greta. I stole Jools's boyfriend.'

'That's right!' cried Jools, slapping me playfully on the thigh. 'You cow! I cried over that for, well, at least half an hour.'

'I was only getting you back for taking my maths assignment home to copy and losing the bloody thing.'

'What about that lemonade stall we had outside Jools's house?' said Sally.

'That's right,' I remembered. 'We said we were raising money for a new school pool . . . we even had a sign! But we were pocketing it for our holiday spending money!'

'Even my mother fell for it!' said Jools. 'Picking the lemons for us and showing us how to make the lemonade.'

'We made a packet,' said Sally. 'Remember?'

'Mum kept asking me when the new pool was going to be built,' said Jools. 'For about a year!'

We erupted into giggles at every memory. I felt as though we were back in class again, going to get told off and separated at any moment.

After two hours of non-stop gossiping, we reluctantly decided to head home.

'You know what?' said Jools, as we were leaving. 'Maybe Greta's life wasn't as perfect as we all thought it was.'

'Maybe,' I agreed. Sally nodded.

After all, I had assumed Sally and Jools would have perfect lives too, and they didn't.

'I wish she was here,' I found myself saying. 'She would have really enjoyed tonight.'

'She sure would have,' agreed Jools.

'She was the one who finally got us together after all these years,' said Sally. 'She always was the leader of our pack.'

We arranged to meet for dinner the following week.

There was still plenty of catching up for us to do. As we kissed one another goodbye we promised not to lose touch with each other again, and something told me we really meant it this time. Life was too short to lose touch with real friends, we decided.

I've missed the two of them, I thought as I drove home, and Greta too, far more than I've ever realized.

Jools

I knew it was my new house as soon as Dad and I pulled up outside. A white cottage with a lovely little garden out the front and a wee porch. It was so cute. In a nice street, in a suburb which was handy to town and on the up.

'Good investment area,' said Dad, who had become a property expert in recent weeks, devouring every property magazine he could get his hands on.

The two-bedroom cottage had been done up on the outside but was still traditionally old-school on the inside. Although it was structurally sound with a good layout, there was still lots of paint and touches to be added. Which was what I wanted. I had no desire to buy a place where all the work had been done and there was no room for me to add my flair. Not that I could have afforded a place like this anyway.

The old lady who owned the place was moving to a retirement village. She'd been living in the house for forty years, and you could tell, in a nice way. Everything was either cream or lemony yellow and was just so. Right down to the fake bougainvilleas in the kitchen.

And after a relatively stress-free period of negotiation between the real-estate agent and myself, the house was mine. (I put it down to the 'talk to the hand' vibes I gave off when dealing with him, even though I was shaking in my sensible flat black shoes.) Four weeks and a quick settlement later, and I was busily unpacking the sky-high pile of boxes in my new home. It was just in the nick of time. I was the size of a small house myself, with my due date a stone's throw away. I immediately launched into getting the most important room in the house up to scratch, the nursery, which Tom insisted on painting.

'You don't have to,' I protested. 'Honestly.'

'I want to,' he replied, bringing around some test pots of paint and letting me choose the colour, a sort of creamy colour with a touch of warm yellow, which sounds disgusting but is really very lovely, and matched the rest of the house perfectly.

As Mum and I set about unpacking the boxes and rearranging the furniture, Tom set about painting the baby's room, only taking a break when Mum or I insisted he stop for a cuppa. I felt a little bit like the pregnant wifey, standing in the doorway and calling her DIY husband in for his morning tea. Only I wasn't a wifey, and Tom wasn't my husband, and the only reason he was here painting the nursery was because we'd been a couple of complete strangers who'd had a one-night stand after drunkenly flirting with each other in a pub. Still, it was nice nonetheless. He looked good with a paintbrush in his hand, I had to admit, sort of like a cross between a young Bruce Willis in *Die Hard* and Prince William (he still had the lovely ruddy-red cheeks). Plus he seemed to know what to do with a paintbrush, which was a bonus.

As I watched him standing on the ladder, brush in hand, I suddenly found myself wondering what he'd be like as a permanent fixture in my new house. He'd asked me out for dinner a few times recently, but I'd come up with a lame excuse each time. I couldn't help myself wondering whether he was only asking me out because he felt sorry for me, being a single, dateless and up-and-coming solo mum.

Perhaps you should just say yes next time, I told myself. What have you got to lose?

Once the nursery was painted I laid out all the furniture, with Mum's help. She was brilliant, erecting a change table like she'd been doing it all her life. Well, I guess she had, but she was brilliant at it nonetheless.

It was fun, picking the colours and placing the furniture, most of which was hand-me-downs from my cousin Cara, but still in pristine condition. Richie and Lydia had bought a beautiful white wooden cot for the baby. I'd had tears in my eyes when they'd turned up with it and Richie had set it up in the nursery. Lydia had even bought beautiful embroidered sheets and a handmade quilt, which she set about putting on the cot, leaving it looking so snug and gorgeous. She had also offered to babysit as often as I needed, surprising me with what seemed to be genuine honesty and enthusiasm. I found myself wondering if perhaps I'd been too hasty in judging her. Maybe the baby would be the link that enabled us to be friends at long last? I hoped so.

As the last boxes were unpacked, I took a look around my new house, hands rubbing my enormous belly as I waddled around each room, a sigh of contentment escaping my lips. No, I decided, it wasn't contentment. It was happiness. I was happy with my home, happy and excited at the imminent arrival of my baby girl. I was happy with my life. It wasn't what I had expected or planned, but I was happy nonetheless. And you know what else? I said to myself, thinking of poor Greta, who was never far from my mind these days. You're also bloody lucky to have it . . . don't you ever forget that.

Sally

Claire had taken the girls to her house for the night to watch videos and have a sleepover, which they were incredibly excited about. Davey was staying over at a friend's house.

Vincent and I were supposed to be going to a dinner to celebrate the launch of his self-help book for men, *The Family Man.*

'Sally, we're going to be late,' he cried, walking into the dining room, where I was sitting, a glass of wine on the table in front of me. 'Have you seen my purple silk tie?' he asked, his eyes focusing on the wine glass.

'Vincent. I want a divorce.'

'Or maybe I should wear the jade one.'

'I want a divorce,' I repeated, louder this time.

'What?' he asked, just realizing I'd spoken.

'I want a divorce,' I said again, looking him in the eyes.

'A divorce? Are you nuts, Sally? We can't get divorced!'

'Yes we can, Vincent,' I replied. 'I want to.'

'But we're a family!'

'The children and I are a family,' I replied. 'And you are someone who lives with us and whose life and values we have to conform to. When was the last time we did something as a family?' I asked. 'Tell me?'

'Sally, we spend every Wednesday and Sunday together in church as a family,' he replied.

'No, Vincent, the children and I spend every Sunday in church sitting there with the rest of your disciples, and then the children and I go out for a hot chocolate together while you stay and bask in the pathetic adoration that you seem to so enjoy. Sitting in church while you stand on the stage and perform for the cameras is not doing something as a family. Do you even know what the kids are up to? Did you know that Davey has his first girlfriend? That she's lovely and he really likes her? Did you know that Elizabeth won the school poetry award last week? Or that Hannah's been selected to play soccer for the under-ten reps?'

The look on his face indicated that he didn't know. How could this be the same man I married? The man I chose to spend the rest of my life with?

'We can't get divorced, Sally!' he cried. 'Just think what it will do to everything, including the book. *Please!*' he begged.

He looked truly pathetic.

'I don't give a fuck about your goddamn image, Vincent,' I replied. And honestly, I didn't. 'And I'm not going to this bloody dinner either, you can go by yourself.'

I stood up and walked out of the room.

'For crying out loud, Sally!' he cried after me. 'Think about what you're doing to us! What you're doing to *me!*'

'I have Vincent,' I replied, looking over my shoulder. 'For far too long.'

He's just like a lemon tree, I thought, dropping bitter fruit wherever he treads.

Kat

For the next few weeks I just couldn't stop thinking about Greta, and how she'd died. So suddenly, and in such a senseless way.

What is the point of planning every step of my life? I wondered. If it could end just end like hers had, in one instant? There's no point.

I phoned Gus.

'I want to sell the house,' I said.

He sounded surprised.

'So you don't want to buy my share anymore?'

'No. Let's put it on the market straightaway.'

'OK.'

'Oh, and you might need to come and give the floorboards a bit of a sand and polish.'

What was the point in staying in a big family home, without the family? It would only continue to remind me of everything I had lost. There was no point in clinging to the past.

The following morning I went into work, as per usual, and met with Martin.

'I want to leave the firm,' I announced.

'What Kat? *Why?*'

He was gobsmacked; there was no other word for it. His gob was all floppy and hanging, as though someone had just smacked it.

'It's time for a change,' I replied. 'I love accounting but I need a break. I want to do something different for a while.'

'Like what?'

'I'm going to enrol in an interior-decorating course. I think I'd like to be an interior designer.'

I figured that with all my furniture rearranging experience, and my passion for décor and colours, I might be quite good at it. Gus and Izzy were always saying I had a knack for decorating, and so was Dan come to think if it. All I knew was that I enjoyed doing it, and surely that was enough of a reason to give it a try?

Martin convinced me to take a year's sabbatical. In other words they would hold my position open for a year, just in case I changed my mind, which they hoped I would. I wasn't so sure; I didn't know exactly what I was going to do with the rest of my life, but I doubted it would involve going backwards.

Izzy was speechless when I broke the news to her. And then she was ecstatic.

'I'm so proud of you, babe!' she exclaimed. 'So bloody proud.'

She insisted on coming around and taking me out for celebratory drinks. And for once I didn't protest. I had something to celebrate after all: my life. I was lucky enough to still have it and I was damn well going to make the most of it.

I changed out of my suit and into a sexy pair of new jeans, a low-cut sparkly red top, and red heels. I felt like wearing something bright that night. And then I took the time to redo my make-up and hair, letting my hair flow down my shoulders.

As I waited for Izzy, I caught sight of my reflection in the hallway mirror, taking a moment to stand in front of it and look at myself for the first time in a very long time. You know what? I told myself. You're a bit of all right, Katherine. You truly are.

And you know what else? I thought, remembering all that had happened to me over the past year, the crap hand I'd been dealt, the heartbreak I'd suffered, and all the changes I'd weathered. It's time for you to make some lemonade, girl. Some good, old-fashioned lemonade.

Acknowledgements

Thank you, thanksalot and a big cheers to all these
fabulous people:

The Gals: Petra, Lauren, Atlanta, Bex, Kirsty, Bobbie,
Claire, Clare, Suz, Jo, Kelly, Mahoney . . . it's good to
know age and babies haven't slowed us down!

My twenty-first-century family: Ma, Pa, Justin,
Ben, Haydon, Faye, Waynne, Jo, Rob, Grandad,
Grandma, Grandpa . . . love you all.

Pamela and Anna, for their love and friendship,
and for being two such inspiring women.

Lorain Day, for her continued encouragement
and *much* patience . . . thank you!

Tracey Wogan, for her ardour, expertise, enthusiasm
. . . and the sharpest eyes in the west.

The rest of the team at HarperCollins NZ, for their
continued support and enthusiasm.

Corinne, for her inspiration, encouragement, radiance
and laughter . . . and for being such a top girl.

Barney, for his support, understanding and truly
amazing spirit. And for being such a wonderful dad
to Jasper Jet, our wee gem of a boy.

My grandmother, Patricia, who passed away while
I was writing this book . . . an amazing lady and
friend, and, without a doubt, my hero.

And to all those people who buy, read and even enjoy
my books — thank you!